SNAKE BITE

SNAKE BITE

CHRISTIE THOMPSON

ALLEN&UNWIN

SYDNEY·MELBOURNE·AUCKLAND·LONDON

First published in 2013

Allen & Unwin
Sydney, Melbourne, Auckland, London

83 Alexander Street
Crows Nest NSW 2065
Australia
Phone: (61 2) 8425 0100
Email: info@allenandunwin.com
Web: www.allenandunwin.com

Cataloguing-in-Publication details are available
from the National Library of Australia
www.trove.nla.gov.au

ISBN 9781743316863
Internal design by Alissa Dinallo
Set in 13.5/19 pt Granjon by Midland Typesetters, Australia
Printed and bound in Australia by Griffin Press
10 9 8 7 6 5 4 3 2 1

MIX
Paper from
responsible sources
FSC
www.fsc.org   FSC® C009448

The paper in this book is FSC certified.
FSC promotes environmentally responsible,
socially beneficial and economically viable
management of the world's forests.

ONE
. . .

Lukey and I were at Kimbo's Body Piercing, in seriously sweet spirits. It was two days after we had finished Year 11, and we were only just coming to realise the possibilities of a whole summer of freedom. We were getting pierced to give a finger to another long year of boring-as-fuck school.

I took a deep breath; the smell of antiseptics made my adrenaline kick in. I loved getting pierced. I had eleven piercings already, one in each nostril, six-mm stretched lobes, and three holes in the top cartilage of each ear, plus a belly ring and a bar through my tongue. *Blood and metal. Yum.* That day I was tossing up between a snake bite—two piercings on either side of my lower lip—and a septum ring, a piercing through the middle bridge of skin inside the nose.

Lying back on the cushioned table, a big metal clamp pinching a fold of skin, the needle being pushed through my flesh—it was all very *Frankenstein* Gothic type shit but like *now*. I knew all about *Frankenstein* because I read it for English that year, when we were supposed to give a talk on a book of our choice. Actually I just downloaded the movie; it was so rad, I really got into it. I loved the bit where Dr Frankenstein goes on about how he's like a scientist who's creating art with flesh and bone. Body modification is like that.

In the waiting lounge we slouched on the hardwood benches, flipping through plastic-sleeved binders that held pictures of different types of piercings. Lukey was stoned, as usual, his face slightly slack and his eyelids drooping at the corners. His face was long and thin, like the rest of his body, and he had dark stubble on his jaw that made him look older. I liked the big silver flesh tunnels he wore in his ears, and the rings through his lower lip. He looked totally scrams.

On the wall above Lukey's head was a poster of a peroxide blonde with massive tits in a fishnet body stocking and huge chunks of metal in her face. Below that was a sticker in the shape of the Australian continent that said, FUCK OFF WE'RE FULL.

Lukey was telling me, in his thick-tongued stoned monotone, about this insane anaconda attack he'd seen on YouTube. A group of zookeepers somewhere in South America were trying to shift the snake into a wooden crate when the snake suddenly snapped around and sank its fangs into one of the men's forearms. It took the strength of all the other men to pry the snake's jaws apart. Awesome. I made a mental note to look it up when I got home.

'I'm going vegan, hey.' Lukey changed the subject.

'For real?'

We'd both been vegetarian since Year 7 after Lukey's anarchist cousin from Melbourne sent him a DVD of footage from animal slaughterhouses.

'Yeah.' Lukey nodded. 'You know how I always puke when I drink milk and shit? Gunna have one last guts on chocolate, though.'

'You'll miss ice-cream.' I pulled my legs up to my chest and rested my chin on my knees.

'Dairy-free gelato? Or soy ice-cream is alright.'

'Doesn't dairy-free gelato have eggs in it?'

'Dunno. Maybe.'

'You're gunna be too fucking hip now.'

'Why?'

'Vegan. It's like a fashion statement, hey?'

'Nah, it's 'cos of my stomach and stuff. Plus the animals.'

'I guess so ...'

'You wanna pig out on chocolate tonight and play Xbox?'

'F'shiz.' I grinned at my best friend.

Lukey punched me lightly on the arm. 'Nobody says that, Jez.'

'We gotta get Rocky Road.'

'Peppermint.'

'You got some weed?'

'Don't I always?'

The door shuddered open and a short, chubby girl with a black Bettie Page fringe and black-rimmed nerd-girl glasses bounced inside, paused briefly to give Lukey and me a once-over and plopped herself on the waiting-room bench next to Lukey. Well, I say next to, but she practically sat in his lap. She grinned widely, her dimpled cheeks sparkling with fake diamond studs. She was so cutesy I swear I could taste vom in the back of my mouth.

'You want a chair there? Lap is good for you?' I queried, ultra polite.

'I've seen you guys before,' she exclaimed, enthusiastic. 'I live up the hill from you, on Sinclair Street. Me and my family just moved here from Melbourne. I'm Laura, by the way.'

'I'm Jez, that's Lukey,' I said. 'I think I saw you on the bus once.'

'That's gotta suck, moving from Melbourne to Canberra,' Lukey observed. 'Why would you move here?'

'Joanie, that's my mum, she works in the public service. I don't mind it here, though.'

'You call your mum "Joanie"?' Lukey sounded impressed. He leaned forward, elbows on his knees. 'Do you call your dad by his first name, too?'

She laughed. 'We call him Mr Sperm. I've got two mums. Joanie is the one who gave birth to me.'

4

Lukey and I nodded. I was thinking, *Wow … I've never met the kid of two lezzas before*, but I didn't want her to think I was impressed or anything.

Laura pulled an iPhone out of her oversized handbag and stared at it for a few seconds, pressed the touchscreen a few times and then put it away again. *Show-off*, I thought.

'It's kind of ugly here,' Laura continued. 'It's so dry. So, like, suburban.' She paused and wrinkled her button nose thoughtfully. 'But it's a novelty for me because I grew up real close to the city.'

'It's boring as fuck here,' I informed her. 'Nothin' to do.'

'What do you guys do for fun?'

'Dunno. Xbox. Swim in the river. Hang around.'

'Back in Melbourne I was always going to all-ages shows.'

'There's shows every now and then,' Lukey said. 'Youth centre stuff.'

'We've got a pool. You guys should come over for a swim.' Laura giggled and then leaned in conspiratorially until her hot-pink-lipsticked lips were close to Lukey's face. 'Have you heard of a Christina?' she whispered, her voice all breathy as though she was trying to be sexy.

'Er, nah. I dunno.' Lukey moved back, embarrassed, blushing. That annoyed me, I don't know why.

'Christina? Is that your other mum?' I asked.

'Oh, my God! No, it's a type of piercing.' She laughed, leaning back. 'I'm not getting a Christina anyway, I'm getting a Marilyn.'

A 'Marilyn' is a top lip, 'beauty spot' piercing, pretty common.

'So what is a "Christina", then?' I asked, almost immediately regretting my curiosity.

'It's a genital piercing, right at the top of your V, above the clit,' she explained, parting her legs slightly and gesturing with her hands.

'Oh,' I said, and I could feel my face getting hot. 'Why would you get that?'

'For pleasure! Well, pain first and then pleasure.' Laura laughed. 'I'll get that one day. You've gotta work your way up to something like that.'

Kimbo swaggered into the waiting room. Two teenage girls followed, looking a little pale yet triumphant. It's weird how tattooists and piercers were always super arrogant. He explained the piercing aftercare to them, really patronisingly, and rang up the sale.

'Who's next?' He sneered at the three of us.

'You go. We're still deciding.' Lukey smiled at Laura. She beamed and hoisted herself from the couch, smoothing out her polka-dot baby-doll dress.

'Piercers,' I whispered to Lukey. 'So up themselves.' I wished I did something cool to be up myself about.

'Fuck that.' Lukey shrugged. 'Doesn't even take talent to be a piercer. You stick a needle through somebody's skin. Big deal. Try computer programming.'

'I don't know shit about computers.'

'Me neither. Old dudes like him know less,' Lukey said. 'Why do you think "nerd" is suddenly cool again? 'Cos everyone knows the cyber world is gunna be as important as the real world one day. The world needs nerds. The world does *not* need more piercers.'

'Why are we even here?'

'Bulk jewellery he buys is cheaper,' Lukey pointed out. 'And my ear got infected when I did it myself,' he admitted, tugging on the cartilage just above his lobe.

I shrugged. 'Yeah, true.'

'So ... she seemed cool.' Lukey looked at me hopefully, blinking his huge green eyes.

'Who?' I asked, playing dumb.

'That chick who was just in here.'

'Pfft.' I made a noise through my teeth. 'Some random flirts with you and you get all typical male on me.'

'She was totally flirting with me, huh? Do you think she was? She kept kind of looking at me funny.' He had this dumb tight smile on his face and he was fiddling with the plastic sleeve of the piercing album, not really looking at it anymore.

'You've got a booger hanging out of your left nostril.'

'You are such a bitch.'

I pretended I hadn't heard him and grabbed the album of piercing photos off his lap, flipping through the pages rapidly. 'Snake bite. I'm definitely getting a snake bite.'

Laura was waiting out the front of the piercing studio for us when we had finished, smoking a cigarette and examining her bright-purple acrylic nails.

7

'Heeey!' Laura exclaimed, stubbing out her smoke. 'Snake bite looks awesome, honey.'

I hated it when people I didn't know called me 'honey', especially when they were my age. To me, it was so smug.

'Do you like mine?' Laura tilted her head to show off her 'Marilyn'.

'Looks great.' Lukey leaned onto the wall next to her. 'I love those on chicks.'

'So you guys want to come for a swim tomorrow? My parents aren't home so I've got the house to myself!'

'Sounds sweet,' Lukey said.

I raised my eyebrows. 'Yeah.' I shrugged. 'Sweet as.'

TWO

. .

The next day Lukey and I met on the street outside Laura's house at the top of Sinclair Street. Lukey lived on the corner of Sinclair and Marconi Crescent and I lived in a little cul-de-sac off Harrington Circuit, which was off Marconi. We were basically neighbours, all in 'da hood', Lukey would say ironically, because it was a relatively safe little bit of Australian suburbia. Well, okay, there'd been a couple of murders, domestic incidents mostly, and a bikie shooting, but compared to the big cities it was the type of place where you could leave the door open on a hot summer night, and just have the flyscreen closed. Laura's house was the same as all the others in the neighbourhood. Brick, one-storey, unremarkable. The native gums that lined the streets provided little shade; the scorching sun created a psyche-delic hazy heatwave effect on the surface of the tarred road.

Laura answered the door in a bright-pink zebra-striped one-piece swimsuit that showed expanses of fleshy dimpled skin. We followed her through the house, filled with packing boxes, to the back patio where Laura plopped herself down at the picnic table. She picked up a lit cigarette from the ashtray and scooped up a handful of potato chips, smoking in between shovelling chips into her gob, and occasionally stopping to fish stray crumbs out of her cavernous cleavage. I gagged involuntarily.

'Got your swimmers on?' Laura asked, her mouth full.

Lukey and I nodded and obediently peeled off our uniform black jeans and whipped off our t-shirts. We exchanged looks and grinned at our skeletally thin bodies, white because we never tanned. Lukey had a dodgy home-job tattoo of a snake, old-school style, winding up his thigh. His anarchist cousin in Melbourne did it for him when he was about fifteen and everyone at school was super-impressed because he was the first person in our year to have stretched lobes and a tattoo. Lukey never thought he was cool or anything, though. He just did shit like that 'cos he liked it.

Laura let out a low whistle and jumped up from her chair. She ran a hand down the snake on Lukey's thigh.

'That is so sexy,' she asserted.

Lukey smiled, chuffed. 'Thanks. I'm gunna get heaps more when I can afford it. Proper ones, I mean.'

'Me, too,' I said. 'I mean, I'm going to get my first one.'

'Yeah?' Laura studied me for a moment. 'What're you gunna get?'

'Dunno. Maybe a swastika right here.' I slapped my shoulder.

Lukey snorted and Laura's eyes widened, then she broke into a grin, realising I was joking.

'Yeah, Nazis are rad!' She giggled.

'And don't you just hate Jews?' Lukey chimed in, deadpan.

It was that kind of cheap *South Park* humour we'd all grown up with. Too easy, but it got the laugh I was looking for. At the same time I wanted to punch Laura in the face for being so pleased with herself for having 'got it' and plus I didn't really think it was funny, laughing at Nazis killing Jews.

'Hey, you guys wanna pinger?' Lukey asked, rummaging in the pocket of his backpack and pulling out a baggie of E.

'Oh, yesss!' Laura squealed. She bounced inside and came back with a bottle of Sprite and three glasses.

We dumped a pill each and washed it down. The lemonade sloshed over my chin. My bottom lip was still swollen from the snake-bite piercing. It hurt but felt great at the same time.

The pool was nothing to write home about, one of those shitty above-grounds. But it was stinking hot and I couldn't wait to get in the water. We bombed into the pool, splashing and doing all the predictable stuff, dunking each other under the water, playing a really short game of Marco Polo because it didn't work in a pool that small.

Within half an hour I could feel the first waves of euphoria from the pill. At first it was a tingling that spread through my torso, then a feeling like I was going to empty my bowels right into the swimming pool, then a kind of numbness in my limbs. We got out of the pool and flopped onto towels spread out on the grass. I could see from the looks on Lukey and Laura's faces—that faraway contented look and slackened faces—that they were feeling the same as I was. They were good pills, floaty and happy.

'Whoooah,' Lukey exhaled.

Me and Laura nodded. He didn't have to explain. It's funny how connected you feel to people when you're high. I never get that in real life. We each dumped another to make sure we had a really long pill and then Lukey rolled a joint and handed it to Laura to light. She took a few deep mouthfuls and let the smoke drift slowly from her lips.

'Yum,' she said and hopped up, passing the joint to me. 'I'm gunna put on some tunes.'

I could taste the faintest trace of Laura's lipstick, fruity and greasy on the end of the joint. She is such a *girl*, I thought, watching her skip into the house, flapping her arms excitedly like a big fat butterfly. I drew sharply on the joint and sucked the smoke deep into my lungs, narrowing my eyes with concentration, letting it out slowly. It caught in my throat and I hacked up, coughing, my eyes spilling tears.

'Slow down, greedy,' Lukey drawled.

I stuck my tongue out at him.

As the first electrifying notes of My Bloody Valentine's 'Only Shallow' floated across the lawn, Laura stepped outside. She started to dance in slow circles, glancing over at us to see if we were watching. I looked at Lukey, who had propped himself up on one elbow, trying to look casual, like he wasn't really paying attention. I suddenly felt like all the blood had drained from my face. The dope. The dope had hit me hard.

I got up and slipped inside and down the hallway until I found the bathroom and locked the door behind me. I absorbed my reflection in the mirror. Longish black hair, with a floppy fringe streaked with silver blonde and pale blue, kohl-black-rimmed eyes that had smudged in the pool giving the panda-eye effect. My dilated pupils seemed to glow under the muted bathroom light. I touched my face. It felt warm, smooth, alive. I narrowed my eyes a little and parted my lips slightly, like the models do on the covers of *Cleo* and *Cosmo*. I looked ridiculous. I mean, like, super-lame ridiculous. I started giggling hysterically until I could hardly breathe and I had to sit down on the edge of the bath with my head between my knees.

'Jez!' Lukey was knocking on the door. 'What're you doing in there? There's a wicked sunset. Jez? I can hear you laughing to yourself and I just want you to know you are the weirdest person *ever.*'

A few minutes later I joined the others on the patio. Against Me!'s 'Sink, Florida, Sink' was playing on the stereo, the sun had dropped to the horizon, blazing bright orange, the sky streaked with pink, purple and peach.

'Did you put this on?' I asked Lukey.

'Laura did.' Lukey grinned. 'I told her this was your song.'

'Our song,' I reminded him, thinking of all the times we'd been high or pilling or drunk and sang along to every word at the top of our lungs.

But we didn't sing along this time. We sat, just listening. I felt so happy and so sad at the same time. Happy because I could feel every part of my body tingling with the ecstasy, and I felt like I was glowing from the inside out; happy because I was with Lukey, my best friend for the last five years. Sad because I knew I would never be able to feel this good without drugs, and sad because it felt like one of those nights where you knew that afterwards nothing would ever be the same again.

When the sun disappeared, we went into the lounge room and sank into the plush cushions of the modular sofa. Laura's house was decorated in that kind of half boho-Asian-eclectic style, with oriental rugs and paisley floor cushions and giant wooden giraffe statues. But it had heaps of other quirky cool shit, like the oak-coloured bass guitar propped on a stand in one corner.

'Whose bass?' I wanted to know.

'Mine.' Laura sounded a little smug. 'I've played since I was thirteen.'

'Jez plays guitar,' Lukey said.

'We should jam!' Laura was eager.

'Where're your parents?' I asked Laura, changing the subject. I wasn't interested in jamming with her.

'In Melbourne. They're getting stuff tied up there and organising the last of Dana's stuff to be moved. She collects vintage bicycles.'

'Heaps rad!' Lukey commented, shifting his head to look at Laura. They were at either end of the larger sofa. She had her feet up on a cushion near his leg, and he was sitting, legs spread wide, kind of facing her.

'Yeah, Dana's a rad bitch.' Laura laughed. 'Heaps more laid-back than Joanie. But I love 'em both.'

'I live with my dad,' Lukey offered. 'He's pretty cool, too. Had me when he was only twenty-one, so he's still young and shit. We smoke joints together and he knows I deal E and that and he doesn't give a fuck.'

'Cool.' Laura grinned. 'I'd hate to have hectic parents. You got any brothers or sisters?'

'Yeah, I got an older brother, Mark, who's a massive fuckin' redneck arsehole. I wanna fucking kill the cunt.'

I twisted my head, surprised by the venom in Lukey's voice. It was true, Mark had always beaten up Lukey and bullied him, but I hadn't heard him talk about Mark like that before, so fully intense.

Lukey changed his tone slightly. 'And I've got a little sister, Ash, she's thirteen. Jez's mum's pretty awesome, too, hey, Jez?' Lukey said, shifting his posture a bit to include me in the conversation.

'My mum is ... alright. She keeps things interesting, I guess.'

'That's heaps cool, but. It would suck to get old and just be boring, too. I just want to party and get messy forever.' Laura sighed.

'Oath,' Lukey agreed.

'Yeah ...' I echoed half-heartedly.

'Hey, you guys want some wine? We've got, like, a couple of bottles stashed somewhere around here.'

'Awesome,' me and Lukey said in unison, and laughed.

'Heeey!' Laura re-emerged from the kitchen. 'Look what I found! Something even better!' She held up a bottle of Absolut Vodka in one hand and a bottle of Coke in the other.

'Yeeeew!' Lukey whooped. 'Let's get loose.'

We went into the kitchen and Laura sloshed vodka into highball glasses, about a third full, and then added a dash of Coke.

'May the best of the past be the worst of the future,' she said, and raised her glass. 'First drink is a skull; loser has to take a shot of straight vodka.'

'That practically is straight vodka,' I observed, holding up my glass full of pale brown liquid.

'Cheers!' Lukey said.

'Cheers!' Laura and I echoed.

We clunked our glasses and bottomed up. As soon as the vodka hit my mouth I knew I was going to lose. My eyes watered.

'Uggghh,' I groaned. 'I can't do it.'

Lukey won. Laura got a shot glass out of the cupboard and filled it to the brim.

'You're up again, Jez.' She handed me the shot.

I held my nose and tipped it down my throat and struggled to swallow. I could feel it burning all the way down to my empty stomach. I mixed myself a third drink, weaker, and it went down easy. My head started to swim almost straightaway. Total buzz.

I swaggered around the living room, kind of thrusting my hips forward as I walked. My vision had softened a little around the edges and I swayed down the hall to find a mirror. After I'd repainted my eyes with soft glittery pale-blue shadow and smudgy black liner I felt sexy, especially next to fat Laura. I went back to the others, grabbed Lukey and pulled him to his feet to dance with me, slinging my arms around his shoulders and laughing louder than I should have at nothing in particular. I danced harder, obnoxiously, and said obnoxious things. I might have even told Laura she might like to lose some weight. I can't be sure if it was something I said or just thought before I bent over double in an armchair, my chin on my own chest.

When I woke up, groggy, the television was on and Lukey and Laura were lying wrapped in each other's arms on the other end of the modular couch. At first I thought they had fallen asleep, too. Then I saw that they were kissing. Laura had one arm up the back of Lukey's shirt and her fingers tangled in his hair. My stomach lurched like I was gunna vom. I might have even made a noise like 'ugh!' then I looked away, got up abruptly, and banged my shin on the coffee table.

'Ooooow fuckety fucking ow!' I hissed, rubbing my sore shin.

Lukey and Laura turned their heads my way.

'What'd you do?' Laura exclaimed with a giddy giggle. 'Jez?'

'Nothing,' I snapped. 'I'm all good. Go back to whatever you were doing.'

'You okay, Jez?' Lukey asked. 'We thought you were asleep.'

'I woke up,' I said, in a matter-of-fact way that probably sounded bitchy, but I didn't care. I just wanted to get the hell out of that room. 'I'm going outside for a smoke.'

I wandered into the kitchen, disoriented. The effects of the E were draining from my body. The bottle of Absolut was still on the kitchen counter, two-thirds full. I grabbed it and took it outside to the patio before collapsing in one of the deckchairs and beginning to swig. And smoke.

I kept expecting Lukey to come outside and join me. He didn't. An hour or so passed. I drank a third more of the bottle of vodka, smoked half a dozen cigarettes out of Laura's packet then moved onto Lukey's pouch of rolling tobacco, chain-smoking until the sky started to lighten to a dull orange.

When I woke up again I was stretched out on Laura's sofa in the lounge room in a pool of hot yellow sunlight, drenched in sweat. I didn't remember how I got there. As soon as I stood up my head reeled. I didn't have a centre of gravity, but I lurched across the room anyway, arms flailing for something to hold onto, my stomach heaving with the sudden forward motion. I rasped up a few shaky burps and shuddered violently. *Oh. My. Fucking. God. I want to die.*

I staggered to the bathroom and threw myself cheek-down upon the cold tiled floor, groaning.

'You orright?'

Lukey appeared in my peripheral vision, slouching in the doorframe of the bathroom, grinning in amusement at me, in starfish mode, on the floor.

'Come down to the kitchen when you're done being a drama queen.'

'You … cunt,' I managed to gasp. 'I'm not being dramatic. I'm dying.'

Lukey doubled over laughing. 'I'm not heaps surprised, hey. You're a vodka pig. And you smoked all Laura's smokes.' He kicked my foot with his sneakered toe. 'Come down to the kitchen,' he urged. 'Laura is making hash stacks, it's her special recipe.'

I rolled over onto my back. 'What the fuck is a hash stack?' I asked.

'Laura's recipe. Hash browns spread with vegemite and stacked with mushrooms in between,' Lukey informed me.

'So no actual hash in 'em.' I tried to sound cool. 'Sounds shit.'

'Could be pretty good.'

'Could be pretty bad.'

'Are you just gunna lie on the bathroom floor all day, then?'

'Help me,' I pleaded, pathetically lifting one limp arm in his direction.

'You're such a whinger when you're hung-over.' He stuck out his hand and pulled me up.

'Be gentle!' I cried. 'My head feels like it's gunna fall off.' I fell against his chest. I breathed in, enjoying the sharp smell of boy sweat mixed with cheap deodorant.

'Piggyback?' he offered, suddenly kind, and stroked my hair.

I met his eyes for moment. He looked away, embarrassed. I felt my face grow hot.

'Yes, please.'

He easily hoisted my fifty kilos of dead weight onto his back and trudged down the hall to the kitchen where Laura, wearing a leopard print bra and boxer shorts, rolls of white fat sitting like kneaded dough around her middle, was plonking down big plates laden with greasy hash browns and mushrooms. She looked up and grinned.

'What's the matter, Jez?!' she crowed. Her shrill voice sounded like a freakin' carillon in my head. 'You look like shiiiit!'

I squeezed my eyes shut and buried my head against Lukey's shoulder. 'Shut up, Laura. I feel like balls, okay?' I snapped. 'Just put me on the couch, Lukey.'

Lukey didn't stop, though. He walked straight out the open sliding doors onto the patio, then across the backyard towards the pool. My slow brain finally figured out what was going on.

'No ... no, please Lukey ... LUKEY!' I was still screaming as he hurled me over the side of the pool into the water, fully clothed.

When I surfaced, coughing, spluttering and blowing water out of my nose, Lukey and Laura were standing on the patio pissing themselves. I death-stared them with my most venomous glare, but it just made them laugh harder.

'You look like that evil dead chick in *The Ring*,' Lukey choked, wiping tears from his eyes. 'Coming out of the murky water with hair all in your face like that.'

'It's not fucking funny, *Luke*,' I spat, hoisting myself out of the pool and collapsing over the edge, still coughing up water from my aching lungs.

'Oooooh, Luke,' Lukey taunted. 'She never calls me Luke,' he informed Laura. 'She's really mad. We better stay out of her way or she'll claw us.'

'You gotta see the funny side, Jez,' Laura giggled. 'You look hilarious, like Cousin It from *The Addams Family*.'

I stripped off my wet jeans and t-shirt and lay on a sun lounger, sulking, in my undies and bra drying off while Lukey and Laura ate their breakfast. I could hear them laughing and chatting and Laura letting out the occasional exuberant shriek over fuck-knows-what. I felt angry little tears pricking the back of my eyelids wanting to escape. I was angry with myself for being such a sooky la la, and the angrier I got the more the tears wanted to fall. Eventually I gave in and hot tears rolled down my cheeks, and I let out a pathetic little sob.

'Jez?' Laura's shadow fell over me. 'It was just a joke, hey. Lukey was just showing off for me. Boys are like that.'

I didn't open my eyes. I was fuming. *Showing off for you?*

'Jez?' I could feel her hefty weight tip the sun lounger, as she perched herself by my side and gently laid one hand on my arm. I wanted to slap it away. 'Jeeeez,' Laura coaxed in a singsong voice.

'What?' I snapped. I gathered my last shreds of dignity and opened my eyes.

'Brought you some ice water.' Laura held the frosted glass out to me with a sympathetic smile.

I took it from her, wordlessly, and gulped it down in five seconds flat and handed her back the empty glass.

'I've gotta get home,' I muttered, and started to pull on my wet clothes.

'Why? If this is about me and Lukey ...' Laura trailed off.

'What about you and Lukey?' I met her eyes defiantly.

'He said you guys are just friends.'

'We are. Best friends. Have been for years.'

'I don't get why you're upset with me, Jez.'

'I'm not upset with you, *Laura*. I just have to get home.' I knew I was being totally OTT and probably a complete bitch, but I didn't care.

Lukey was still sitting at the kitchen table. I stalked past him without a word.

'Where are you going, Jez?' he called after me.

The lump in my throat was so huge I knew any attempt to speak would come out as a wail. I slammed Laura's front door behind me and ran all the way home.

Mum was spreadeagled on the brown corduroy couch that she refused to throw out even though it was older than me, wearing a greying and pilled nightie, watching info-mercial telly, one arm above her head, and the other dangling into a box of crackers that were spilling out onto the coffee table.

'Jezza ... Why are you all wet?' Mum slurred.

I marched over to the coffee table and picked up her coffee mug and sniffed it. 'Are you fucking drunk?!' I screeched. 'It's not even lunchtime!'

'Not drunk. Hung-over. I'm having an Irish coffee without the coffee,' she said, clearly tired, and half smiled.

'You are pathetic,' I sneered at her.

'What the hell is the matter with *you*?!' she yelled after me as I went to the bathroom to take a shower.

I peeled off my wet undies and bra and stepped under the lukewarm water. I leaned against the cold tiled wall, nauseous, and vomited down my chest, then moved under the shower's flow to rinse it off. I looked down at my small, pointed breasts, and long flat stomach, pierced with a silver belly ring. I cursed myself. *You are such a fucking* idiot *fuck-up.* I bashed my head once, hard against the shower screen, and let out a small cry at the pain.

I could hear Mum let herself into the bathroom. I opened one eye and saw her perched on the edge of the tub.

'I've got the right to a social life, Jez. I don't deny you one.' Mum sounded upset.

Go away, go away, go away.

23

I stepped out of the shower, dripping. And started to cry.

'Awww, Jez. I'm sorry. I literally just woke up about an hour ago and felt like absolute shit. I had a little nip of Jameson's to take the sting out of my hangover.' Mum wrapped a towel around me gently and sighed. 'I'm working at the club again tonight. There're some of those tofu nugget things you like in the freezer.'

I started crying harder because Mum was being so nice to me and I didn't deserve it.

'Lukey ...' I choked. 'Lukey has a girlfriend.'

I didn't actually know if that was technically true, but I didn't want Mum to think I was crying over something trivial.

'A girlfriend, huh?' Mum said, shaking her head. 'Geez ...'

'And I hate her!' I exploded. 'She's annoying and fat and wears these short little dresses that show how fat her legs are and she thinks she's so great just because she's got lesbo mums and she's from Melbourne and all like,' I put on my best high-pitched 'girly' voice, 'I'm a big city girl moving to suburbia, what a freakin' novelty.'

'Whoah.' Mum put her arms around me, pressing my wet head down into her breasts. 'That sucks, babe. This girl beat you to it, hey?'

I stepped back and wiped the tears from my eyes. 'What do you mean?'

'Lukey. He's basically all you talk about.'

'He's my best friend, Mum. Since Year 7.'

'Just friends?'

'Yes! Oh, fucking hell, Mum. You just don't understand anything.'

Mum did that wounded child face where her mouth turned down at the sides and made her double chin deepen and it always tore me into two, part of me wanting to slap her and part of me wanting to squeeze her in a tight sympathetic hug.

'Aw, Ma. Don't be like that.' I kind of patted her arm. 'You wanna watch a movie or something before you go to work? *Dirty Dancing*?'

'It always makes me cry,' she reminded me.

'Everything makes you cry.' I rolled my eyes but said it lightly so she wouldn't pull one of her sad-sack heads again.

THREE
• •

After Mum left for work that night I couldn't sleep so I dragged her laptop onto the couch and read *Harry Potter* fan fiction on the net until my eyes bled. My favourite was one where Draco Malfoy and Potter are secretly bumming in the Forbidden Forest every night; a lot of great puns involving 'wands'. I gave this the two thumbs up.

Mum came home from her shift around three in the morning, acting a little spaced. She dumped her keys and bag on the coffee table and just kind of muttered goodnight and then went to bed. I was guessing she'd had a few staffies after close-up.

I grabbed one of Mum's smokes out of her handbag. I stared into the fridge for a while, thinking about eating something, but there wasn't anything there: a jar of mayonnaise, milk, a few cans of Pepsi Max. I made myself a cup of instant coffee with two sugars and extra milk, went out onto the back porch and sat there thinking about stuff. Lukey and Laura, my mum ... and serious First World problems like, *Am I ever gunna get a boyfriend?*

I've never had sex. It's not like I didn't want to or I was like dried up down there or anything; I'd hooked up with a few guys. But I was gunna be eighteen the next year and it seemed like everyone was doing it except for me and that really broke my crayons because it made me feel like maybe I was ugly or smelled weird or something. So Laura coming along all wobbly cottage-cheese thighs and more rolls than Baker's Delight macking on with *my best friend* ...

Then there was Mum. It's not like she had always been such a bad drunk. It happened after we moved into this house, after she left my dad. At first it seemed like everything was gunna be okay. We were so excited to have a house just for the two of us. I mean, it's a pretty shitty old house and a govvie rental. The front of the house is still the same—grey brick trimmed with peeling forest-green paint on the eaves and gutters, a little more weatherworn than when we first moved in, one tiny half-dead shrub drooping sadly in a mound of dirt next to the front step. But to us it was *our new house* and, for the first time in years, Mum appeared to be happy and she was so fucking proud, too, because she'd scammed the housing department into giving us a three-beddie on account of her asthma being so bad she couldn't climb stairs to an apartment. I remember the day we moved in she started jumping around like a lunatic, crying and laughing at the same time.

She started talking in excited 'gunnas'—*I'm gunna fix up the backyard, Jezza. A vegie patch for me, a swing set for you. I'm gunna paint the lounge room, replace those ugly old brown wood panels with a bright-red feature wall. You'll get a new doona cover and we'll get one of those big tellies and and and . . .*

Then Mum invited all the girlfriends she'd known since high school over for a housewarming—Shaz, Linda and Kaye came over, crowding our driveway with their battered Datsuns and Geminis and sprayed the orange-and-brown-tiled kitchen with cheap sparkling wines. While frost settled on the grass outside, I hugged the heater in my flammable fleece nightie, enjoying the way it made me feel all drowsy and floppy, until my mum reminded me for the hundredth time, *Don't get so close to the heater, Jez, you'll catch fire*, and then I moved to the couch and watched Mum and her friends dance around the living room singing along to Pearl Jam's 'Better Man' at the top of their lungs.

None of that ever happened, all that bullshit Mum said about fixing up the place. The backyard is still unused; I was too old for a swing set anyway. The ugly wood panels are still in the lounge room behind the old brown corduroy couch and I sleep under the same pink-and-purple lady-bugs doona cover

I've had since I was four. We did get a new telly, though … And when Mum started drinking, like really drinking heavily, she'd park herself in front of it, sipping from cans of JD, shovelling crap into her gob like a zombie.

So I sat in the backyard that night just kinda thinking about all that. Like I said, First World problems. Then as the light started to turn grey there was an old tabby cat near the back fence that looked up at me guiltily. I could see it toying with something under its paws: a mouse broke free and ran a little way. The cat just watched it run for a bit and then pounced on it again. This isn't some metaphor for how I was feeling or anything gay like that, it's just what happened. I lit the smoke and watched the cat play with the mouse for a little while longer, finished my coffee, then went inside to bed.

FOUR

• •

'Yo yo, biatch! 'Sup?'

'Hey, Casey,' I answered, sliding my mobile phone between my ear and my pillow and stifling a yawn.

'Somebody wake up on the wrong side of the bed?'

'Nah. I'm just tired.'

'Man up, Jez Pez! I still haven't slept! Best night ever.'

'What'd you get up to?'

'Come over. Can't talk for long on the mobile.'

'Why didn't you ring off the landline?'

'Landline!' Casey snorted. 'What is this, nineteen ninety-six?'

'Gimme, like, half an hour.'

'It's freakin' midday! I'll give you fifteen.'

'What are we doin'?'

'Mad hangs, fuckin' mayhem, fuckin' whatever. Come over.'

I hung up the phone and groaned. I'd cocooned myself in a single bed sheet, an electric fan aimed at my face. The curtains were closed and my bedroom was lovely and dark, but the cracks of light that seeped under the bottom of the curtain warned of another scorching hot day outside.

I pulled on my black satin kimono-style bathrobe, popped a piece of strawberry bubble gum in my mouth to get rid of my shitty dry mouth and wandered down the hall to my mum's room. She was still in bed, sprawled out on her stomach, limbs in rock-climbing position. Even though her arms were over her head, the folds of fat on her back looked like Uluru under her orangey satin camisole. I flopped belly-down next to her.

'Muuuum,' I whispered, leaning close to her ear. 'Mum. Wake up!'

'Eeeeer,' Mum grunted. 'What time is it?'

'Time to get up,' I said, flattening the bubble gum on my tongue so I could blow a bubble.

She sniffed. 'Bubble gum for brekkie, Jez?'

'Technically I think it's lunchtime.'

'Really? Ugh. I've got to stop sleeping so late. I've got washing to do. You going to help me? I noticed you've just about filled the hamper.'

I avoided her question. 'You want a coffee?'

Mum opened one eye suspiciously. 'Yeeeeah. Why are you being so nice?'

'No reason,' I spoke quickly. 'But if you'd be so kind as to spot me a twenty, then that would be super rad of you and I'll love you forever and I'll do the next two loads of washing.'

'When are you gunna start looking for a job, Jez?'

I sighed loudly. 'I finished school, like, two weeks ago. After New Year, okay? I promise.'

Mum pulled the doona over her head and sighed. 'What's the money for?' Her voice was muffled from beneath the bedding.

I knew she was anxious to make amends for our argument the day before. Mum was like that. I would get angry with her for drinking, then she would get upset, then I would ignore her for a day or two, and then she would feel guilty and everything would be okay again for a little while.

'I'm just going out.'

'So you've made up with Lukey, then?' She re-emerged from under the doona.

'I haven't heard from him. I'm goin' next door.'

'To Casey's?' Mum said, raising her eyebrows.

'She's alright.'

'You reckon?' Mum grunted.

Casey Holland has been my next-door neighbour since Mum and I moved into the neighbourhood about a decade ago. Casey was a bit older than me, just turned eighteen, and the type of girl whose own parents referred to as a 'handful', but other parents and authority figures referred to as 'trouble'.

'So can I have some money, puh-leeeese?' I begged.

'Take a twenty from my purse …'

'Thank you, Mummy! I love you!'

'But that's it for the rest of this week. Milk and two sugars!'

I was already halfway down the hall to the kitchen. 'Shower or coffee first, Mum?' I called behind me. I stopped in front of the stereo and slipped in a CD.

'Shower!' Mum yelled over the crescendo of guitar, drums and bass that belted out.

While Mum was in the bathroom I tugged on a pair of stovepipe black jeans and a faded grey singlet and put my hair in a ponytail. I went out to our little patio table that was set up on the back porch and pulled my legs up under my chin, lit a smoke and started reading this awesome graphic novel that Lukey had loaned me, *Preacher*. I had only started getting into comics about a year earlier; mostly I got into reading fan fiction, which was my number-one way to waste a few hours. I loved that all these strangers could hop on the net and share their imaginings of another world. I also liked that being a total nerdlinger (in an ironic way, obviously) was becoming cool again, mostly because I was so shit at sport, and not great at book-smart stuff either. Maybe I could have been smart. I mean, I was okay when I was in primary school, kind of creative, too. But that was back when Mum would (could) help me with my homework. I think it got too hard for her. I'd take home maths and she'd be, like, 'Fuuuuu …' and shake her head kind of embarrassed and go, 'Can't you go look it up on the net?' That was also around the time Mum started working nights at the club so I would dodge homework for hangs with Lukey. So maybe I could have been smart, but stuff doesn't always work out like that.

Mum joined me on the porch, her hair wet and combed back, her face still not made up. She looked older than her thirty-three years, her fat face still blotchy from the heat of the shower. Probably hung-over, too.

'Reading on the school holidays? Don't you have more constructive ways of spending your time?' Mum teased as she lowered herself into a deckchair.

'I'm scoring heroin later today,' I said drily.

Mum ignored my sarcasm and sipped the coffee I had made her. 'Mmm. Good coffee. Thank you.'

'You're welcome.'

Mum shielded her eyes against the sun. There wasn't much of a view from our yard. We could see the roofs of our neighbours' houses; a large pine that grew in the corner of Casey's backyard. In the distance, if you stood so you were looking between houses and powerlines and trees, you could see the purple silhouette of the Brindabella Mountains in the distant landscape. The yard was basically an oblong of sparse yellow grass, about thirty centimetres high in patches. A small shed stood in the corner. A concrete path led from the porch to the Hills Hoist, decorated with multi-coloured plastic pegs, which creaked with the hot breeze, joining in a chorus with the annoying squawking of cockatoos and chatter of the parrots, which I would probably take a gun to if I wasn't so staunch on animal rights.

'We should do something with this yard,' Mum murmured.

She said this too frequently for me to take it seriously. I picked up a bowl of soggy frosted cereal from the table and shovelled an oversized spoonful into my mouth.

'Thish schereal ish sho grosshh,' I said, spitting flakes across my lap.

'Nice,' she commented.

'Meh.' I shrugged and flicked my fringe out of my eyes. 'You working tonight?' I asked.

'As always,' Mum confirmed. 'I've got Sunday off, though. You want to do something? Dinner? DVDs?'

'Uuuum. Yeah, maybe.'

'Oh, okay.'

Mum's disappointment crossed her face like a shadow.

'We'll hang out Sunday,' I assured her.

A grateful smile lit up her eyes. When she smiled and the fat on her cheeks kind of stretched out a bit, I could see how we kind of looked alike, the same small noses that turned up slightly, eyes set just wide enough to look a little weird. We had the same curled upper lip that rested upon a set of large, square front teeth—one of the things I hated most about my face. When I got nervous, I held my hand in front of my mouth to hide the bunny chompers. Most of the time I felt lucky to have my father's build—gangly, long-limbed and stupidly thin—whereas Mum was short and big-boobed and had an arse like the back of a bus.

Our novelty doorbell chimed 'Waltzing Matilda'.

'I'll get it.' I hopped up.

Lukey was on the front-door step looking freshly showered and shaved, his long black fringe combed over his eyes. He was wearing long shorts and an Embrace t-shirt. He glanced up briefly then looked at his black Volleys, his hands shoved deep in his pockets.

'What're you doin' here?' I asked. I fished in my jeans pocket for another piece of bubble gum, unwrapped it and popped it in my mouth.

'Just seein' what you're doin'. Goin' over to Laura's for a swim.'

My hand flew up to tug on my hair, irritated as fuck but trying sooo hard to act casual. 'You're goin' in the wrong direction, then.'

'Seeing if you wanna come.'

'Nah, I'm hanging with Casey today.'

'Casey? No shit. How's she?'

'Dunno, haven't seen her yet.'

'So you wanna hook up later?'

'Maybe. Chuck me a message or sumz.'

'Cool.' He shrugged and searched my face, waiting for me to say something. 'Well, see ya,' he said before turning to leave.

I shut the door and went down to my bedroom and pulled on my faded green Converse high-tops. I shoved my mobile, the twenty bucks from Mum and pot of choc-peppermint lip balm in my pockets.

'Mum? I'm heading. Later!'

'Don't do anything stupid!' Mum stuck her head inside the sliding door.

'Nah. All good.' I half smiled and nodded.

FIVE
• •

I loved Casey's front garden, maybe because I knew that the rest of the neighbourhood hated it. Casey's mum had potted plants, shrubs and cacti in all sorts of weird receptacles she'd collected: toilets bowls, sinks, bathtubs, beer kegs, ice-cream containers, buckets and old tyres cut to resemble swans. In the middle of the garden, the centrepiece—the body of an old Valiant which hadn't been worked on for years—rusted on bricks.

'Case?'

The front door was open and the flyscreen was unlocked. I let myself into the house and walked to the family room that adjoined the kitchen at the back of the house. Casey was on the couch wearing a canary-yellow spaghetti-strapped dress, her white stiletto heels up on the coffee table, legs spread so I copped an eyeful of a scant pair of panties barely covering her, no doubt, immaculately waxed crotch. Her body gleamed with shimmering bronzer which looked extra orange against her white-bleached hair extensions. She was watching *Dr Phil* on the huge wall-mounted plasma.

'Shhhh,' she whispered and leaned forward. 'I just want to hear this bit. Dr Phil is gunna take this bitch *doooown.*'

'What'd she do?' I asked, not really interested. I plopped down beside her, picked up a copy of *Who Weekly* from the coffee table and started idly flipping through it.

'She decided she's a lesbian after twenty years of marriage, but she wants to stay married to her husband for the sake of her children when meanwhile she is having affairs and going out to all these lezzo clubs at night and taking drugs and shit. Totally fucked up! Look at her. What a fugly bitch. There is no way I would eat *that*. She probably has a big fat flabby grey vag.'

'Gross, Casey. I was just gunna ask if you had any food, but now I've lost my appetite.'

'Yeah, help yourself. But I mean, really. Look at her. A massive *gunt*. You'd have to lift up that fucking flesh apron to find her clitoris.'

'Casey ...'

'Nah, I'm totally serious.' Casey gave me an earnest look. 'If you are gunna be a lesbian, be a lipstick lesbian. I mean, I've hooked up with chicks before but they were hot. I'm not gunna fuck a butch dyke with tattoos and a shaved head. Might as well sleep with a man if you're into that.'

'Yeah, good point.' It was useless disagreeing with Casey when she was on one of her rants.

I went to the fridge and scanned its contents. The Hollands always had the best food, and a well-stocked kitchen full of cheeses, jars of pickles and marinated vegetables, soft drinks, dips, biscuits and chips. I took out a can of Coke and a bag of cheddar cheese cubes, went to the pantry and located a box of Jatz, then took my bounty back to the couch.

'Om nom nom!' Casey eyed off my loot. 'Dude, it's a miracle you aren't a heifer eating shit like that. Gimme some of that.' She leaned over and cracked open my can of Coke and took a long swig.

'Hey!' I protested. 'I'm starving. There's, like, bread in our house. That's about it.'

'My house, my rules, bitch.'

'That was the last Coke, fucktard.'

'I'm chronically hung-over. I need the sugar and caffeine.'

'Dude, you actually stink. Have you even bothered to wash lately?'

Casey grinned. 'I did the walk of shame at ten o'clock this morning from some random dude's house. Walked two freakin' suburbs in these heels in thirty-degree heat. Total bun and thigh work out, hey.'

'You don't smell pretty,' I observed.

'You want some of this, bitch?' Casey lifted up an arm

and dived on me, pressing an acrid and warm sticky pit against my cheek until I shrieked in submission.

'Fuckin' hell! Investigate getting some purse-sized deodorant.'

Casey cackled. 'Sweat is good for the complexion.'

'So?' I said. 'Tell me all the goss. Haven't seen you in ages.'

Casey and I have never been close friends. We've been convenient friends. Casey had been somebody to play Barbie dolls with in primary school (Casey used to make Ken sexually assault Barbie and then the other dolls would be crime scene investigators). We were occasional sleepover buddies in early high school when Casey would get me to read out 'Dolly Doctor' advice requests from *Dolly* magazine and then she would make up mock answers. For example, Q: My vagina doesn't look like pictures I have seen in magazines. My labia are much bigger. Is this normal? A: (Casey) 'You are a fucking freak, biatch. Turn lezzo pronto 'cos no dude is gunna go down on those fat lips.' Since she'd turned eighteen and started going out to pubs and clubs, we pretty much only saw each other in passing. Even though she was kind of shallow, plastic pretty and totally self-obsessed, I found her entertaining.

'So,' Casey echoed, her eyes gleaming. 'I got a job!'

'*You* got a *job*?' I exclaimed. 'Get fucked. Doing what?'

'Guess!' she said, and leapt up, pulling one of the chairs from the kitchen table. 'Duh duh da de duh ...' She threw a leg over the chair, facing backwards, and arched her back until her hair brushed the floor.

'No way!' My jaw dropped.

Casey came up to me and gave me an impromptu lap dance, shaking her small bra-less boobs in my face. I turned my face away and pushed her off me.

'Jesus, Casey.' I shook my head. 'Seriously, you need to take a fucking shower.'

'So what do you think, then?' Casey asked. 'I'm making a motza in tips. I've been working for three weeks and already have enough to buy myself a new car. Pretty sweet, hey?'

'Yeah, cool, I guess. I don't know how you can do it, though.'

'What? Strip? Easy. It's just like dancing, except naked. It's a total buzz, too.'

'Meh. A bit icky, I reckon.'

'Why?!'

'Stripping is a bit sluzza, that's all.'

'There's nothing sluzza about making a fat lot of cash, honey!'

I cringed. There was that old 'honey' chestnut again.

'Pull my finger.' Casey shoved her index finger in my face.

'Fuck off!'

'Do it!' she cried. 'DO IT!'

I pulled her finger and she farted loudly. We both giggled helplessly for several moments.

'Alright, deary. I'm gunna go get freshened up.' Casey sashayed out of the living room, hips moving as though she was on a runway.

I spat out my gum and ripped out a page of *Who Weekly* to

wrap it in. Then I tore open the box of Jatz and bag of cheese and started washing down the salty chunks of snack with swigs of Coke.

'Nice eating style, Jezza.'

I almost choked on a cracker.

SIX
. .

'Cash!' I exclaimed, clearing my throat and blowing a chunk of half-chewed food across the room. 'What are you doing here?!'

Cash slung his green canvas army bag off his shoulder and leaned against the kitchen counter. 'Got back yesterday. Been up north working on fishing boats and that. It's been good. Hard work, but.' He grinned, his eyes twinkling light blue against his deeply tanned face.

Cash, Casey's big brother, had the same bleached white-blond hair as Casey, shaved but longish around the collar, giving him a punkish kind of look. *Cash*. On anybody else it would have been a total bogan name, but he wore it well. I didn't know Cash very well; he'd left home when me and

Casey were still kids, stolen his dad's car and driven it across the Nullarbor before the cops caught up with him in Perth. Ever since, as far as I knew, he had never stuck in the same place for more than six months at a time.

'Is that my fucking feral brother?!' Casey screeched from the bathroom. She skidded across the tiled family-room floor, a towel around her chest, still dripping wet.

'AAAAAHHHHH!' she screamed. 'You mother*FUCKER*! I didn't know you were coming back!'

'Don't get too excited, only till Christmas.'

Casey leapt on Cash, kissing him full on the mouth and hugging him. Cash looked mildly embarrassed as he detangled himself from Casey's clinch-hold. He raked his fingers through his hair.

'You're still one crazy girl, huh?' He grinned down at his sister and then up at me.

'What the fuck are you wearing?' Casey examined Cash's clothes, wrinkling her nose. 'You look like Mad Max.'

He was wearing ripped black jeans and a blue wife-beater that revealed tanned and heavily tattooed arms and chest, and a denim jacket that had the sleeves cut off, with patches sewn all over it. I thought he looked super rad.

'How've you been, Jezza?' Cash smiled at me. 'You've grown up heaps.'

'Of course she has!' Casey exclaimed, throwing herself down on the couch next to me and squeezing my leg. 'It's been two freakin' years since we've seen you, you bastard!'

'I wanted to surprise you. I got here last night but you were out.'

'Where're you staying?'

'Here. I was catching up with old mates last night, but I'm gunna pitch my tent in the backyard tonight.'

'Tent?' Casey shrieked with laughter. 'You can sleep in the house, y'know?'

Cash shrugged, grinning. 'It'd be weird sleeping in a bed. I like it outdoors.'

'We need beer!' Casey was up again. 'Go get a case, Cash! We are gunna get *smashed*!'

Cash smiled at me again. 'She hasn't changed.'

'Nah, not much.'

'I'm gunna get dressed!' Casey yelled over her shoulder, already bouncing down the hall to her room. 'Backyard beers! Fuck yeah!'

Cash pushed himself off the kitchen counter. 'You wanna come get this case? You're gunna have to. I'll need you to hold it on the back.'

'That's right, you have a bike.'

'Moto Guzzi,' Cash said, proudly. 'Let's go.'

Cash's motorcycle was parked in the driveway. I hoped my mum wouldn't come out the front of our house; she'd probably have totally flipped her rag if she'd seen me on the back of a bike. Cash handed me his passenger helmet and helped me strap it under my chin.

'I'm kind of nervous,' I confessed. I was more excited than nervous. I felt like a little kid on Christmas morning.

'You'll be right,' Cash assured me. 'Just hold on to me and lean in with me on the turns.'

I nodded. Cash kick-started the bike and I climbed on behind him. I could feel the power of the engine beneath my body as Cash revved a few times. As he accelerated I felt my stomach lurch backwards. I threw my arms around his waist and pressed my cheek against his shoulder. The denim of his jacket was stiff with motor oil and sweat. The combination of smells and the vibrating machine made my heart beat a million times faster. The wind whipped against my face.

'The best, huh?' Cash yelled over one shoulder.

I couldn't stop grinning. I hoped we would ride past somebody I knew so they would see me riding with Cash. Well, anybody but my mum.

We pulled up at the local shops. I loitered out the front while Cash bought us a case of beer. He emerged a few minutes later and nodded towards the park over the street.

'Let's have one now. Casey will be ages getting ready.'

A concrete path led from the shops to a tunnel that passed under the road. It stank of piss and shit and had a giant cock and balls spray-painted on the wall. At the park we sat on the dried-up yellow grass next to a derelict children's playground that was covered in scrawls of texta and graffiti, under a gum that did nothing to shield us from the sun.

Cash opened the case, cracked open a stubby and handed it to me.

'Thanks.' I took a long sip.

'Tell me what's been going on in Jez World.' Cash took a stubby for himself.

'Not much. Same old.'

'You still kickin' with little Lukey Johnson?'

'He's not so little anymore. He's taller than you.'

'For real?' Cash raised his eyebrows. 'He your boyfriend?'

I shook my hair into my eyes. 'Nah. He's kind of hanging with this chick, Laura.'

'Yeah? What's she like?'

'Short. Kinda chubby. Big boobs. Piercings.'

'I mean, what's she *like*?'

'Oh. Um ... I dunno. Nice. Real friendly and that.' I didn't want to sound bitchy.

'Sounds like a sweet chick, man. Good on him.' Cash grinned lazily and stretched back, propping himself up on his elbows. 'So what about you, Jezza?'

'What?'

'Got a boy?'

'Nooooo ...' I shook my head.

'You're kidding?' Cash took a gulp of beer and wiped his mouth with the back of his hand. 'Casey had a bunch of boyfriends when she was your age.'

'I pashed Martin Carroll at the Year 10 formal,' I said. 'It was gross. Spearmint gum breath. I hate spearmint, it makes me wanna vom.'

Cash laughed. He had an awesome laugh, like a dry-throated cackle kind of thing. His whole face changed and you could see all the little wrinkles around his eyes and his front tooth, chipped on one corner.

'What about you?' I asked.

'Girls?'

'I mean, when you were my age.'

'Fuck, Jez. I'm not that much older than you am I?'

'Nah, not at all. I didn't mean that,' I assured him.

'I wasn't heaps into girls. I was into motorbikes and punk rock and getting myself into shit.'

'Yeah.' I laughed. 'I can remember. So what about now?'

'I like girls.' Cash grinned.

I laughed again. 'I wanna hear about your travels. Must be sweet just travelling around and that.'

'It's unreal. I mean, I was working the fishing boats for a while but before that I was just cruising up the coast with my swag, crashing on beaches, meeting people, busking for cash with my guitar.'

'Wow. Sounds amazing.'

Cash shrugged. 'Anyone could do it. Livin' the good life, saying "fuck you" to the man.'

'I wanna say "fuck you" to the man.'

'Do it.'

'Mum'd never let me. She wants me to get a job, start chipping in for bills 'n that.'

'A job, huh? What kind of job are you gunna get?'

'I have no fucking idea.'

'What do you want to do?'

'I have no fucking idea,' I repeated, laughing like I didn't give a fuck.

Cash nodded appreciatively. 'Nobody does when they're your age. I just wanted to get fucked up.'

'Yeah, I wanna do that.' I smiled.

Cash finished his beer. 'You ready to roll?'

When we got back to the house, Casey was back on the couch, eyes glued to *Oprah*, in a gold bikini top and denim shorts. Her feet were up on the coffee table with cotton balls stuffed between each of her gold-painted toes.

'Beer!' Casey exclaimed, not taking her eyes off the telly. 'Gimme, gimme!'

'Nope.' Cash started unloading the case into the fridge. 'Not till you turn that telly off and come outside.'

'Jesus, Cash. You sound like Mum,' Casey grumbled. She got up and hobbled outside, cotton balls still intact, a magazine tucked under one arm. Her shorts were cut so high I could see a couple of inches of butt cheek peeking out.

The Hollands' backyard was shady, with a small paved barbecue area that was lined with ceramic garden animals. Under the pine tree, a huge bullfrog with bulging eyes sat, smoking a cigar, next to a pair of life-sized pelicans whose beaks rested on their chests. Cash handed me a beer and I straddled the tyre and rope swing that hung from the pine tree, facing Cash and Casey who sat at the wooden picnic table. I pushed off with one toe and swung a little way, spinning around.

'I remember Dad putting up that tyre,' Cash mused, shielding his eyes from the sun as he observed me swinging. 'I was about ten or eleven. Where are the olds, anyway?'

'At work.' Casey yawned. 'They'll be late tonight, I reckon.'

The Hollands owned a bathroom installation business, Bathing Beauty, and worked long hours out in Fyshwick. Mum says the Hollands are 'cashed-up bogans', but I reckon she's jealous because they own their own house while she's in a govvie.

Casey started flipping through her magazine. 'Jesus fucking Christ! Givenchy heels!' she screeched, stabbing a page with her finger. 'Why must you make me so *wet* when I will never be able to afford to wear you!'

'Yeah, that's the key to happiness, Casey, a pair of fucking shoes,' Cash teased.

'Oh, screw you and your anti-consumer bullshit. This is 2009, *bro*! Get with the program. A pair of Givenchy heels is more important than you realise.'

'It's just a pair of shoes,' I agreed with Cash.

'If I wore *this* pair of heels, then people are gunna look at them and think, who is that rad bitch who knows how to dress and can afford to wear designer shit. I will therefore attract other people who know how to dress and can afford designer shit. Success abounds!'

'That easy, huh?'

'Ah, fuck it.' Casey chucked the magazine down on the table. 'I'm not gunna bother explaining the importance of couture to you two fucking *ferals*!'

'I'm not the one who smelled like a football player's crotch this morning!' I retorted.

'You weren't the one *on* a football player's crotch this morning!' Casey crowed.

Cash held up both hands. 'I don't wanna know.'

'Oh, brother dear. Don't act so innocent!' Casey's grin was wicked.

My mobile vibrated. I dismounted the tyre swing and fished in my pocket. A text message from Lukey: *Sup? Keen for hangz?*

I typed back: *Already drinking with Casey and Cash.*

'Who's messaging ya?' Casey asked. 'That Lukey? Tell him to come over.'

'He's hanging with this chick, Laura.'

'No shit? I can't picture Lukey with a girl! That is too funny!'

'I'm a girl,' I pointed out.

'You know what I mean! A *girlfriend*. He is such an emo fairy!' Casey shifted her weight on the wooden bench seat. 'Hey, Jez, did I tell you I seen him out the front of his house washing his dad's ute with no shirt on and I rode past on my bike on the way to the shops and was all like, "Woot woooo!". Oh, my God, Jezza, you should've seen how fuckin' red he went. So fuckin' funny.'

'Too funny …' I murmured, still playing with my phone.

'Invite him over! It'll be hilarious. I reckon he used to have a crush on me, y'know.'

'You think every guy has a crush on you, Casey,' I observed.

'Lukey did! I caught him staring at my tits so many times. Ring him up!' Casey urged.

'Maybe Jez doesn't want him to come over,' Cash commented, glancing at me.

I looked up at him quickly. 'Nah, that's cool. I'll text him.' I started a new message and typed, *Come over to Casey's.*

'So what's Laura like anyway?' Casey wanted to know.

I sighed. I didn't want to talk about Laura. 'She's alright. From Melbourne and she's got two mums. Lesbo mums.'

'GET FUCKED!' Casey's eyes widened. 'Just like on *Dr Phil* today!'

'Jesus, Casey.' Cash shook his head.

'I dunno, Case. I've never met them.' I sighed again.

'That is far out, but!' Casey said eagerly. 'I've never met anyone with lesbian mums. That is so fucking *now*, hey? Like, you wouldn't have got that twenty years ago.' Casey let her eyes settle on some distant point, deep in thought.

Cash and I looked at each other and laughed.

Twenty minutes later, the back sliding door opened and Lukey and Laura turned up, hand in hand. Laura beamed at his side, with pink bow hairclips on either side of her head and a purple sundress cut just above the knees.

'LUKEY PUKEY!' Casey squealed and bowled him over with a hug, messing up his hair with her acrylic-nailed fingers. 'I can't believe you've finally lost your freakin' cherry, you bad boy!' She smacked him on the backside.

'Fuckin' hell, Casey!' Cash exclaimed. 'You're fucking unbelievable.' Cash got up and shook Lukey and Laura's hands. 'I'll get you guys a beer.'

'Hey, Jez.' Lukey smiled at me, embarrassed.

Laura came and perched on the other end of my wooden bench seat. She squeezed my shoulder and grinned.

'How are *you*?' she asked, way too brightly.

'Fine.' I looked at her levelly. 'And you?'

'Aaaawesome,' Laura drawled before meeting Lukey's gaze. 'Really, really sweet.'

'Oh, well that's *sweeeet*,' Casey said, narrowing her eyes slightly.

I glanced at Casey who was busy sizing up Laura, giving her a twice-over. Suddenly I felt myself warming up to the idea of putting Casey and Laura at each other for several hours. Casey would totally rip Laura a new one.

Laura addressed Casey's evaluating gaze. 'So, Casey, what are you into?' She smiled eagerly.

'Oh, you know …' Casey shrugged, coolly, and shot me a look that said, *tell no one*. 'Bit of this and that.'

'Bit of lying on the couch gasbagging on the phone and watching telly?' Cash said, emerging from the house with another six-pack.

We all laughed.

'Owned,' Lukey said, punching Casey on the arm.

Casey poked out her tongue at Cash. 'Not everyone can be a walkabout bum like you, brother!'

'Whew. How hot is it?' Laura observed, fanning her face with her hand.

'Stinking,' I agreed. 'You guys been for a swim yet?'

'Nah, we were just sitting in the air con watching Foxtel,' Lukey said. 'Lazy day.'

'Come over later for a swim if you want, Jez,' Laura offered. 'You guys, too,' she added, turning to Casey and Cash.

'Jezza's hanging with me today! Ain't that right, Jezza?' Casey ran around the table to my side and plonked herself in my lap, hooking an arm around my neck.

'It's too hot, Casey. Get off!' I complained.

'Well don't wear stupid tight black jeans in thirty-five-degree weather!'

'Fuck you!'

'Kiss this!' Casey bent over and backed her butt up near my face.

I pretended to make a grab for her butt and she shrieked and leapt away, squealing, 'Fucking lezzo!'

Casey and I glanced at Laura quickly, and I'm pretty sure I blushed a little. I wasn't sure if that was a super uncool thing to do, to make lesbian jokes when Laura had two mums. But Laura just laughed.

We sat in the afternoon sun, drinking, talking and smoking cigarettes. It was another searing hot day, and the beer was going straight to my head, making me drowsy and slurring my speech. Casey was becoming louder and looser. She brought out a portable iPod dock and put on The Black Eyed Peas. Casey started dancing around, writhing her hips to 'My Humps'.

'C'mon, Cash, dance with me!' Casey shrieked, pulling Cash to his feet, despite his protests.

'I'll dance!' Laura jumped up, her arms and legs jiggling.

Lukey looked at me and smiled wryly. We weren't the dancing type. He shifted seats closer to me.

'So … you seemed kind of pissed off at me and Laura when you left her house yesterday …' he began, looking at his hands.

'Nah. I was just heaps hung-over, hey. Needed to go home and have a vom and crash.'

'Yeah, right.'

'So what'd you guys get up to last night?'

'Not much, chilled out and watched movies. Got a bit maggot.'

'Did you sleep with her?' The words slipped out of my mouth before I gave myself time to think about it, and I immediately wanted to take them back. *Don't answer, I don't want to know!* the voice inside my head screamed.

Lukey started playing with his lip ring with his tongue, something he did all the time. *He has nice lips*, I thought. They weren't fat or salivary, just normal lips and a nice pale pink colour. I started wondering what it would feel like to kiss Lukey, with both of our lip and tongue piercings. I remembered when we were thirteen and had gone to Kimbo's together to get our tongues pierced. Lukey had to hold my hand I was so nervous, but he was really sweet about it and didn't make fun of me or anything. After we left the piercing studio Lukey bought me frozen custard and when I drooled down my chin he leaned over with a serviette and caught the drips. We had to wait for about an hour in the bus interchange for our ride home, so Lukey rolled a joint and we got high. It hailed that night, marble-sized pellets of ice pounded onto the concrete so hard we couldn't even hear each other talk, so we just sat there poking out our newly pierced tongues at each other, watching the storm. On the bus we sat right up the back in one corner and huddled together to get warm, Lukey's arm around my shoulders, my head tucked under his chin, listening to The Smiths on his MP3, one earphone each. When I think about that night, I see us from the outside: two skinny kids with long black hair and piercings, dressed in black, our faces drawn into expressions of practised boredom and gloom. But I also remember what I felt like inside: radiant and perfectly contented.

'Well? Did you?' My voice didn't sound like my own.

'Would it matter to you if I did?' Lukey looked up at me and frowned.

I swallowed hard. I could see the confirmation written all over his face. His words just kind of hung in the air between us.

'Nah, that's cool. I don't give a fuck, hey,' I said. 'Just wondering.'

SEVEN
• •

When I got home later that night I called out *hello*, but there was no answer. Mum had gone to work. I smiled a little; it was nice to be home alone, to have some peace. I went on the internet and browsed Facebook for twenty minutes or so, reading through the status updates: this 'friend' *is enjoying summer*, that 'friend' *smoked a mad doob of chronic hydro and greened bright-orange Dorito voms.*

Yaaawn.

I went to my room and closed the door, stripped off into my bra and undies, turned on the electric fan and pulled my cherry-red fender strat into my lap. Idly, I plucked at the strings for a while, then I pulled my practice amp out of the closet and plugged in my guitar and started thrashing out some power chords. My spine tingled. It felt amazing.

I went over to my closet and pulled on a floaty little white baby-doll dress that my mum had given me on my thirteenth birthday along with all her old punk tapes, old late eighties and early nineties grungy shit, which I fell head over heels in love with. The dress had a torn hem, and when I wore it, I totally looked like Courtney Love in old-school Hole, except not blonde, obviously ... I sat in front of my mirror and painted my face with wine-red lipstick and heavy black eyeliner, teased my hair into sixty different directions and then stood, wide-stance, in front of the mirror, my guitar slung low across my hips, beating out the chords to Babes in Toyland's 'Swamp Pussy', sneering and snarling into the mirror, lost in my own wild, furious eyes. Fuck Lukey and his little girlfriend.

In my bedroom, home alone, I ruled the fucking world.

EIGHT

When I was a little kid, four or five, and my dad and his brothers were drinking beer and playing cricket at the oval on a Sunday afternoon, my mother and I would spend the time in the kitchen at Nan's house. Nan was my dad's mother. My mum had been a foster kid and after she had me she didn't have any contact with her carers. While Mum and Dad were still together, Nan was sort of a mum to my mum. She died a few years ago, of lung cancer.

I liked the kitchen table at Nan's house. The bench chairs and table were built into a nook, so it was like a booth you'd see at McDonald's. Nan would ask if I would like a glass of cordial. She always made it way too weak so you could barely tell what

flavour it was. Then she would set out an afternoon tea: ham
and butter sandwiches cut into triangles, jam sponge roll from
Woolies and Honey Jumbles from a packet. I thought the butter
in the sandwiches was cheese. It was cut thick, straight off the
block, deliciously firm to the tooth when bitten into.

I was used to Mum and Nan squabbling and bitching and
gossiping. Nan was what Mum used to call a 'big personality'.
To me that just meant Nan was loud and smoked a lot. Her
voice was scratchy from smoking too many Marlboros and
she would sit in the kitchen booth, her back to the window,
one elbow propped up on the table, with a lit durry dangling
from her stubby yellow fingers, every second sentence opening
with, *I'll tell you something about* ... or *I'll tell you this much
for free* ...

That particular Sunday, Nan was telling Mum about Pop,
who had died in a car crash just before I was born.

'I'll tell you something about Paulie's father,' Nan rasped to
Mum. 'He wasn't a perfect man. He drank too much and spent
far too much time at the club. But he was good with the boys
and he put food on the table. And that's all you can ask from
a husband or father.'

Mum lowered her head. 'I want more than just the food on
the table. Sometimes we barely manage that much.'

Nan threw her hands in the air. 'What do you want, Helen?
The flippin' fairytale?! This is the nineties for godssake. You've
got a kid to consider, so you can't go worrying yourself in knots
because your marriage isn't all roses and honeymoons.'

'Things just aren't right between Paul and me anymore.' Mum gripped her mug to her chest, her knuckles white.

I remember staring at Mum's hands. She had, and still has, beautiful hands. Soft, not too slender, with long white-tipped nails. On this day they were wrapped around a blue-and-purple pastel mug with a picture of flying kites on the front.

'That's the problem nowadays. You want everything to be instant, easy.'

'We've tried to make it work, Kath. Honestly, we have.' Mum struggled to control her voice.

'No tears, please, Helen. Not in front of Jessica.' Nan cut me a slice of jam roll and handed it to me on a serviette. 'Here you go, honey. Eat up, or it will go to waste.'

'I'm going to move out,' Mum said.

'On your own? What about Jessica?'

'She's coming with me.'

'Paulie isn't gunna want that.'

'He doesn't know yet. I'm gunna tell him tonight.'

'Where will you live?' Nan demanded. 'What about *Paul*?'

'We fight all the time, Kath. He comes home drunk most nights. He smokes around Jez no matter how many times I ask him not to.'

'He's still a boy, Kath. He's only twenty-two, for God's sake. You expect too much of him,' Nan scolded, and sucked hard on her cigarette. 'Stick it out for a few years and things will settle down.'

'Last weekend he didn't come home at all! Three nights in a row!' Mum shook her head bitterly.

'I don't know what you want me to say, Helen. He's my son.' Nan sighed and brushed her greying honey-coloured hair behind her ears. 'He has a good heart. He adores that little girl.'

'Oh, bullshit!' Mum spat. 'He's at work or he's at the tavern or he's at a mate's place or he's feeding our grocery money into those bloody pokies. He's never home long enough to *know* her and —'

'That's enough!' Nan raised her voice.

I shoved the last piece of cake into my mouth and slid out of the kitchen table booth. This conversation had become boring to me. I went over to the bird cage that hung in the corner of the kitchen, near a sunny window, and peered in at the little yellow canary hopping back and forth along its wooden perch. The bottom of the cage, lined with newspaper, was covered in little green-and-white droppings. There were two little feed tubes clipped to the wire on the side of the cage, one for water and one for birdseed.

Nan's house smelled like old people. Mothballs, antiseptic cleaning products, lavender toilet spray. The pot pourri of fragrances made me feel dizzy. The bright light from outside, although muted by white gauzy curtains, hurt my eyes and I had to look away. My belly started to hurt and I felt hot all over. I turned back to the kitchen table, still seeing bright white spots in my vision.

'I feel sick, Mummy,' I said, urgently. 'Mummy? I don't feel well.'

Mum and Nan were in a heated debate, their voices barely controlled as they fought to be heard. I walked to Mum's side and placed my head in her lap.

'Mummy, please.' I tugged at her elbow, looking imploringly up into her eyes. 'I don't feel well, Mummy.'

My mother looked down at me, blankly, her eyes red-rimmed. 'We'll be going soon. Just let me finish my conversation with Nan.'

'Can I go outside?' I asked.

'No, darl. We'll be going soon.'

I sat on the linoleum floor under the canary cage, and plaited and unplaited the fringe of a worn grey rug, which is where, several moments later, my glass of cordial, ham and butter sandwiches and jam roll came back up.

'Oh, Jesus! Jessica!' My mother exclaimed.

'I told you I was sick, Mummy,' I whispered, tears rolling down my cheeks.

NINE

• •

Mum started working at the club part-time when I was about twelve or so and since then she was down there nearly every day whether she was working or not. I suppose it made her feel like she had a life. She took me out to dinner there on Sundays because she said we were too broke to go to Chinese. The club had big bistro meals, pretty much everything deep fried, with an all-you-can-eat salad bar for ten bucks, and Mum got a staff discount. The salad bar was so shit—nothing fresh, just coleslaw, pasta salad, potato salad and tinned beets. I don't know why they even bothered really. It was just a token effort for anybody who wanted to eat 'healthily', but I totally think the same trays of salad sat there all week.

We put our orders in at the bistro and found a table outside so we could smoke. Mum bought me a lemon squash with bitters and herself a glass of white wine. I wished I could have a beer or a glass of wine, but Mum was all about keeping up appearances in her workplace. She handed me a cigarette, though, and I smiled gratefully.

'Just don't make a habit of it,' Mum said.

We lit our smokes and leaned back in our chairs, puffing away in silence for several moments.

'So …' Mum tapped her cigarette ash into the ashtray. 'Feels like ages since we've done this, hey?'

'Has been,' I said. 'So busy with school this year. I fucking hated it.'

'You did well.' Mum smiled. 'I've been meaning to say that since I got your report card.'

'I tried.' I grinned. 'Well, sort of. Telly took a high priority. So did Facebook.'

'Yeah, yeah. And hanging out with Lukey, playing computer games, listening to music.' Mum ticked off on her fingers. 'You still did okay, though. Imagine what you could do if you *really* tried.'

I shrugged.

'I wanted to ask what you were thinking about for Chrissie this year,' Mum said. 'We could have a lunch at our house?'

'Yeah, sounds okay.'

'What about your pressie? Anything in mind?'

'A puppy!' I put on my best pleading face, even though I already knew the answer would be 'no'.

'You're barely home, Jez!' Mum sighed. 'I'd be stuck feeding the damn thing, training it, playing with it. And what about all the vet bills? Puppies are so expensive and ...'

'Yeah, yeah.' I sulked. 'I've heard the speech a zillion times, Mum.'

'Is there something practical you want?'

'Yeah,' I said, being a smartarse. 'Socks and undies, please. I would just love socks, undies and maybe a new toothbrush.'

'Are you going to give your dad a visit?' Mum asked, ignoring my sarcasm.

I paused, using my straw to poke ice cubes down into the bitters that had settled at the bottom of the schooner glass.

'I guess so. If he wants to catch up.' I shrugged again. 'Have you heard from him?'

'He's more likely to ring you than me.'

'I haven't heard from him.'

'Well, send him a text and see what he's up to.'

'Yep, I will.'

My dad liked me to call him Paul, or Paulie, mostly because it made him feel more like my 'mate' than my father (gag). He lives in Queanbeyan with his girlfriend, Tanya, and their two Rottweilers, Bonnie and Clyde (really original, I know). I don't even really know what Paul did for a living. I know that he works in the public service, something to do with building services or maintenance or some shit. He was always moaning about the long hours he worked, dropping hints about how much he was being 'robbed' by Child Support, and asking me questions about what Mum spent her money on, trying to catch her out for fuck-knows-what. Paul and Tanya were totally obsessed with money, not that they had a whole lot to show for it except for the usual middle Australia shit: an eggplant-coloured lego house decorated with Fantastic Furniture package deals, a car each (second-hand, but fairly recent models), and a holiday at Batemans Bay once a year. Woop de doo. They were really just total bogans who happened to have landed themselves decent-paying public service jobs, so they thought that gave them the right to act super self-important and above me and Mum, and that was like shit on my shoe.

When I was a kid, I enjoyed going to visit my dad because he would take me out to Maccas or KFC and to the movies. This stopped after I started high school. Firstly I stopped eating meat and secondly Paul started feeding me the line of 'you're old enough to entertain yourself'. It's like he figured my childhood days were over so he was relieved of parental duties that involved actually *trying* and I didn't want to spend time with him just because we were related, or feel the need to *like* him just because we were related. But I must have had a soft spot for Paul because I couldn't quite bring myself to tell him to fuck right off (a scenario I'd played through in my head more than once). I think it was because he wasn't really a bad person, just deluded and self-absorbed and a bit of a douchebag. It's kind of ironic that Mum left him because he was an alco but now he's doing the whole middle-class bit and Mum is a total booze hag. Seriously though, I reckon I'd rather be a drunk than spend my life with my head up my own arse.

Our meals arrived. A bean burrito for me, a chicken schnittie with veg and chips smothered in diane gravy for Mum.

'Yuuuum,' I stuck my knife and fork into the burrito and disembowelled it; tomato sauce and kidney beans spilled all over my plate.

'Good?' Mum asked.

'Greasy as fuck,' I said. 'Good shit. How's your dirty bird?'

'Greasy.' Mum nodded and smiled. 'We better walk this off tomorrow morning.'

Mum ate one-handed, mashing the food with her fork and shovelling it into her face, chewing as she loaded the next forkful.

'Yeah.' I looked at her sceptically. 'I doubt it.'

'You got your father's genes.'

I didn't really like being reminded of being half my dad's creation, but I suppose it was better than being fat. 'How's work going?'

I didn't really know what else to talk to Mum about. I could tell sometimes she struggled to find common ground with me, too. It's kind of weird because we were close in age for a mother and daughter. Mum had me when she was seventeen and raised me almost single-handedly. But we weren't like those mums and daughters you see on telly, like the ones on *Gilmore Girls*, where Mum is Daughter's bestie and it is so freakin' lovey it makes you want to vom.

'Work's good,' Mum said. 'We've been busy, so I've been getting rostered on five or six nights a week.'

'Yeah, cool.'

'And the work Chrissie party is next weekend.'

'Oh, nice.'

'You could probably come if you wanted to.'

'What night?'

'Next Saturday.'

'Aw … Saturday night …'

'Yeah, yeah, I get it. Something better on.' Mum smiled tightly.

'It would all be oldies, anyways. I'd be bored shitless.'

'Actually a few people are bringing their kids. I thought maybe I could introduce you to Katie Jamieson's kid, he's a year older than you, right into skateboarding and stuff.'

'I know Scott Jamieson, Mum. He's a total douche.'

'He's a good-looking kid.'

'A good-looking douche. And the douche cancels out the good-looking so he's just a douche.'

'Okay.' Mum raised her palms in resignation. 'I was just saying.'

'Why don't you take Shaz to the Chrissie party?'

'Well, actually I already invited her over for Christmas day at our house.'

I let my jaw drop open exaggeratedly to display my disdain. Shaz was Mum's super bogan friend whom she'd known since high school, a nasal-voiced old booze hag with acrylic nails and a spiral perm who, in her own head, was freakin' Samantha from *Sex and the City*, but to everyone else was just a tactless trashbag who spent way too much time talking about dick than was tasteful for a woman in her mid-thirties.

'Are you serious?' I whined. 'Why does Shaz have to come?'

'She doesn't have anybody, Jez.'

'That's her fault for being a gross mole ...'

'Jez.' Mum's tone became threatening. 'Don't start. She's been a good friend to me.'

'A good friend to get shit-faced with and tart onto gross club bogans.'

I never liked Shaz, not even when I was a kid. Until they popped out kids of their own and stopped hanging out as much, Mum's other friends, Linda and Kaye, treated me like their little sister. I was allowed to stay up after *Sex and the City* had finished on the telly and drink 'mocktails' made of red cordial and Sprite and ice, and Linda and Kaye would get out their make-up bags and paint my face with blue eye shadow and red lipstick. But Shaz, when she thought I wasn't listening, would ask Mum, *When are you gunna offload the kid so we can have a proper night on the town?* And she was forever trying to get me into bed and to sleep so they could 'really get the party started'. I wished Linda and Kaye would hang around with Mum again, and Shaz would find herself a hubbie and spawn. Fat chance of that happening.

Mum downed the rest of her wine. 'I'm going to go get another.'

I stifled a sigh and shifted the corpse of my burrito around my plate with my fork. It had gone cold. Within minutes Mum sat back down with her glass of wine and, without saying anything, picked up her fork and continued to eat.

'Aren't you going to finish that?' Mum gestured to my plate.

'Had enough.'

'You hardly ate anything.'

'Had a big lunch.'

Mum raised her eyebrows slightly but didn't say anything. I folded my arms over my stomach defiantly. I was still a little hungry, but I didn't want to get fat.

'Hey, isn't that Lukey's brother?' Mum said suddenly and pointed over my shoulder with her fork. 'He's three sheets. Fuckin' hell.'

I looked behind me, through the glass windows to the bar service area. Lukey's older brother, Mark, was standing, swaying, almost bent over double, one hand on his schooner glass that was sitting on the bar counter.

'He's been kicked out of here more times than any other member, I'd reckon,' Mum observed. 'He'll be banned soon.'

'Hang on a sec.' I was glad for an excuse to get up from my seat. 'I'm just gunna go see if he's alright.'

'Maybe you should stay out of it, Jez,' Mum said.

'One sec!' I insisted.

When I reached Mark's side he was having an argument with Jeremy, one of the bartenders.

'You're cut off, Mark,' Jeremy was saying. 'That's it for tonight. Go home or I'll have security escort you off the premises.'

'Oi'm nah drunk,' Mark slurred, struggling to hold himself upright. 'Oi've had about ... four beers all night.'

'How many did you have before you got here?' Jeremy folded his arms.

'Faaaarkk oooffff. Oi'm nah *drunk*!' Mark pounded his schooner glass on the bar.

'Mark!' I interrupted. 'How's it going?'

Mark slowly swivelled to face me, his face slack and eyes unfocused. 'Jez. Wass ya doin' here?' Mark stumbled towards me and I caught him by the shoulder.

'Having dinner with my mum. Just thought I'd come say g'day,' I said, trying to push his weight off me.

'Friend of yours, Jez?' Jeremy raised his eyebrows at me.

'Friend's brother,' I told him, still grappling with Mark.

'He's had enough for tonight. You want to get him in a taxi?'

'*Oi'mnahgettininnahfarkintaxi!* I wan anudder farkin' beer!' Mark bellowed, spitting his words.

'Mark, you want me to call somebody to come get ya?' I asked him.

The club's security guard, a gigantic Samoan man dressed in black pants and a white shirt, came over to the bar and grabbed Mark by the elbow.

'That's it, mate. You're out of here. Come with me.' The security guard prodded him towards the door like a farmer herding a cow into a milking shed.

'Fark youse all, ya farkin' poofter cunts! Kick me out fa what? What'd I do?!' Mark could be heard screaming all the way to the front doors of the club.

I reached in my pocket for my mobile.

''Sup?' Lukey answered.

'Hey. Just saw your brother, he's getting kicked out of the club.'

There was a pause on the other end of the line.

'Thanks for the heads up,' Lukey said.

'No worries.'

'You doin' much tonight?'

'Dinner with Mum. You?'

'Nothing much at all, hey. You want to come over after dinner?'

I hesitated. 'Hmmmm ... yeah, okay. See you round nine.'

'Sweet.'

Mum appeared by my side in the bar area and nodded towards the bartender and gave him this gross flirty smile, and to my disgust, he winked back.

'Another house white, thanks, Jeremy.' She turned to me. 'What're your plans for tonight, Jez? You right to walk home? I think I'm going to stay here and play the pokies for a while.'

'I'm gunna head over to Lukey's. I guess I'll walk.'

'Okay, well I'll see you at home, then.'

'What are you going to do with the car?' I wanted to know.

'This will be my last drink.' Mum seemed irritated that I'd asked. 'Just Coke after this.'

'Yeah, cool,' I said wearily. 'Well, I'll see you later.'

'Here.' Mum fished in her handbag for her purse. 'Why don't you go past Woolies and get some choccies or something?'

I took the twenty dollars and gave Mum a kiss on the cheek. 'Thanks.'

On the way out of the club I passed a skinny platinum blonde, frizzy hair pulled tight back into a bun, in too-tight high-waisted blue jeans and cropped suede boots. She was leaning over the counter, flirting with the bodyguard who had just kicked out Mark. I would have recognised those late eighties duds a zillion miles away.

'Shaz …' I nodded at her, coolly.

'Jeeeez!' Shaz cooed and leaned over to kiss my cheek. I flinched at the feeling of her pock-marked skin against mine. She stank of cigarettes and cheap perfume. 'Just meetin' ya Mum for a couple.'

'She's cut off after this one, okay?' I sidestepped Shaz on my way to the front doors. 'If she's driving, she can't drink.'

'Oh, sure, honey. We're all adults here,' Shaz whined in a nasal drawl, hands on hips. I met her gaze levelly. *You brainless bimbo*, I thought, and turned and left without saying goodbye.

TEN

It was still hot as I walked to Lukey's. The sun had only just set and the air was thick, not even the slightest breeze. I could feel the sweat dripping down the back of my knees inside my black jeans and I just wanted to rip them off and walk in my undies. I got to Lukey's house and let myself in through the front door. Mark was on the couch in through the living room, shirtless, clutching a VB tinny to his chest, his huge hairy beer gut hanging over the front of his footy shorts. The electric fan was on full blast. He didn't look up as I passed him to go to Lukey's room.

'Hey, how's it going?' I shut Lukey's bedroom door behind me.

Lukey was sitting on his blue check-sheeted bed, several pillows propped up behind him, eyes glued to his little boxy analogue telly, playing *Grand Theft Auto*, a mini desk fan propped on his chalky stomach. I flopped onto the bed beside him and helped myself to one of his cigarettes.

'Hey,' Lukey greeted me. 'Put the towel under the door before you smoke that. Dad's been trying to get us to smoke outside.'

I sighed then got up and jammed a towel in the crack under the door.

'What's been goin' on?' I asked him.

'Not much. Fucking hot. I wish we had air con.'

'Totally,' I agreed. 'Last night I had to wet a tea towel and stick it over me.'

'Ha,' Lukey grunted appreciatively. 'Up here for thinking. I'm dregging hardcore. Smoked about a quarter today, I reckon.'

'Been hanging out with Laura?'

'Yeah, a bit.'

'I've been hanging out with Casey a bit.'

'She's a nut job.'

I laughed. 'In the best way.'

'Cash is cool, though.' Lukey paused his game and leaned over and took the lit cigarette from between my fingers.

'Yeah, Cash is awesome,' I agreed.

Lukey examined my face for a moment. 'You got the hots for Cash?'

I shrugged, trying to stop myself from smiling. 'He's okay.'

'Laura reckons you do.'

'Laura should shut her fat pie hole.'

'You *do*.' Lukey took a drag of the smoke and handed it back to me.

'Fuck off,' I said. 'I don't.'

'No point anyway. He's about ten years older than you.'

'Six years older ... Maybe seven.'

'Illegal.'

'What's it to you, anyway?' I asked, annoyed.

'Nothing. Do what you want. Cash will be the one who ends up in jail. Folsom Prison.'

'Nobody is going to jail. I'm not gunna ... Oh, lame joke, arsehole.'

'Meh.' Lukey shrugged. 'I was just sayin —'

'I'm seventeen, idiot. It's not illegal.'

I finished the cigarette and stubbed it into the ashtray on Lukey's bedside table. I lay back against his pillows, my eyes wandering over his postered walls and shelves full of junky knick-knacks. Old chains, melted wax candles stuck in wine bottles, a stuffed gorilla wearing boxing gloves that Lukey had won at the Canberra Show and named Mike Tyson.

'You got anything to drink?' I asked him.

'Yeah, there's a six-pack of tinnies in the fridge,' Lukey said. 'C'mon, let's go sit out back. It's too hot in here.'

We went down the carpeted hall to the small kitchen. The layout of Lukey's house was almost identical to mine except it was slightly bigger, a four-bedroom whereas my house was a three-bedder. There was a combined kitchen and dining with a sliding door to the backyard. Lukey's house smelled like fried eggs and sausages; there were plates piled high in the sink and crumbs and toast crusts on the countertops. Lukey went to the fridge and bent over to look inside.

'Fuckin' hell.' He looked up at me. 'I had a six-pack of tinnies in here. There's two left.'

'Were they VB?' I asked.

'Yeah.' He reached in and held up two cans still stuck in the plastic ring holders.

'Your brother was drinking VB tinnies when I got here.'

Lukey's face darkened. He slammed the fridge shut and marched through the dining to the living room with me following at his heels. Mark had stretched out along the length of the couch and was propped up on one elbow, sipping from a tinny. Three other empty cans were on the coffee table in front of him.

'Mark, you fat fuck!' Lukey stood in Mark's line of vision in front of the telly. 'You're drinking my fucking beer.'

Mark squinted at Lukey, one eye closed. 'Wha?'

'You're drinking my fucking beer!' Lukey leaned over and snatched the tinny out of his brother's hand.

'What da faaark!' Mark slurred. 'It's my beer you lil' poofter. Who bought it?'

'I gave you the money.'

'Who's da one what bought it for you, you farkin' fairy. Get da faaaark out of moi face.'

'You bought it with my money, you fat fucking piece of shit!'

Mark swung his legs around and hauled himself up off the couch, staggering over until he stood toe to toe with Lukey. They stared each other down. Mark was about twice as wide as Lukey, and a head taller. I reached out and tugged Lukey's elbow.

'Forget it, Lukey,' I urged. 'Don't worry about it.'

'What's goin' on?'

I turned around. Ashleigh, Lukey's thirteen-year-old sister, stood in the arch between the kitchen and living room in boxer shorts and a singlet, a mobile phone in her hand that had little plastic charms dangling off it.

'Hey, Ash,' I greeted her. 'Nothing's going on. Where's your dad?'

'At his mate's. What's goin' on?' she repeated, looking back and forth between Mark and Lukey, who were still staring each other down.

'Nothing,' I said. 'Right, *Lukey*?'

'LUKEY!? Lukey, Lukey … Are you a fucking FAGGOT, Lukey? Your name is *Luke*, you fucking homo.' Mark laughed cruelly.

'Chill the fuck out. Let's call a truce.' Lukey shrugged and took a step back. 'No big deal.'

Mark paused, his face darkening. 'Nah, nah, nah!' he bellowed. 'You called me a *liar*.'

'What the fuck?! No I didn't,' Lukey protested.

'Yeah, ya did,' Mark insisted. 'Ya came in here and called me a farkin' liar.' Mark swayed drunkenly, his lips wet with saliva.

'He never called you anything,' I tried to interject.

'You're a fuckin' mental case, Mark.' Lukey shook his head and tried to brush past his brother.

Mark put his palm on Lukey's chest and gave him a shove. Lukey grabbed him by the wrist and with his free hand shoved Mark backwards; the back of Mark's calves hit the coffee table and he fell over, crashing into the couch.

'You're gunna farkin' regret that, you farkin' pissant,' Mark hissed and charged at Lukey, taking him around the waist and knocking him into an upright lamp. The stained-glass lamp-shade hit the window and smashed, showering the carpet with little fragments.

'Jesus fucking Christ,' I muttered, my teeth clenched in panic. 'C'mon, Ash.'

I dragged the protesting girl down the hall to her bedroom, shoved her inside and pulled the door over.

'Just stay here, dude, okay?' I touched her arm briefly, to try to reassure her.

She looked at me wide-eyed and nodded, but didn't seem too unsettled. I was guessing she had seen it all before.

When I got back to the living room, Mark was back on the couch, panting heavily, his gut heaving up and down. He looked at me and then back at the telly.

'Nobody calls me a liar in moi farkin' house.'

You fucking fat piece of shit! I fumed inwardly and raced through the kitchen, out the sliding door.

The backyard was dark, but I could see Lukey's pale naked torso gleaming in the moonlight, where he was doubled over on his knees near the Hills Hoist, and I could hear him gasping for air, sucking it in and then letting it back out in ragged sobs.

'Luke?' I approached him slowly, trying to think of what to say.

'Get the beers, Jez,' he panted. 'Please.'

I dashed back inside and got the last two beers. I stared at them dismally for a moment before heading back outside. I was sort of ashamed of myself for wanting one so badly after all the trouble the six-pack had caused. I cracked one for myself anyway, and handed the other to Lukey. He pressed it against his forehead and collapsed back on the grass, still breathing heavily. I sat cross-legged near his head and put one hand on his shoulder. He reached up and grabbed my hand and squeezed it hard, and then rolled over into a foetal position and started to cry silently.

'Are you okay?' I whispered.

Lukey didn't say anything for ages. I sat quietly in the dark. I could smell the honeysuckle bush that grew along the fence. When we were younger, like thirteen or something, we'd get ripped in his backyard and pull the stamens out of the honey-suckle flowers and lick the sweet nectar.

Five or ten minutes passed before he sat upright, cracked his beer open and drank from it greedily. I could hear his lip ring gently tapping against the rim of the tinny. He met my eyes and kind of half smiled.

'I want to kill that cunt.' He shook his head and laughed humourlessly. 'I really do.'

'Forget him.'

'How can I forget him, Jez?' Lukey exclaimed angrily. 'He lives in the room next to mine. I see the fat cunt every day. He's always drunk out of his fuckin' skull.'

'Tell your dad ...' I trailed off.

'Dad?!' Lukey spat. 'Dad doesn't give a fuck. "Sort it out amongst yourselves." That's his solution. And he's hardly here anyway.'

Lukey's mum had died from breast cancer years ago, when Lukey was about eight or nine. He didn't really talk much about her, except to say that his family had been a lot different when she was alive, and things had kind of fallen apart since she'd gone. There were a few framed photos of her in the front hallway and in the living room. She had Lukey's big green eyes, but she was chubby like Mark, and had long wavy brown hair like Ashleigh.

'You know what Mark used to do? When Mum was dying?' Lukey asked, as though reading my mind. 'He'd steal her fucking pain medication. That fucking *prick* was stealing her pills and selling 'em at school.'

I nodded. 'I think you told me before —'

'And you say just forget about him?!' Lukey snorted.

'I dunno ...' I didn't know what to say. 'You can always come crash on our couch?'

'Really?' Lukey looked up at me, his eyes hopeful. 'Your mum wouldn't mind?'

He leaned forward suddenly and grabbed both of my hands in his, guided them up to his cheeks and placed them there, gently. Then he took my face in his hands.

'Have you been drinking tonight?' I whispered, my face close to his.

'No,' he whispered back. 'It's not like that.'

I stroked his jaw, rough with unshaven stubble, and then moved my hand up to his hair, which was surprisingly silky and smooth beneath my fingertips. My heart was racing so hard I thought I might have a heart attack. Lukey leaned in and put his lips on mine; I almost gasped as I felt the cool metal of his lip ring press against my skin. We kissed for a moment and then he parted his lips slightly and gently traced my bottom lip with his tongue. Suddenly, he pulled back.

'Whoaaahhh,' he exhaled. 'Intense.'

I nodded, and pulled my hands away and into my lap. We sat, half facing each other, cross-legged under the clothesline, avoiding each other's gaze but subtly trying to read each other's expression.

'You got a smoke?' I asked him.

'Yeah.' Lukey reached into his pocket and pulled out a crushed packet of Winfields.

'Thanks.' My hands were shaking as I lit a cigarette.

'Stay here tonight,' Lukey's voice was low. He touched my knee. 'Okay?'

'What?' My voice came out harsher than I intended.

'Stay with me,' Lukey repeated, slightly embarrassed. 'I want you to sleep here.'

My stomach heaved. I got to my feet and ducked slightly to move clear of the clothesline. Lukey stood and tried to grab my hand. I shook him free.

'Forget it,' I snapped. 'If you want a root, go ring up your fat little *girlfriend*. Remember her?'

'Fuckin' hell.' Lukey threw his hands in the air. 'It's not like that. We've crashed out heaps of times together.'

'Ooooh. So you just want a cuddle buddy to rub your little back until you sleep, is that it? Well, fuck that.'

'Why are you having a massive *sargasm*?' Lukey narrowed his eyes. 'What the fuck *do* you want?'

'Nothing from you, *buddy*,' I spat. 'I don't need somebody to *cry* to.'

We were both silent for a moment. I could hear crickets chirping and a dog barking in the distance.

'You fucking bitch.' Lukey shook his head angrily.

I drew a sharp breath and exhaled slowly. 'I'm sorry.'

'Forget it,' Lukey said, turning away from me and skulling his beer. 'Just go home.'

'I said I'm sorry.'

Lukey half turned and looked sideways. 'Yeah, I'm sorry, too.'

I nodded. 'So what do you wanna do now?'

Lukey shook his head and muttered something under his breath.

'What?' I took a step closer. 'I can't hear you.'

'I said, I hate this fuckin' shithole,' Lukey seethed. 'I hate my fat fuckhead brother, I hate my dad … Ashleigh's okay … but I hate this fucking town and every cunt in it, y'know?'

I nodded. I knew.

'Except you, Jez.' Lukey met my eyes then quickly looked away.

'And Laura?'

'I just met her, for fuck's sake,' Lukey cried. 'How the fuck should I know?'

'So you're just using her for sex, then? Is that it?'

'Why're you talking about Laura all the time? Who cares about Laura? I'm talking about *me* leaving this shithole.'

'Serious?' I ventured. 'You're gunna leave?'

'Fuckin' oath, I'm gunna take off.' Lukey stared straight through me with a scary intensity. 'As soon as I have the cash, as soon as I move some more pills, I'm just getting on a bus and going.'

'When?' I whispered, feeling a little sick.

'After New Year's,' Lukey said. 'I'll move a heap of pills on New Year's.'

'Cool,' I managed to say. 'I mean … that's good. I'll probably get out of here, too, one day … I'll get a job and save up some cash …'

Lukey stepped over and took my face between his hands again. 'Come with me,' he said.

My head spun. I wanted to say, 'Yes!', but I was hot and

dehydrated and still reeling from the intensity of the kiss a moment before. I wanted him to kiss me again.

I leaned in towards him, but he didn't meet me halfway and I ended up resting my head on his shoulder.

'Come with me,' Lukey whispered again and put his arms around me, crushing me against him until I grunted for air.

I pulled back and half shook my head. 'Can we talk about this later? I need to think … You want to play some Xbox or something?' It was probably the lamest thing I possibly could have said.

Lukey dropped his embrace as if his hands had been burned. 'Nah, I'm probably gunna go to bed soon, hey.' He pouted, scuffing his sneaker into a tuft of grass.

'It's only ten thirty,' I pointed out, glancing at my red plastic Elmo watch.

Lukey shrugged. 'Tired.'

'Okay, that's cool. I'll see ya later.' I didn't want to leave, but I turned and headed for the gate at the side of the house.

'Laters.'

ELEVEN
• •

As I walked home I felt irritated, mostly with myself for being such an angry little troll. I walked a little way and then sat down in the gutter and pounded my palm into my forehead and squeezed out a few angry tears. *Stupid stupid stupid*, I cringed, remembering the harsh words I'd spoken to Lukey. What totally pissed on my parade was that I couldn't stop thinking that I just wanted to rewind the whole last scene, to the part where me and Lukey were sitting under the clothesline, our hands on each other's faces, lips touching.

I cut across our front lawn, dragging my feet, digging in my pocket for the door key. And then I stopped suddenly.

Oh. My. Fucking. God.

The front door was wide open, so was the flyscreen, but there were no lights on in the house. I whipped around quickly to check to see if Mum had driven home; her white Toyota hatchback was parked in the driveway. I took a few steps until I was standing just outside the front door.

'Mum?' I called. 'MUUUUM?'

I hooked one arm around the doorframe and ran my hand along the wall inside the house, searching for the light switch, and turned on the front hall light.

'Mum?' I pushed the front door open a little wider; I was half shaking and I was aware of my full bladder.

JESUS!'

The first thing I saw was Mum's strappy sandals, strewed half a metre apart in the front hall. The next thing I saw was Mum's bare feet, at angles, underneath the archway that separated the front hall and the living room. My heart leapt into my mouth.

'Mum!'

Frantic, I kneeled at her side. She was fully clothed, belly down on the carpet, her arms at her sides. I leaned close to her face. I could hear her breathing. And I could smell the alcohol on her breath. Bundy and Coke.

You fucking useless cunt!

I collapsed backwards against the archway frame and pulled my knees to my chest and rocked myself back and forth, choking back sobs. Then I realised I must have looked like I was a bad teen actor in a scene from *Home and Away* or

Neighbours or some other lame soap. I cursed myself because
this wasn't a lame soap, it was real life, so I forced myself to
get up and step over Mum. I went to the fridge in the kitchen
and found two West Coast Coolers, *perfect refreshment for a
summer night*, I thought, not without some irony. Then I went
back to where Mum lay and gently unhooked her handbag
from her shoulder and eased it out from under her right breast.
I took her packet of Benson and Hedges and forty bucks from
her wallet.

Mum didn't stir.

I couldn't stay at the house. I needed out. I needed to go for
an epic walk, something I almost never did because I was lazy
and blessed with the skinny gene. So I walked and walked,
sometimes I broke into a jog, my head down, my legs pumping
beneath me until I reached the eastern edge of Kambah, the
foot of Mount Taylor. I crossed Sulwood Drive and slipped
under the wire fence and climbed a little way up the hill, stumbling over rocks and clumps of yellow grass in the darkness,
until I reached a small clearing. Even from this height, I could
see the whole suburb, and beyond to the Tuggeranong Valley,
in twinkling lights. It actually looked kind of nice at night-
time. Peaceful, and you could fool yourself into thinking every
little light was a family in their lounge room, watching DVDs
and eating microwave popcorn, laughing and joking. The view
in the daytime gave away what a shithole it really was; houses
in orange, white and mission brown lining curvy crescents and
cul-de-sacs, ghost-grey and green gum trees providing sparse

shade. A sunken pit of suburbia surrounded by yellow hills with a giant muddy man-made lake and shopping mall smack in the centre of the Valley.

Kambah used to be a sheep station before it was turned into a big fat shitty suburban sprawl in the 1970s. There are two dead obvious clues to this: firstly the old Woolshed that has been converted into a family barbecue area (and a place for kids to get mashed at night-time). Secondly, the flock of metal sheep sculptures that 'graze' on the hill in front of the Kambah Village Shopping Centre. If a million monkeys tried for a million years they couldn't replicate that level of tack, I swear that much.

I read on the internet that most people in Australia live in suburbs. Automatically I got this image in my head of an infinity of square brick houses, wooden and aluminium fences, lawns, gardens, porches, backyard barbecues. What I wasn't able to picture was the people who lived there. If I tried, I kept coming back to this family I'd seen on an advertisement on the telly, I think it was for a bank or a car or something: mum, dad and three kids, a boy and two girls, standing out the front of a house in the suburbs, all smiling happily, their arms around each other. I think they had a dog, too—a border collie with its tongue hanging out. I don't know any families like that. I truly fucking don't.

I reckon people would have been happier back in those times when Kambah was a sheep station, when everyone lived on farms and stuff. They wouldn't have had telly to show them advertisements of all the stuff they were missing out on—posh cars, Nintendo Wiis, health insurance, life insurance and the latest value meal from Maccas. I look at the suburbs now and the way people live and it's like, they go to their boring-as-fuck paper-pushing or menial-labour jobs to make money to go to the shopping centre to buy crap that temporarily makes their lives more bearable so they can face going to their boring-as-fuck jobs. So stupid. At least there are heaps of drugs available these days. But even that doesn't really work. My mum is living proof of that. Sure, she can forget about her problems for a while when she's pissed, but when she wakes up the next day she's still a fat single mum working a dead-end job living in a shitty govvie in a craphole suburb in woop woop Australia, but with a pounding hangover to boot. I don't want to end up like her. I would rather DIE than end up like *her*.

I stumbled back down the hill, half sliding down the gravel-dirt path, ducked under the wire fence and crossed the road back into the suburb. My legs were tired. I was torn between not wanting to go home and needing a place to stay the night. At the end of my street I paused and lit a cigarette. Then I walked over to Lukey's.

There was light coming from his bedroom at the front of the house so I tapped on the window.

'Lukey,' I hissed. 'It's me.'

He pulled back the curtains and looked surprised, then guilty. I looked past him to where Laura sat on the end of his bed, lighter in one hand, bong in the other, looking stoned and uncomfortable as she met my eyes. I felt like I was gunna vom.

Lukey pulled the window open. 'Hey,' he said. 'What're you doing here?'

'Nothing, man,' I said. 'Just seeing if I could crash, but it's all good.'

'Serious?' Lukey shifted his weight and glanced over his shoulder at Laura. 'You could take the couch? You okay? What's going on?'

'Nah.' I shrugged, swallowing hard. 'Like I said, all gee. I'll catch ya round.'

I turned and hurried away into the night before Lukey had a chance to reply, but I must've half hoped he'd call after me because the sound of his window sliding shut was like a knife in my back.

When I got home Mum'd moved from her floor coma. I could hear her snoring as I passed her bedroom. I slipped into bed, still fully clothed, and cried until I fell asleep.

TWELVE
•   •

Cash and Casey rang my doorbell around eleven in the morning a couple of days later while Mum was out grocery shopping at the Village. Cash was leaning against the door-frame, looking as relaxed as a cat sleeping in the sun. He was wearing black jeans and his denim jacket with the cut-off sleeves, bare-chested. Casey stood a few metres behind him, distracted, frantically working her thumbs on her Barbie-pink mobile.

'Wanna come for a swim down the river?' Cash asked.

I rubbed my eyes tiredly, but instantly had butterflies in my stomach.

Casey looked up from her phone and rushed forward, throwing her stick-thin arms around my neck. 'I got a new fuckin' *CAR*! Well, it's second-hand, but it's so haaaaawt. Oh, my God, wait till you see it!' she squealed excitedly, adjusting the straps of her fluoro-pink bikini top.

'Sure,' I said. 'Let me get my swimmers on.'

Ten minutes later we were zooming at one hundred and twenty kilometres an hour in Casey's yellow Suzuki 4x4 convertible down the Kambah Pool road, past cow paddocks and farmland and the golf course that sat next to Glen Eagles Estate, one of the only rich areas in the Valley.

'Yeeeeew!' Casey whooped as she accelerated faster, a cigarette dangling from her bottom lip, one hand on the wheel and one hand in her purse, rummaging for a lighter.

Cash turned his head and grinned at me. I was crammed in the back seat, the wind blowing so hard in my face I could barely keep my eyes open. Ahead of us grey-green escarpments rose against a perfect blue sky dotted with white clouds. We rounded the turn and descended into the reserve known as Kambah Pool. The Murrumbidgee River snaked through shallow canyons, providing picnic areas and swimming holes.

Casey pulled into a car park, slamming on the brakes. The parking lot was half full with families unloading yelling kids and eskies, and teenagers hanging around cars, puffing on cigarettes and looking bored. The smell of smoking barbecues and sizzling sausages floated up from the picnic areas. Heads turned as Casey, Cash and I walked through the car park: Casey in her bikini, lycra miniskirt and wedge sandals; Cash with his punk mullet and denim; both of them with white-blond hair and golden tan. Then there was me, trailing behind, white as Dove soap behind oversized sunnies, a layer of sunscreen, an old red trucker cap, wearing tight black jeans and a black vintage Blondie t-shirt.

'Let's hike a little way down river. There's a pretty good swimming hole,' Cash suggested.

The river was looking dismal. It hadn't rained in months. There were a few stagnant pools of muddy brown water, and rocky areas where the river flowed more freely. I remembered coming down to the Kambah Pool when I was a kid and swimming in clear amber-coloured waterholes where you could see yabbies skittling across the sandy bottom. The bushfires of 2003 had wiped out heaps of the bush and even houses on the west side of Canberra, and the river was closed for swimming for years after.

Cash, Casey and I marched single file, further downstream. There was a nude bathing area, marked with a sign. From the walking path through the casuarinas, I caught glimpses of old men's pale fleshy bodies by the water's edge. I nudged Casey and gestured silently in their direction. Casey clapped one hand over her mouth to smother her giggles.

'Real mature.' Cash rolled his eyes.

'Take a photo!' Casey exclaimed, fishing in her beach bag and finding a digital camera.

'Casey!' I hissed. 'You can't take their photo!'

'Not of *them*! Of us next to the sign!'

We took turns posing next to the 'Nude Bathing Area' sign, Casey puffing out her breasts and pouting, me and Cash pulling stupid faces.

'These are going straight up on Facebook!' Casey said gleefully.

We walked for another hundred metres or so and found a small beach near some slow-flowing rapids. Cash ripped off his vest and jeans, wearing only plaid cotton shorts underneath, and sprinted into the shallow water and dived under, then emerged, shaking droplets off his hair like a dog. Casey crinkled her nose.

'I'm going to sunbathe first,' she said, and spread out her oversized beach towel. She got out the latest copy of *New Weekly*, a bag of sour gummi worms and a can of Fanta.

'Damn.' I eyed her sugar stash enviously. 'I wish I'd thought to bring some food.'

'Lucky I know what a pig you are!' Casey dug in her bag and handed me a packet of peanut M&Ms.

'You're the best, Casey!' I singsonged and threw myself on her for a hug.

'Yeah, yeah … You want a magazine, too?'

'Come for a swim, Jez!' Cash called, perched on a rock on the other side of the river.

'You gunna swim?' I asked Casey.

She rolled over and fluttered her fingers next to her eyes. 'Don't want to ruin my eye make-up. I'll just bake.'

I shoved a handful of peanut M&Ms in my mouth. 'I'll be back,' I told Casey. I stood up to peel off my jeans and t-shirt.

I could feel Cash's eyes on me as I waded into the water, carefully avoiding rocks and sticks. When the water was up to my thighs I dived forward and swam to where Cash was sitting.

'Let's go up the rapids to the next pool.' Cash pointed. 'It might be deeper.'

I shaded my eyes with one hand as I looked up-river. There was a set of small rapids bordered by huge grey boulders separating us from the next waterhole, which was lined with casuarinas and escarpment, inaccessible from the walking track.

'Yeah, okay,' I agreed.

We swam against the current to the rapids, and then clambered up the rocks, practically on all fours because they were so slippery. My foot got wedged between two big rocks and I fell forward, banging my knees. I cursed loudly, '*FUUUUUCK!*' Cash turned around and looked at me, lying face forward over the rocks, the river water hitting my chest and face causing me to cough and splutter. He stuck out his hand.

'Fail!' he said, laughing. 'You want some help?'

I grunted and accepted his hand. He pulled me up and into his body, and wrapped his arm around my waist.

'I'm okay now,' I said, moving away from him slightly. 'Just tripped on those stupid rocks.'

'What the hell are you guys *doing*?!' Casey screeched from the beach, propped up on her elbows. 'You're crazy, Jez!'

'We're exploring!' Cash yelled, and grinned down at me.

'Huh!' I grunted again, my knees still aching from hitting the rocks.

'When we used to come down here years ago the water was so deep you could bomb off rocks and cliffs that were, like, three or four metres high,' Cash remembered.

'Totally!' I said. 'I used to jump off the highest platform at Bombing Rock. My mum would nearly be having a heart attack.'

'You're a pretty tough chick, hey?' Cash raised his eyebrows.

I smiled, all false confidence. 'I guess not much scares me.'

'You want to keep going?' Cash gestured up-river.

We waded upstream, Cash holding out his hand to help me negotiate the slippery rocks, until we reached the next pool of still water.

'Watch,' Cash said, and climbed out of the water onto a big grey boulder, about two metres above the waterhole. 'Yeeeeew!' he yelled as he bombed off the rock, knees tucked to his chest.

I pushed off into the deeper water, breast-stroking in the maple-coloured river until I reached the shore, a shady crescent of sand just behind some overhanging pines.

'Nice spot,' Cash called from where he was treading water. 'You wanna bum there for a bit?'

'Bum there?' I pretended to be shocked.

'Ha!' Cash snorted. 'Bum around. Hang.'

'Sure.' I was a little hesitant. We were far enough upstream now that we were out of Casey's sight.

Cash waded out of the water and collapsed onto the grainy beach a couple of metres from where I was perched on a rock, my knees pulled up to my chest. I shivered and rubbed my goose-fleshy arms.

'Cold out of the sun,' I commented.

'Yeah, it is a bit.'

'So, what're you gunna do after you leave here, like, after Christmas or whatever?' I asked, trying to sound casual.

'I've got some options. Got a bit of cash at the moment so I'll probably head down to Victoria round Daylesford area. I've got some mates living on a property down there.'

'That sounds awesome,' I said. 'I'm jealous.'

Cash shrugged. 'I get itchy feet.'

I nodded. 'I'm starting to know the feeling.'

'It's peaceful out bush. Heaps of my mates are into bikes so I help 'em out fixing up old bikes and get a free bed.'

'I've never even been out of New South Wales,' I admitted.

'If you wanted to come ...'

I looked up at him, surprised. 'Are you serious?'

'Sure.' Cash shrugged. 'Why not?'

'I don't have any money,' I pointed out. 'And my mum would kill me. And school starts again in February.'

'Yeah, true.' Cash propped himself up on his elbows and ran his hand through his tangled hair. 'But if you really wanted to, you'd just do it.'

'I s'pose ...'

'It'd be fun travelling with somebody, too. Gets kinda boring being out on your own. I mean, I've met heaps of people from all over, but it'd be cool to travel with somebody.'

'Yeah?'

'The first time I took off my mate Jeremy came with me.'

'Jeremy who works at the club?'

'You know him?'

'My mum still works there.'

'Yeah. We got to Albury and he freaked out that he'd get in heaps of trouble. Caught the bus back home.'

'Did you get in much trouble? That time you took your dad's car?'

'Dad didn't press charges, if that's what you mean.'

'But didn't you end up in jail? That's what Casey told me.'

Cash laughed. 'Don't stand between Casey and a good story.'

'So you didn't?'

'I've spent nights in holding cells here and there.'

'What's it like?'

'Alright. Just a bed. Blanket. Toilet in the corner. They take your shoes and all of your shit, even take the earrings out of your ears, I dunno why, but you get it all back in the morning.'

'Fuck ...' I exhaled, a little awed. 'I don't think I've met anyone besides you who's actually been to jail.'

'That's a bit weird, coming from Kambah, isn't it?'

'Actually, Lukey's brother ...' I admitted.

'See, I'm not the only bad boy.'

'You're not that bad.'

Cash got up and sat next to me on the rock. 'You know, Jez, even when you were younger you were always different to Casey.'

I laughed. 'Me and Casey are both girls … that's where it ends.'

'I dig it.'

I nodded, holding my breath. 'Thanks.'

'Can I kiss you?' Cash asked, picking up my hand and holding it in his.

I nodded again and turned my face towards his, my eyes closed. I could feel his breath, warm on my neck, as he kissed beneath my ear, and then along my cheek, then down to my mouth while his arm slid around my waist.

Whooooah! This is AWESOME!

This was a totally different feeling to kissing Lukey under the clothesline a few days earlier. With Lukey it had been sweet, tender and gentle. Cash's kisses were hot and wet and urgent and made me feel dizzy and euphoric and blazingly *turned on*.

So this is what it feels like …

Cash pulled back.

'You okay?' he whispered, leaning in and sort of giving me a little hug.

'Of course!' I squeezed him back, and buried my face in his chest so I could catch my breath.

His armpit, close to my face, smelled like strong body odour, but not the gross type where you feel like you want to vom, but that intoxicating sweat smell. We kissed again. Cash slid his hand along the outside of my breast and I nearly fucking lost it.

Cash and I were still kissing when something caught the corner of my eye. A flash of white gleamed in the sun from across the river.

Oh. My. God.

I scrambled to my feet and ran to the water's edge. There was another flash of chalk-coloured flabby skin as the old man ducked behind a cluster of boulders and scraggly tree roots.

'I can see you, you fucking pervert!' I screamed across the river.

'What the fuck?!' Cash exclaimed. 'Who is it?'

'Some old pervert with his hand on his cock!' I muttered, trying to pinpoint where the old man was exactly.

Cash covered his face, trying to smother a laugh, unsuccessfully.

'It's not *funny!*' I seethed. 'It's *disgusting.*'

'You want me to go bash him?' Cash grinned, putting his arm around my shoulders.

'*I* want to go bash him.'

'Don't worry about him, hey. Just a dirty old man getting his rocks off.'

'Don't worry?! It's sick. Why do they have a nude bathing area here anyway?'

'A place for the perverts to go, I guess.'

'Right near where kids are having picnics.'

'Yeah.' Cash shrugged. 'Should we write a letter?'

'It's not funny! It's really fucked up!'

'Sorry, Jez,' Cash said, but his eyes were shining with laughter.

'We should probably get back to Casey, hey,' I said, suddenly feeling awkward, my cheeks burning.

Cash slid his hand to my lower back while he studied my face. 'Yeah, if you want. Hey, cheer up.'

Cash leaned in as though he was going to kiss me again, but I stepped away from him towards the water. 'Let's go, then.'

I felt so hot all over that I was almost surprised the water didn't make a hissing noise as I waded in; the muscles in my legs had liquefied.

It was sort of the same way I felt the first time I got really stoned. It was seventh grade, and Lukey and I were about to walk home when Martin Carroll called out to us, *Hey, Jez, Lukey! Wanna go for a smoke?*, and held up a little brass-coloured tin. We walked across the oval and then sat in some of the long grass that separated the school from the residential area. Martin pulled a dirty sock out of his backpack, from inside the sock a plastic bag, and then unwrapped a home-made bong—a metal stem forced into a melted hole in the side of a Clearasil bottle. He filled the Clearasil bong with water from his drink bottle and then packed the cone piece with chopped up weed spun with tobacco and handed it to me. *Just cover the shotty, here, with your thumb and suck on the top, here, while you light the cone.* I got giggly with excited anticipation; it took me a minute or two before I could compose myself enough to light the bong. I sucked as hard as I could and the lit weed fell through the funnel of the cone piece. I could feel my chest expand with the large lungful of smoke. It tickled my throat so I had to splutter it out, coughing. Lukey and Martin laughed and high-fived me. *You took it in one toke, dude ... Awesome.*

Cash made me feel the same giddiness that being stoned did. My limbs were getting all spaz and unco and my head felt like it had filled with helium. I dived underwater and held my breath, opening my eyes so I could see. A couple of metres below, some small fish flitted past. I let out a lungful of air and watched the bubbles rise to the surface.

As I emerged Cash ran into the river after me and belly-flopped, splashing me with water. I grinned and pushed both of my hands along the water's surface, spraying him in the face. *It is so much better*, I thought, *just mucking around like this*. I felt like things were moving too quickly.

We slid down the little rapids on our butts, pushing ourselves along with our hands, helped by the weight of the current, Cash yelling, '*Yeeeeew!*' as we skidded over the last of the rapids, into waist-deep water, one after the other.

Casey stood up as we paddled over to where she was on the beach.

'Where have you guys been?!' she moaned. 'I'm so over this shithole.'

'We haven't been here that long, Case,' Cash pointed out, as we waded out of the water and grabbed our towels.

Casey had the attention span of a ferret, never satisfied with what she was currently doing, always looking for the next excitement. I guess I could kind of relate. When I was at home it wasn't uncommon for me to be found on the couch, laptop on with several browser windows open, listening to music, watching telly, drinking a cup of tea and distractedly gasbagging to Lukey on my mobile, usually saying something like, *God, I'm sooo fuckin' bored* ...

'Let's go see if Stu's home!' Casey said.

'Who's Stu?' I wanted to know.

'An old mate of mine who Casey has the hots for.' Cash rolled his eyes. 'He's a bit of a derro, I gotta warn you.'

'He is hot!' Casey said, her eyes gleaming. 'And he has a pool! Which is better than swimming in this stinking cesspool. Seriously, you guys smell, and I don't want river smell in my new bikini.'

'What do you reckon, Jez?' Cash asked.

'Sure.' I shrugged. 'Whatever.'

'Oh, my God, Jez!' Casey started giggling. 'You look like you've shat yourself! You've got mud and crap all over your butt!'

'Where?' I twisted around, stupidly trying to see the back of my bikini bottom.

'Cash!' Casey doubled over, hooting. 'Yours is even worse! Fuckin' hell!'

'Ah, fuck it!' Cash laughed. 'We had fun, hey Jez?'

I half nodded and pulled my jeans and t-shirt on over my wet, sandy swimmers, shifting uncomfortably at the grit stuck up my crotch.

The car park was swarming with people when we got back to the car, mostly teenagers competing for airtime with their bass speakers, blasting out extremely lame psy-trance and happy hardcore. So fucking nineties. They stood in clusters around souped-up Holdens, Fords and Mazdas, smoking cigarettes. The boys wore baseball caps, long shorts and brand-name tees; the girls denim miniskirts, short shorts and singlets, every colour of thong on their feet. It was blazingly hot and everybody seemed to move in slow motion, as though it were a struggle to move or talk. I couldn't wait to find a toilet to rinse the river bed out of my bikini pants.

'Britney!' A guy with short brown hair and a bright yellow t-shirt yelled in our direction, his mates looking on, interested. He and a couple of his friends started walking towards us.

'Oh, God,' Casey swore under her breath and shot me an urgent look. 'Let's go!'

'Are they talking to you, Case?' Cash looked at her quizzically. 'You want me to sort 'em out?'

'I look like every blonde.' Casey lowered her sunglasses over her eyes, flicking her hair. 'They've got the wrong person.'

'Hey, Britney!' The guy came closer and grinned, nudging his mates. 'It is you. Remember me? James? You gave me a lap dance the other night for my birthday.'

'Not me, honey.' Casey started the car. 'You've got the wrong person.' She stuck her tongue out at the boys as she put the car in reverse.

'Wait a sec! We just wanna talk to ya!' James leaned through the driver's side window.

'Get your fuckin' hands off the car, dickhead,' Cash warned. 'Drive, Casey.'

'Oi! Give us a free fuck, ya fucking whore!' James slapped the hood of the jeep.

'Drive, Casey!' I urged her.

She nodded, dazed, and began backing out of the car park.

One of James's mates ran alongside the driver's side window of Casey's jeep, screaming, 'BRITNEY! I LOVE YOU!'

I could hear their shouts of of laughter fade behind us. Casey's shoulders were hunched over the wheel. I reached out and touched her arm.

'You okay, dude?'

She shook me off with a flick of her wrist. 'Yeah. Fuckin' idiots, that's all.'

Cash glanced back at me and then to Casey.

'You know those guys?' he yelled over the rushing wind.

Casey moved one hand down, crunching the 4x4 into top gear. 'Just leave it, Cash! Fuckin' hell! Should we pick up some beer or what?'

Cash looked back at me one more time but said nothing.

THIRTEEN

Ten minutes later, Casey pulled the Suzuki onto the dirt out the front of a square grey brick house trimmed with dark-green gutter guards. A row of sparse lavender bushes and thirsty azaleas lined the dirt beds at the front of the concrete porch. I could see the white curtains in the front room part slightly. A face appeared briefly then disappeared again.

Casey bounded up the front steps and bashed her fist on the front door, then opened it and stepped inside, Cash and I following closely.

'Helloooo? Stu?'

'Stu's outside.'

A bored-looking Goth girl sat on the floor, wedged between an old couch and the coffee table. Two similarly anguished-looking boys with greasy hair shaved at the sides sat on the couch behind her with Xbox controllers in hand playing *UFC* on a big boxy analogue television set. The room stank like stale cigarettes, bongs and Lynx deodorant. They each glanced briefly at us and looked back at their game.

'I'm Casey, this is my friend Jez and brother, Cash. Cash is an old mate of Stu's.' Casey took a couple of steps inside the darkened room.

'Stu's outside,' the Goth girl repeated.

'Okaaay.' Casey was pissed off. She wasn't used to being ignored. She walked through the world as though she were in a Pussycat Dolls video clip.

We stepped out into the backyard. The rectangular in-ground swimming pool that took up most of the yard was littered with floating debris, beer cans and leaves, and surrounded by a rusting pool fence. New School metal blared from a small three-walled shack constructed from wood and corrugated iron that stood at the end of the driveway at the side of the house. A huge muscled guy with tribal tattoos wearing a Nike singlet and Adidas tracksuit pants was seated on a plastic deckchair. A smaller dude was perched on a fold-out camp stool while the muscled guy hunched over him, tattoo gun in one hand, scrunched-up piece of paper towel in the other. As we approached, the bigger guy took his foot off the tattoo gun pedal and grinned.

'Cash! Fuck me dead.' Stu, the big dude, stood up and shook Cash's hand. 'Casey, how are ya, beautiful? Who's your mate?'

Casey slipped under Stu's arm. 'This is Jez, our neighbour. She wants a tattoo, don't ya, Jez?'

'Well, yeah, but probably not today.' I swallowed, looking at the spots of blood emerging from the line work on the skinny guy's arm.

'This is John,' Stu introduced us. 'What'd'ya reckon 'bout his tatt?'

I leaned closer to examine the picture through the smudges of blood and ink. It was a Celtic-style cross that took up most of his arm. I thought it was pretty tacky.

'Love ya work, Stuey,' John said, lighting a cigarette. 'Finish this tomorrow, ya reckon?'

'Yeah, come back tomorrow for sure.' Stu nodded.

John left, pressing a wad of paper towels over his tattooed arm.

'Pull up some chairs,' Stu said to us, gesturing towards a stack of dirty white plastic chairs inside the pool gate.

'Stu, you need to clean your pool. I sooo wanted a swim,' Casey complained as Cash passed us each a chair. 'I wore my new bikini and everything!'

'I would love to have you lying around my pool in a bikini, babe,' Stu said raising his eyebrows.

'Oi!' Cash interjected with a grin. 'That's my sister.'

'Doesn't mean she ain't hot,' Stu said, accepting the beer Cash handed to him.

Casey glowed, loving the attention. I narrowed my eyes a little and took a long sip of beer. I didn't know what Casey saw in Stu. He looked like a big gorilla to me. His forehead sort of hung over his eyes, making them look like squashed sultanas. *Gross.*

'So what can I do you for, Jez?' Stu said, nodding towards his tattoo gun and inks. 'Nice little heart or something?'

'Ummm ... nah, nothing ...' I mumbled.

'Go on, Jez!' Casey's eyes gleamed. 'It doesn't hurt!'

'You don't have any tattoos, Case,' I pointed out.

'I'm still deciding what I want,' Casey said.

'Some other time, maybe?' I said to Stu. 'When I decide what I want?'

Stu shrugged. 'Suit yourself.'

'So, who're the *Children of the Corn*?' Casey asked Stu. 'The little Goth brigade inside?'

'*Children of the Corn* were blond, Case,' I pointed out.

'Whatever.' Casey shrugged. 'The freak kids.'

Stu laughed. 'My cousin, Katie. Doesn't get along with her parents so I let her hang around. She's pretty cool.'

'Meh.' Casey sniffed. 'It's a beautiful sunny day and they're sitting around like Marilyn Mason just died or something.'

'Marilyn *Manson*,' I said.

'Seriously, Jez, if you don't stop correcting me I'm gunna fucking bitchslap you!' Casey shrieked. 'This isn't high school.'

I laughed. 'Good, 'cos you would *fail*!'

'*Again*,' Cash noted, grinning.

'I hate you guys sooo much,' Casey said dramatically.

Casey had positioned herself so that she could poke out her tits to their best advantage, her arms wrapped around the back of the chair, legs folded luxuriously in front of her. Stu could barely keep his eyes off her and Casey knew it. Every now and then she would rake her nails through her hair and then let her hand fall 'casually' to her chest and run her fingers down the centre of her torso. I wondered how many times she'd practised that move in the mirror.

'Nothing wrong with Goth kids,' Cash said. 'Just expressing themselves.'

'Oh, my God, Cash!' Casey cried. 'Next thing you'll be saying it's okay to worship Satan and sacrifice goats and all that other gross shit Goths are into!'

'I'm pretty sure my cousin doesn't sacrifice goats, Casey,' Stu hooted.

'You never know.' Casey raised her eyebrows.

'Actually, Katie hired this fucked-up movie last night.' Stu shook his head. 'Fuckin' hell. It was, like, serial killers hanging people up on hooks and then raping their corpses and then the corpses turning into fucking zombies and all kinds of fucked-up shit.'

'Seeeee!' Casey hissed, poking Cash in the leg. 'Gross shit!'

'Me and Lukey watch some stuff like that,' I admitted. 'Horror and stuff.'

'Well, I already knew you and Lukey were weird, Jez, so no big surprise!'

'Serious?' Cash looked at me. 'Why'd'ya watch shit like that?'

'It's not real, it's just entertainment. I dunno.'

I remembered when me and Lukey started watching horror movies I was so grossed out and terrified, but I always pretended I enjoyed watching them because I didn't want him to make fun of me. But after a while they weren't scary anymore; I learned to anticipate what was going to happen— the classic climaxes and twists of the genre were nearly always played out, and I could remind myself that the blood and guts were just awesome make-up artistry or special effects. Watching horror every weekend, soon I found other types of film boring (except for *Harry Potter*, of course). I used to watch heaps of telly when I was younger. I've cut back a lot. The shows I liked the most when I was little were things like *Friends* and *7th Heaven*, because the people in them were always smiling and happy and lived in really awesome big houses and had loving families. When I got older and wiser I realised that those shows were just a load of shit and happy people like that don't even exist. At the end of a horror film you can go, *well, my life is totally lame but at least I'm not on a hook in some psychopath's basement having my breasts hacked off with a handsaw.*

'They're just movies,' I said.

Casey shot me a withering stare. '*Weirdo*,' she emphasised.

'Aren't we all?' Cash said, smiling at me.

'Cash ... Puh-lease,' Casey drawled. 'Horror movies are for big fat nerds with acne who will never get a date. I guarantee you that if you did a survey of the people who watch horror movies they would be the fattest, ugliest, most pathetic losers. Can you imagine Paris Hilton sitting home on a Saturday night watching zombie corpse rape or whatever over a plate of chicken nuggets and oven fries?!'

'Paris Hilton was in a horror movie!' I pointed out.

'Exactly.' Casey threw up her hands. 'She was on the other side of the camera, probably wearing something totally hot before her character got killed. Where she was *not* was on the couch shovelling chocolates into her gob.'

'Why the fuck are we talking about Paris Hilton? Who cares what Paris Hilton would do?' Cash asked.

'Paris Hilton is a skanky whore. I'd tap that,' Stu chortled.

'Jesus,' I muttered. 'Maybe we should all run out and make sex tapes, then?'

Casey leaned forward, narrowing her eyes. 'Do *not* take the piss out of me, Jez. Seriously.'

I sighed inwardly. Casey was getting into one of her bitch moods, but I wasn't going to buy into the argument.

'Not taking the piss, Case,' I said mildly, sipping my beer. 'I'm just not a fan is all.'

'She became world famous after that sex tape, anyways. I reckon she's a pretty smart bitch.' Casey settled back into her chair.

'Hey, Stu, you still got that Honda?' Cash asked.

The guys went inside the shed to look at Stu's motorbike.

'That was pretty hectic with those guys at Kambah Pool in the parking lot, hey?' I said carefully, measuring Casey's reaction.

Casey laughed shortly. 'Dickheads. But hey, I haven't told my parents yet, okay? They would go mental or something. Probably kick me out of home and shit.'

'What about Cash?' I asked.

'Meh.' Casey studied a fingernail. 'Dunno. He acts cool but I dunno what he'd think 'cos I'm his sister and stuff. Figure it's best not to tell him either.'

'I won't tell him,' I assured her. 'What's with "Britney"?'

Casey's mouth stretched into a grin. 'As in Britney Spears! Hottest trashy bitch ever. My stage name.'

'Oh.'

'So.' Casey smacked me on the arm. 'Did you mack on with my brother or what?'

I could feel the blush rising in my cheeks. 'Yeah,' I admitted, giving her a dopey grin.

'You guys were gone for a while.' Casey wiggled her eyebrows. 'Did you ...?'

'*No!*' I exclaimed. 'No ... we just kissed a bit.'

'Duuude. I don't give a fuck if you fuck my brother. Go for gold.'

'I don't know. We'll see.'

'Jez ... Are you still, you know? A *virgin*?' Casey stage whispered.

'Fuck uuuup!' I was embarrassed.

'I just assumed you and Lukey would have done it by now.'

'Lukey? No!' I could feel my face reddening.

'Oh, my gaaaawwwd!' Casey hissed. 'You're a fucking virgin! Aren't you?'

'None of your business!'

'That is amaaaazing. You are like prime real estate to guys, you know that?!'

'Oh, gee, thanks.' I rolled my eyes.

'No, it's a good thing! But babe, you don't want to hold onto that thing for too long. Firstly, there are way too many hot guys out there and you need to start a-fucking. Secondly, you don't want people to think you're frigid.'

'I don't really care what people think, Casey.'

'Okay, maybe not. But guys aren't going to want to go home with the girl who pecks them on the cheek and then runs away. That's called being a cock tease, honey.'

'Then they just use you for sex, though!' I protested.

'So you go out and find another cock! Plenty of cock to go around!'

'Maybe.' I wanted to drop the subject.

'Your problem is low self-esteem, Jez. You don't even know how pretty you are and how much power that gives you straight off, up front. I'm not joking.'

At that moment I looked up and caught Cash staring at me from over the top of Stu's blue-and-silver Honda. Casey followed my eyeline. Cash broke into a grin as he realised we were clocking him, and he kind of shook his head, embarrassed, and looked away.

'Seeee?!' Casey urged. 'He is totally hot for you. Your move!'

'Okay, okay.' My tone told her to change the subject.

'Did I tell you I'm gunna get fakies?' Casey gripped at her chest.

'Fake boobs?'

'Totes. As soon as I can afford it.'

'Why? Your tits are okay.'

'Mine are freakin' A cups!' Casey exclaimed. 'I'm gunna get large Cs at least.'

'What for?'

'Jez!' Casey rolled her eyes. 'Don't be a moron. Guys don't go for flat-chested chicks. I'll make three times as much money with fake breasts.'

'Who cares what guys think?'

'I care, stupid!' Casey retorted. 'I'm a stripper not a scientist. I'm gunna make heaps of money off being a hot bitch.'

I couldn't think of anything to say. For some reason I felt like I should be against boob implants, like I should be saying it was wrong and that men should like women for how they look naturally. But this was Casey. If she wasn't stripping, what would she do for a living? She would probably get a job in retail and work really long hours for really crap money, or at best land some sort of desk job, where she would be bored out of her tiny brain. Or she'd get hitched to some bloke and pop out kids and be a really shitty mother because she is way too self-obsessed to give a fuck about another person's needs. That really got me thinking—a lot of that femi-nazi shit is fine for chicks smart enough to go to university and get proper jobs. And then those smart women with good jobs still whinge about how men get all the better paying jobs or whatever. *What are the rest of us supposed to do?* I wondered. *What the fuck am I going to do?*

'Go for it,' I said, feeling kind of moody all of a sudden. 'Yeah, I reckon just go for it.'

I looked up at Cash again. He was leaning over Stu's bike, his tattooed biceps flexed, stomach rippled, concentration in his sky-blue eyes. *Go for it*, I repeated to myself, and then had to clench my guts for fear of the butterflies bringing up a bellyful of warm beer.

FOURTEEN

• •

It was in the tent in the Hollands' backyard, a few days later, with Cash. It was just another sticky afternoon. Casey, Cash and I were drinking beers, me straddling the tyre swing, Casey stretched out on a towel catching the last few warm rays, when the wind started to pick up and blew a storm over the Valley.

'Fuck! Rain!' Casey squealed, grabbing her towel and dashing inside the house.

'Hey, Jez! Tent!' Cash motioned to me and then pointed to his tent.

I glanced back at Casey standing just inside the glass sliding door, grinning knowingly and poking her tongue between her forked index and middle fingers.

I dashed across the yard towards Cash, who was kneeling inside the tent, holding up the flaps, looking at me expectantly, saying, 'C'mon, Jez! You're getting soaked'. I half fell into the tent behind Cash and he caught me in his arms and kissed me.

Cash fumbled around for a moment then clicked on a pen-light. It lit the tent in a mild grey-yellow glow. The rain started coming down so hard we had to yell to hear each other. So we didn't bother talking.

Cash stripped off my wet t-shirt and jeans and balled them up in the corner of the tent and started kissing my belly, his breath warm on my goose-fleshy skin. I was drunk, stoned, only half conscious. Too out of it to care much whether I was doing things right or putting on a performance or whatever. I was curious to see Cash's naked body, as I'd never really seen a man up close like that before, but his form was all shadows and warmth flashing back and forth across my vision, and then a weight on top of me, uncomfortable and heavy.

Having sex for the first time—the pain wasn't that hekkers or anything. When Cash entered me (such a horrible way of putting it, but how else can I say it? Started fucking me? Started making love to me?) I remember thinking, *Well. There you go. You're not a virgin anymore.* After that, while he thrust away on top of me, my mind started wandering. *Is this supposed to feel good? Am I going to have an orgasm?* I don't remember anything else except that when he finished (came? blew his load?) I heard the snap of rubber as he pulled off the condom. Done.

Cash rolled off me, his arm slung across my waist, his face burrowed into my neck. He kissed me a few times—on the cheek and on my ear. Then I could hear his breathing growing heavier and soon he was snoring. I turned my head so he wasn't next to my ear, pulled my bikini back on and lay awake for a while, curled up under the sleeping bag, rubbing myself to try to keep warm.

'Jez! Jezza!'

I woke half aware that my head was wet, took in a sharp breath and gurgled on some water then shot upright into a sitting position, spluttering and shaking the water from my hair.

'The tent is flooding,' Cash's voice came out of the darkness, but I could hear the laughter in it. 'C'mon. Inside.'

Cash unzipped the tent, and we crawled out into puddles of earth. I could feel the hard mud scrape my knees and shins as I scrambled to my feet and dashed across the yard, through the rain, towards the light coming from the house. Cash opened the sliding door for me and I stepped into the house, skidding on the tiled floor and grimacing at the arctic gush of the air conditioning against my flesh as I stood, in my bikini, while Mr and Mrs Holland looked up, startled from where they reclined on the leather lounges, watching telly.

'Hi,' I said weakly, peering at them through thick clumps of hair plastered over my face, my hands automatically swooping down to cover my bare body.

'That you, Jessica?' Mrs Holland leaned forward against the glare from the telly and squinted at me. 'What on earth …?'

'Been for a swim, Jez?' Mr Holland boomed, clearly amused.

'Uh, no …' I stammered before looking at Cash desperately. He just stood there in his shorts, elbowing me in the ribs, grinning like a maniac.

Mrs Holland wrinkled her face in distaste as she surveyed our sodden, dirt-caked bodies. She threw her hands up in the air and let out a dramatic sigh as if to say, *What am I going to do with you kids?!*

'Stay there,' she said in her no-nonsense 'Mum' voice, her tuckshop lady arms jiggling as she gestured. 'Don't get mud in the house. I'll get you some towels. You'll need to go straight into the shower.'

I stood at the door, shuffling miserably from one foot to the other. I'm pretty sure if anybody could have seen my face it would have been burning scarlet. Mrs Holland emerged from the hallway with two big towels and wrapped one around me and started rubbing me down, briskly.

I'd always been a little in awe of Mrs Holland. She was a short, fat lady, with an intimidating presence, but was as fiercely protective of her kids as a lioness with her cubs, which was kind of ironic because Cash and Casey were two of the wildest kids I knew. Mum and I once watched from the front yard, on one of the several occasions the police came to question Cash about something, as Mrs Holland stood, hands on hips, shaking her finger, red-faced, saying, *He's not the bad egg you think he is!*

Which I found super amusing at the time because I'd never heard anybody say 'bad egg' before.

'You shower first, Jez.' Mrs Holland ushered me down the hall to the bathroom. 'What the hell have you two been up to, anyway? Doing a bloody rain dance?'

'Rain dance!' Cash hooted from where he was drying himself in the living room. 'Nah, tent flooded. Must've got a hole. I didn't realise. Haven't seen rain for a while.'

Mrs Holland fixed me with one more bemused stare before closing the bathroom door behind me, but a smile itched around the corner of her mouth to let me know she wasn't really angry.

After showering I stepped out of the steaming bathroom, a towel wrapped double around my body, damp bikini in hand, and felt the air conditioning blast against my skin again, refreshing this time. I tapped on Casey's door.

'Case?' I let myself in.

She was sprawled on her bed, pink-cased laptop about thirty centimetres in front of her face. She broke into a sly smile when she saw me.

'So?!'

I shrugged and tried not to grin like a maniac. 'It was good,' I lied, trying to be all casual but secretly ecstatic to have her attention and admiration.

'High fives!' Casey raised her palm.

'What's happening?' I asked, meeting her hand and plopping down on her bed.

'Facebook,' Casey replied, looking back at the screen. 'Borrow some clothes.' She gestured vaguely to her cupboard.

I went over to her white laminate tallboy and pulled out a pair of cotton shorts and a singlet, and wriggled into them under my towel, too self-conscious to get completely naked in front of Casey. I took a look around her room while I was dressing. Her carpet was cream coloured, clean and plush under my feet. There were only a few knick-knacks on top of her dresser, and a half-open drawer stuffed to the brim with accessories and junk jewellery. There was no dust, only clean surfaces. I thought of my own bedroom, like a pirate's cave, every surface overflowing with dust-laden shit, burned-out candles and incense holders. I was betting Casey's mum still cleaned her room for her.

'I'm starving,' Casey announced, sitting up. 'Want a snack?'

'Sure,' I said.

I followed Casey to the kitchen. Her parents were still on the couch. Cash lazed on the floor rug, his back against the coffee table. Their faces glowed blue and purple from the light of the flat-screen television, and they helped themselves to bowls of nuts and rice crackers.

Casey emerged from the kitchen with a bag of Doritos, salsa, and two cans of Diet Coke. She pressed one into my hand and then crossed the room to the sofa and flopped down between her parents. Mr Holland casually slung his arm around his daughter's shoulders and sneakily reached into the bag of corn chips and nicked a couple.

'Oi!' Casey shrieked with a giggle. 'Hands off, piggy!'

'I paid for them chips.' Mr Holland grinned, crunching a handful of Doritos in his mouth.

'You don't need any chips, Bruce,' Mrs Holland admonished. 'You're getting fat!'

'Me?' Mr Holland rubbed his beer gut. 'This is all six-pack, love.'

I stood awkwardly in the kitchen observing the scene that was being played out before me. I came to the conclusion that this type of event was unusual for the Hollands. I'd known their family for almost a decade and had never really seen Casey and Cash hang out with their parents. It seemed to me they were role-playing the 'happy family' thing, and I wondered if they would have bothered if I hadn't been there as an audience. Casey kept looking over at me as she chatted to her dad, and Cash would occasionally smile in my direction while he talked with his mum. It was as though they needed me there to reassure themselves that they had an inner family circle of which I could never be a part. Or maybe they felt a little self-conscious because they knew that I was the poor girl from next door with the alcoholic single mum who lived in a govvie house and they were experiencing some of that class guilt that people get. I didn't care, really. Truthfully, sometimes when people treated me differently I felt a little special because I knew I'd had a 'tough' upbringing. Then I'd go home and the fridge would be empty and Mum'd be drunk or stoned with Shaz, both of them cackling like hyenas listening to loud music trying to pretend they were still young, and then I'd feel so bitter and twisted up inside I just wanted to scream or cry or throw a hard and pointy something at my mum's skull.

Cash caught my eye and patted the carpet next to him. 'Sit down, Jez,' he urged, smiling.

'Oh, that's okay, maybe I should get going …' I was smug in my knowledge that somebody would urge me to stay. And I wanted to stay. The Hollands role-playing a family unit was something I could participate in. If they had been a genuinely tight family, I might have felt more weird about it.

'Yes, for goodness sake, stop hovering over there.' Mrs Holland nodded reprovingly. 'Come and have something to eat.' She held out a bowl of rice crackers.

I gave Mrs Holland a smile, which she returned with a quick nod.

'What are you guys watching?' I asked, as I crossed the room and knelt on the carpet next to Cash, my hand already in the cracker bowl.

FIFTEEN

The next few days dragged oooon and oooon and it became too hot to even consider going outside in the daytime. Heatwave. Like, forty fucking degrees or something. I spent hours at a time lazing on my bed in front of the fan with a wet tea towel over my head, surfing the net on Mum's laptop, checking Facebook every half an hour and staring at my mobile phone, willing it to ring. I wanted Lukey to ring, but he didn't. He wasn't even posting on Facebook, and I should know because I was lurking his page, looking through his photos, a lot of them of him and me, identical in our long black fringes and silver-studded faces, mouths drawn into little pouts. 'Cos I was, like, sooo experienced at sex by then (sargasm) I even started fantasising about what it might be like to have sex with Lukey. But then I'd think of fat Laura and it really killed the buzz.

When I wasn't Facestalking Lukey I thought about Cash, and how it had been THREE WHOLE DAYS (six hours, seventeen minutes) since the night in the tent and he hadn't so much as fanged me a text or anything. Even though it was scorching, I pulled on some shorts and a singlet and sat on the porch hoping to catch a glimpse of Cash over the fence. I didn't see him.

I went back to my room and flopped onto the bed. The place smelled stale from the cups of half-drunken instant coffee that were growing awesome little mould gardens and there were crumbs between the sheets from all the biscuits I'd been nibbling over Mum's laptop, too hot and lazy to fix myself something proper to eat. I flopped my legs open and kind of played with myself a bit, buzzing again on the sex thing, this time picturing Cash's face, body, smile … the smell of petrol and dry sweat. It was like when you're a kid and you discover a new game on the Playstation and you just have to play it, like, twelve hours a day. I'd discovered my vagina and I wanted to use it.

I didn't want to call Cash. I was too nervous about sounding desperate. So I rang Casey and the call went to voicemail.

'Hey, Case, where are you guys? I'm bored shitless. Call me back.'

'Jez?' Mum's head peeking around the edge of my bedroom door made me bolt upright and clamp my legs together.

'What?!' I snapped, hurriedly pulling the bed sheet up around my waist.

'Mail for you.' Mum held up a postcard. From across the room I could see a white sand beach dotted with palm trees.

'Mail?'

I never got mail. Who sent mail these days? Only old people. My nan used to mail me a birthday card with ten bucks enclosed every year before she died, and she only lived a few streets over.

'Can I come in?' Mum had her sad-sack head on, and I knew straightaway it wasn't good news.

I sighed and sat upright. 'Can you pass me a t-shirt?'

Mum picked a t-shirt off the floor and tossed it into my lap. I pulled it over my head as she perched on the end of my bed picking at the postage stamp on the corner of the card.

I put my hand out and Mum placed the card in my palm, sort of reluctantly, I thought. I turned the card over and recognised my dad's handwriting, bending back and forth across the page like a drunkard trying to walk home from a big night at the pub.

'Did you read this?' I demanded.

'I couldn't help it, Jez,' Mum said defensively. 'I saw it was from Paulie.'

Annoyed at her, I turned the card over and began to read.

Hey Jezza,
Sorry I didn't have time to call before we left, a bit of a Christmas present to ourselves, me and Tanya are enjoying a bit of a break

in Phuket! It was a last-minute deal. You'd love it here. Lots of cheap shopping, nice beaches, too—almost as good as Batemans Bay! Another bit of good news, we are now husband and wife! Amazing what a few cocktails in the sun will do to you. Wired a fifty to your mum's bank account for your Chrissie present, don't spend it all at once!
Love, Paulie

Before I finished reading the words I could feel the rage and betrayal rising in my gut.

'That fucking faggot!' I screamed, scrunching the postcard in my fist and hurling it across the room. 'Selfish fucking piece of shit!'

Mum tried to move closer and hug me. 'I know, honey, I know. I feel so mad, too —'

'Mum, just ...' I wriggled past her. 'Get off me!'

'Jez, you're not the only one —'

'MUM! That postcard was addressed to ME. I don't want to hear about how YOU feel. Why do you have to make everything about YOU all the time. Go drink a fucking bottle, booze hag!'

I regretted my words as soon as they left my mouth and Mum's face twisted like she'd sucked a sour Warhead. I turned my back so I wouldn't have to see her and tugged on my jeans.

Mum spoke quietly. 'I know it's not just about me. He's an arsehole, Jez. He's always been selfish, you know that.'

'Yeah,' I muttered, searching my shelves for a stashed smoke.

'Where are you going?' Mum asked.

'Outside. For a fag.' I looked up to see her staring into her lap, looking a bit dazed.

She hoisted herself off my bed. 'I'll join you.'

After a cigarette Mum and I sat in the kitchen in front of the fan drinking icy-cold Diet Coke. We bitched about Dad, trying to outdo each other with stories about how much of a selfish dickhead he was and how much he'd fucked us over.

'Remember the time when I was five and he missed my birthday party for his mate's housewarming?'

'I remember when you were still a baby and your dad got so maggot he passed out in the bathroom and got his stupid fat head lodged behind the S-bend of the dunny. I just left him there. *Stuff him*, I thought.'

I kind of smiled at that story, in spite of myself.

'C'mon.' Mum wriggled up out of her chair. 'No point sitting around here in this hothouse. We need some retail therapy.'

'Shopping?' I kind of brightened a little. Mum hardly ever forked out money for new clothes and stuff like that. It never really bothered me 'cos me and Lukey would go 'clothes-line shopping', hopping back fences and pinching stuff we liked off lines.

'Yep.' Mum nodded. 'Let's go. At least we'll be in the air con.'

As we entered the shopping centre, the sight of every store and walkway packed with pine trees and tinsel and baubles, teeming with Christmas shoppers, school holiday crowds of kids and their fat-arsed mums pushing prams kind of put a weird cheer in me. Like, I can be a total cynical bitch about the Valley where I live, and how people buy shit to make their boring shitty dead-end jobs more meaningful, 'cos they can go 'Oooh, look, I have a nice telly and a shiny car, so it doesn't suck that much to flip burgers at Hungry Jacks', but at the end of the day, I guess either I am a total hypocrite or my life is just as fucking boring and dead end, 'cos seriously, put me in a store full of shiny new things and a fat stack of cash in my paw and I'm a happy camper. There's something really soulless about a shopping centre that I like, 'cos it doesn't pretend, y'know? The people who live in the suburbs who play happy families and try to pretend they're something they aren't, *they* are the ones that cheese me off. Shopping centres are all just a soulless shiny veneer of promised happiness packaged into a box and labelled 'Made in China'. I dunno why I find that comforting, but I do.

I was also thinking, *I really hope nobody from school sees me at the Tuggeranong Hyperdome Shopping Centre with my mum.* That sounds mega bitchy, but people who haven't seen her before always have that *'That's* your mum?!' expression on their dial and it really gets my goat because I can tell they are thinking why is she so fat when Jez is such a string-bean. But really, compared to some of the trogs hoofing around Tuggers, Mum wasn't that fat. She did have a big arse, though. A definite apple.

'Where to first?' Mum asked. 'Kmart? I dunno about you, but I need new undies.'

'Oh, God,' I groaned. 'Please don't make me come look at undies with you. Please.'

Mum looked distracted. 'We splitting up, then? You got some cash?'

'I'd love some cash.' My mouth kind of slipped into a goofy grin at the thought.

This is what I mean about shops. You can try to be all anti-consumer because you realise western society is, like, brainwashed into needing a whole bunch of shit that apparently makes life easier, but really makes it so complicated. But I like having money and stuff, so sue me.

Mum opened her wallet. 'That fifty bucks from your dad, and fifty from me, too. An early Chrissie present.' She pressed it hurriedly into my hand while looking over my shoulder. I turned and followed her line of vision.

'Ha!' I snorted. 'It's fucking Jeremy.'

Mum and I stood and watched Jeremy the bartender from the club, wearing a Balmain Tigers jersey and carrying a bunch of shopping bags. He lifted one arm full of bags in a wave.

'He is such a dork.' I giggled.

'Jez!' Mum hissed. 'Be nice.'

'Ladies.' Jeremy nodded self-consciously. 'Doing your Christmas shopping?'

It was amazing to me that Jeremy was the same age as Cash and that they'd been best mates in high school. Jeremy had two patches of receding hair on either side of his temple that left a small circle-shaped island of hair in the middle of his forehead.

He also had the beginnings of a beer gut, terrible dress sense, vaguely smelled of sweaty socks and just generally was a bit of a gronk. Nice guy, though, I guess.

'Just gunna get a few bits and bobs,' Mum said, sort of all bashful and hugging her handbag to her belly.

'Same,' said Jeremy, holding up his shopping.

There was an awkward silence as Mum and Jeremy shifted their feet and tried to hide the little smiles that were tugging at the corners of their lips. I looked from one to the other, drinking in the body language—the way Mum was clutching and rubbing at her arms as though she was cold, the way Jeremy swapped the bags from one hand to the other to redistribute the weight of his shopping. If somebody had told me this morning that I was going to witness this today I would have laughed and told them to get fucked! But here it was, in front of me, plain as Arrowroots next to Tim Tams! My mother and Jeremy the bartender (who had to be, what, eight years younger than her?!) were fucking.

I looked at Mum, and she looked up and met my eyes and then she knew that I knew, and we both looked at Jeremy and he just stared back with his gob hanging open slightly.

'So … erm … Can I buy you a coffee, Helen?' Jeremy burbled.

'Yeah,' I said raising my eyebrows and giving her the hairy eyeball. 'You should go have a coffee.'

'Okay then.' Mum's eyes flitted to me and then to Jeremy and then to me again, the rounds of her cheeks tinged with pink. 'Sounds good.'

'Well, then,' I said, all cold so my mother could see how mega annoyed I was. 'I'll message you for a lift home?'

'Yep,' Mum mumbled, unable to meet my eyes.

I turned on my heel and stalked away, past the centre court and vaguely towards the food hall, but sort of stumbling without thinking about any destination, pushing past shoppers and tripping over kids and prams. I felt shocked and disgusted with my mother. *How long had she been seeing Jeremy?* I tried to think back to all those nights she came in late, drunk, passed out on the couch. Now that I think of it there were some nights when she didn't come home at all and I'd just assumed she'd crashed at Shaz's. *That sneaky little bitch!*

I stumbled into Hungry Jacks and ordered a large fries and a Diet Coke and then sat in one of the booths and nibbled at the end of a chip, but they were all limp and oily and felt gross in my mouth so I pushed the box of fries away and just sat there sipping on my Coke. It was lunchtime and the place was packed with young families, mums who didn't look much older than me, feeding the faces of toddlers as they squirmed in their chairs and squealed and unwrapped their Happy Meal toys and then roared past me, screeching with joy. Amazing the number of fat arses that waddled past, their trays loaded with burgers and fries and chocolate sundaes. Troglodytes and evolutionary throwbacks. Where did all these breeders even meet each other? I sank lower in my seat and clutched at my head, feeling as energetic as a sack of spuds.

It wasn't like I was angry that Mum had been fucking

(which was icky to think about), it's more that it was such a shady fuck, a *cougar* fuck, and that she'd hidden it from me. Mum had never really had boyfriends—scrap that, she had *never* had a boyfriend, not since she got divorced from Paulie. Turns out, funnily enough, that men don't go for single mums who list telly, binge eating and getting maggot as their hobbies. Imagine that as an ad on eHarmony.com!

My mum was more the type to *talk* about men to make it seem like she was still in the game. I remember when I was a kid, on Monday nights Mum, Shaz, Linda and Kaye would watch *Sex and the City* on our sixty-centimetre analogue cube telly. If they drank enough vodka and cranberry mixers they could forget they were four women in a lounge room in Kambah, wearing ripped jeans and Converse sneakers and threadbare cardigans and suddenly, by common bond of being single and fast approaching thirty, they were Carrie, Charlotte, Samantha and Miranda (minus the careers, money, clothes and bodies) when really all they had in common with the characters was that they talked a lot about men and men's cocks and relationships and drank like desert camels.

Men who they had dumped were 'immature' or 'not ready'. Men who had dumped them were 'selfish', 'shit in bed'. Men they were currently seeing 'had potential'. Then there were the men about whom they fantasised—their ideal men who were sensitive, considerate, romantic and funny—that none of them seemed to actually know, but were more like mythical creatures they'd heard about from telly or other women. To find one of these men seemed to be the secret quest of the single woman. I also came to understand that to be a single mother, like my mum, meant you had less time to spend pursuing men, or that the 'good' men were turned off by the fact that you'd already had a child with another man. As a gangly nine-year-old, with teeth that seemed too large for my mouth and eyes that were set just far enough apart to look a bit weird, I decided that I would never be like my mum and have a kid on my own.

It was around that time that Kaye and Linda both got pregnant within a year of each other. Shaz had announced loudly, pointedly staring at me, that now the party was *really* over. And she was right. Kaye and Linda stopped coming around to our house for drinks and gossip and dinner parties. And when they showed up months later with softly wrapped bundles in the crooks of their arms, they seemed like different women. They didn't take their eyes off their bundles, craning their necks and tilting them under their nose for another sniff of the downy tufts on top of their little heads. The conversation with Mum was over a cup of tea, and involved talking about how little sleep they got, but the complaints were always accompanied by smug little smiles, as if to say *but I wouldn't trade sleep for this ...* Linda came accompanied by a large man with the muscles of a rugby player and a big lippy grin, introduced to me as 'Davo'. He hovered constantly at Linda's side, a second pair of eyes glued to their newborn boy. I knew it was understood that Linda had special status among the group now. I could also see the envy in my mother's eyes. She tried not to show it. She would say things like, *You are the love of my life, Jez* and *Who needs boys when we've got each other, hey?*, but even as a kid I'd watched enough movies to know that ours wasn't the model of a perfect family. There was supposed to be some *Jerry Maguire* moment when, even though my mum was thirty-something, overweight, single, with a kid, 'Jerry' came through the door and looked her straight in the eye and said, *You complete me.* But that never happened.

Maybe I should have been happy for Mum, if rooting Jeremy made her happy, but honestly I couldn't have felt more sorry for myself at that moment, sitting alone in Hungry Jacks with a box of sodden shoestring fries and a watery Coke. *Fuck my life! Fuck the world!* The little voice inside my head was seething. And just when I thought my day couldn't get any worse, I heard a shrill-as-fuck voice calling out my name.

'Jeeeez!'

SIXTEEN
• •

Get fuuuucked.

I bunched up my mouth into a pained expression of really really obvious *get the fuck away from me*, but Laura, teetering on kitten heels, carrying a full tray of food, was totally oblivious and plopped herself into the booth seat opposite me.

'The vegie burgers are so delicious!' Laura exclaimed, tearing the paper off her burger like a five-year-old opens a Chrissie present. 'Oh. My.' Laura took a massive bite. 'Gaaarsggghssh.'

She chucked her burger back on the tray and took a giant slurp of her drink and a handful of fries with the other hand.

'How are you, Jez?' Laura asked as if suddenly remembering that I was there. 'I'm starving. Dana and Joan have been dragging me around Christmas shopping for, like, *hours*! My feet actually hurt.'

'You're wearing heels,' I pointed out. 'To the Tuggeranong Hyperdome,' I added to stress how ludicrous she looked.

Laura giggled. 'All my friends in Melbourne dress up.'

'You're not in Melbourne,' I spoke slowly, as though talking to a child.

Laura grimaced and ducked her head under the table to look at my Havaianas. 'So thongs, then?'

'Thongs in summer, Ugh boots in winter,' I said dryly. 'It's like an unwritten law or something.'

'Oh, well, I'll keep that in mind.'

'So how's Lukey?'

Laura blinked. 'He's okay. You haven't seen him?'

'Not much since *you* arrived.'

'Have you called him? He'd probably be keen to hang out with you.'

'Been busy.' I shrugged. 'Not like we're joined at the hip, y'know.'

'He makes out like you are.'

'You can't trust men, can ya? They think with their dicks.'

'That's what Dana says, too.' Laura nodded, then she added, playfully, 'You sure you aren't a lesbian?'

'Fuck off!' I scoffed.

'Nothing wrong with lesbianism.'

'If you're into muff. And I'm not.'

'So you like cock?' 'Cock' sounded wrong coming from her cutesy little round face.

I shrugged. 'Not as much as you, obviously.'

Laura opened her burger and pulled out the pickle and flicked it against the wall of the booth. It stuck on the white plastic surface for a few seconds and then we both watched as it peeled off and fell onto the table.

'Nice,' I said. 'Somebody's gunna have to clean that up, you know.'

'Why are you so cold towards me?'

I sipped my watery Diet Coke.

'Is it just because of my thing with Lukey?' she persisted.

I started examining my fingernails, chipping off little flecks of black polish.

'If I'd known you liked him, I wouldn't have gone there.' Laura lowered her voice and I could feel her eyes on the top of my scalp. 'I'm not out to cut your grass or whatever.'

'Well maybe you just moved in like a big slut before you had a chance to check the situation.' My stomach flipped a little as I saw the pain register in her eyes, magnified behind her lenses.

'Right.' Laura shook her fringe out of her eyes. 'I'm a slut now? Because I have sex with a guy. He wanted it too, you know. He never told me otherwise.'

'Yeah, well he's a seventeen-year-old guy. If there's a hole to stick his dick into ...' I shrugged.

'But I'm the slut?' Laura's pitch raised. 'Haven't you ever had sex before?'

I swallowed. This conversation was really grinding my gears.

'Of course I have,' I said quickly. 'Not that it's your business. But I didn't meet him, like, that day.'

'So you've never had a one-night stand?'

'Look, whatever. I don't care, okay?'

'You've never bothered to get to know me, y'know, Jez —'

'I don't want to,' I interrupted.

'I really wanted to be friends with you —'

'I don't want to be mates with you.'

'— but you just shut me down every time.'

I stared at her sullenly. 'Look, nothing against you, but maybe you're just not my type of person.'

'You haven't given me a chance. Lukey talks you up all the time, like, ohh, Jez is awesome and funny and so much fun, blah blah blah. But to me you're just a bitch.'

I shrugged. 'I've got enough mates.'

'Really?' Laura raised her eyebrows. 'Like Casey?'

'She's one of them.' I folded my arms, defensive.

'Yeah, right,' Laura said slowly, loading her words with meaning. 'Casey.'

'Laura!'

Two slim women in jeans and singlet tops approached our table. The taller of the two had dark-brown curly hair and a tattoo of a sun, done in black ink on her upper arm. The shorter woman had a childlike face, with round blue eyes and short-cropped platinum-blonde hair and studs dotting the length of her ear, all the way up to the cartilage. A pair of Ray-Bans was perched on the top of her head. So these two were Laura's mums.

'We're heading off, hon. What're you up to?' The shorter one spoke directly to Laura, not even glancing in my direction, which annoyed me.

'Yeah, I'm coming. This is Jez.' Laura waved a hand in my direction.

'Oh yeah?' The shorter woman turned her sky-blue eyes to me with a critical interest. 'I'm Dana, this is Joanie ... Joan. We've heard a lot about you.'

'Hi, Jez.' The older-looking woman, Joan, had a whispery soft voice.

'Likewise.' I tried to sound bold. 'Likewise, I've heard about youse, too.'

'Laura hasn't met many people since we got here. She said you guys might be able to play some music together?' Dana continued, her eyes searching my face. 'We're busy this afternoon organising for a rally, but maybe you could pop over sometime this week.'

'Maybe Jez would like to help paint some signs for the rally?' Joan nudged her partner in the ribs. 'We could always do with extra hands.'

'Jez?' Dana asked.

'What's the rally? I mean I'm busy today I think, but —'

'Equal marriage rights. We're joining a demonstration tomorrow in the city.'

'Marriage for ...?' My question trailed off.

'Gay and lesbian couples.' Dana said it so matter-of-factly that I felt a blush rise in my cheeks.

'I'm not a lesbian or anything.'

'You don't have to be. I take it demonstrating is not your thing?'

'Demonstrating?' I couldn't hide the scepticism in my voice. 'There's nothing I want to demonstrate against.'

'Oh, really? So you're apolitical?'

I felt flustered because I didn't know what apolitical meant. I was guessing Dana meant that I didn't have a fucking clue about politics and she would be right.

'I'm vegetarian,' I answered lamely. 'I care about animals.'

'Well, that's something. I'd love to talk to you more about that. Can you join us for dinner sometime?' Dana asked.

'C'mon, let's go home, can we?' Laura interrupted, squirming out of the booth, her voice pleading. 'I'm so tired.'

As we exited Hungry Jacks, Dana pressed me. 'So when can you pop around?'

'I guess … maybe this weekend?' There were only so many times I could avoid her invitations. Not that I had any intention of actually going.

I spotted my mother over Dana's shoulder, waddling towards me with purpose, her figure bent in the middle to accommodate the load at her rear, like a toddler dragging around a full nappy.

'I gotta go,' I said quickly, hoping to get to Mum before any introductions needed to be made.

'Je-eeez!' Mum hooted in a yoohoo sing-song tone.

'I gotta go,' I repeated, edging away.

Laura, Joan and Dana all turned to look as Mum approached us, breathless, her cheeks flushed.

'You must be Jez's mum,' Joan said, winning the 'State the Obvious' trophy.

'Yep.' Mum squeezed me around the waist, as though we were besties. 'That I am.' She stuck out her marshmallow paw. 'I'm Helen, nice to meet you.'

'Joan, and this is my partner, Dana, and daughter, Laura.'

Dana and Laura nodded their hellos.

'They moved here from Melbourne,' I said.

I bit my lip and inwardly pleaded for Mum not to repeat anything I'd told her about Laura or her lesbian mums, but then I remembered that this was my mother, the lady who, countless times throughout primary school, forgot what time school ended and left me waiting in a deserted schoolyard for a lift home. Mum had the memory retention of a stoned goldfish.

'I've just invited Jez over to our house for dinner Friday,' Dana said. 'I hope you'll be able to join us, too, Helen?'

Mum looked surprised and chuffed. 'Oh, suuure!' she gushed to these women she'd known for all of five seconds. 'That sounds lovely, doesn't it, Jez? A girls' night out! I'll get my shift covered at the club.' Mum gave me another pinch around the waist.

All right, that's it.

'We've got to go.' I pulled Mum in the direction of where we'd parked the car.

'Really? We just got here ... Have you spent all that money already?' Mum was grilling me as I tugged on her arm.

'Six o'clock Friday, okay?' Dana called after us.

'Great, fine!' I sounded so fake, even to myself. 'See you then!'

'Why are we going home, Jez?'

'I'm just … sick of this place. I want to go home, okay?' For some horrible reason my throat started tightening up like I might start to cry. 'Where'd *Jeremy* go?'

'Was that the girl you were telling me about? Lukey's new girlfriend?'

'Yessss,' I hissed. 'Well, no. She's just a girl. Not his girl-friend. Don't change the subject!'

'Jeremy went home. He's keen to come for dinner one night. Or we could all have dinner at the club Sunday night?'

'Not a chance, Mum. Seriously. You and him. So gross.'

'Just give him a chance, Jez. That's all I ask. I knew you'd be this way, that's why I didn't tell you about him. Now you know, so please, try to be cool —'

'Cool? Mum, you're not a teenager!'

'Whatevs, you know what I mean.'

'*Whatevs?!* Mum, seriously, sometimes I feel like I'm your freaking parent.'

'So tomorrow night, huh? Going to Laura's for dinner?'

'No, we're not.'

'Well, we are now, Jez. I just told her mum we are.'

'I'm *so* not going.'

'Yes, you are. What if I bump into her mum at the shops or at the club? That would be a bit embarrassing, wouldn't it? Plus they seem like lovely people.' Mum paused, musing to herself. 'Wait, which one is her mum?'

'They are both her mums.'

'*Both* her mums? How does that work?'

'Oh, *Mum.*' I marched two steps ahead of her, keeping the pace all the way to the car. 'You don't understand *anything.*'

Mum turned up the radio full blast as she peeled out of the car park, windows wound down, singing Nickelback at the top of her lungs. I sunk way, way down low in my seat in case anybody I knew saw me.

SEVENTEEN
• •

I was pissed off right into that night. I felt bored. Restless. I lay on my bed and thought about Cash and Lukey and sex and my dad and then thinking about my dad was killing the thinking about sex buzz so I just tried to think about Cash and the sex. I wanted to do something. I wanted beers and chats and some sort of mad times. I thought about who I could call up. Lukey—no, I was still annoyed about him and Laura. Plus, I wanted him to call me. It was a matter of pride.

I thought about calling Cash. It had still only been a few days since we had sex in the tent. I feared rejection. Maybe the sex hadn't been good. How would I know? It was my first time. To me, it had been disappointing. He was really good-looking, hot even. I liked the thought of him. I liked the thought of me and him riding off along the highway to Daylesford, both of us dressed in black denims and leather, me clutching onto him as the wind whipped through my hair. But the sex had been average. It was just … something that happened.

I shut the bedroom door and pulled my dresser in front of the door to block it. I stripped naked and lay on my bed and took out a small compact mirror and held it up to my vagina. It looked sexy to me. I'd shaved. My pubic hair was pretty sparse anyway, but I'd shaved it on both sides and trimmed it back so I had just the 'landing strip'. I examined the folds of moist skin between my legs and sort of touched myself. It felt good. I felt … sexual. And excited. I wanted to fool around with a guy. Not Cash … Not Lukey … Somebody not so close.

I rang Martin Carroll.

'Martin?'

'Yeah? Who's this?'

'Jez.'

'Oh, hey. What're you doing? How've you been? Haven't seen you in ages.'

'What're you doing tonight?'

'Nothing. My parents went to the coast. I'm looking after my dog.'

'Yeah right. I'll come over? I've got fifty Mum gave me for Christmas, we could get some goon?'

'Yeah, for sure.' Martin was enthusiastic. I knew he liked me last year and it sounded like he still did. I felt relieved;

I really wanted this. 'Save your money, though. My parents' liquor cabinet is well stocked.'

'Even better.'

'See you in what, half an hour?'

'About an hour.'

'Sweet.'

I went into the shower and washed and re-shaved my vagina, suddenly wondering what I was supposed to call my genitals. Genitals sounded too . . . like, doctor-like. Vagina, I'd learned in science class, wasn't really the outside bit. It was the inside bit. The actual hole. The outside bit was called 'labia'. But nobody I knew said 'labia'. They said 'lips' or 'flaps'. Once I heard a couple of guys in my year talking about a girl one of them had rooted. The second guy asked the first guy, 'What were her flaps like? Wizard's sleeves or mouse's ears?'

Pussy? That sounded like something cooked up by people who made porno films. *Oooh yeah, lick my pussy* . . . It was weird. I had these bits between my legs that were meant for reproducing, for sex, for pleasure, but I didn't even know what to call them. I'd heard heaps of stupid words in the classroom. Muff, minge, flange . . .

Once when we were in science class and watching some sort of sexual education video, this girl named Rachel Jacobson stuck her hand up and went, 'Can a chick get preggers when she's having the time of the month in her vajayjay?' We all laughed. Vajayjay sounded like some sort of energy drink. *New! Vajayjay with guarana!*

I got dressed. Black lace undies and bra from Target and my usual black jeans and t-shirt over the top. Then I did my make-up: thick black eyeliner and mascara and hot-pink lipstick. I didn't bother with my hair. It didn't take long for me to walk to Martin's house.

Martin seemed nervous when he opened the door. He looked freshly showered; the ends of his hair hung wet around the collar of his t-shirt.

'Hey, bitch,' he said. I knew he was trying too hard to sound cool, but I also knew he was doing that to impress me and I kind of liked that.

'Hey, punk.' I gave him a quick hug. He smelled of Lynx deodorant and soap.

I strolled into the lounge room, feeling Martin's eyes on me. I knew he was already thinking about sex. With me. It made me feel powerful. I had something that he wanted.

Martin was tall, but not as tall as Lukey, and kind of solid, like you could tell he would get fat when he was older, and had that sort of arrogant swagger that heaps of boys at my school had. Martin was always trying to be funny, but he wasn't that witty, and always trying to be the loudest and drunkest. I'd gone to the Year 10 formal with him, but it wasn't really a date. Me and Lukey and Martin and a few other kids went as a group. We didn't bother hiring cars and all that bullshit. Our formal was held in the school gymnasium, so we walked there, smoking joints and swigging from bottles of Jameson's. I was drunk and high by the time we arrived, my head was like a helium balloon, bobbing along and pulling the rest of my body with it. The teachers who were chaperoning the dance were eyeing off our group, huddled together in the corner, falling into each other, laughing and sneaking sips from hip flasks. This other friend of ours, Caroline, pulled Lukey onto the dance floor. They spun around like idiots, trying to make each other dizzy. From behind me I felt Martin's breath in my ear. *Come outside for another joint, Jez?* I motioned to the others. Martin grabbed my elbow. *I've only got a bit left. Just me and you.*

We walked out onto the school oval and sat on the dry, dirt-patch ground near the concrete cricket pitch. There had been a drought that year. It seemed like most years there was a drought. Green grass was something you only saw on the lawns of Parliament House.

Martin had sat down close to me and straightaway leaned in and started kissing me. I responded. I was drunk and curious. I'd macked on with a few guys before, at parties and stuff. It was always interesting, seeing how guys kissed. Martin was all about the tongue; he pushed his straight past my lips, hard and aggressive, until he was practically licking my tonsils. He tasted liked spearmint Extra. I hated spearmint. It totally made me wanna vom. Looking at him now I hoped he'd got better at kissing.

Martin opened his parents' liquor cabinet, which was an actual wood and glass cabinet in the dining room. His house was huge compared to mine, further up the hill in Kambah, even further up than Laura's house. Martin was an only child, but he lived in a four-bedroom house and his parents had converted one half of the double garage into a den with couches and a telly. We sometimes smoked bongs in there and played PS3, it was a totally sweet hang spot. Martin was the type of kid my mum would call 'spoiled'. But he was nice enough, and really smart, too, because his dad was a teacher and could help him with his homework.

'You want to sit up here or in the bong lab?' Martin asked me. 'PS3 is in the bong lab.'

'Yeah, let's go to the bong lab, then.'

He'd nicknamed his garage haunt 'the bong lab' because he'd nicked all these beakers and glassware from the science labs at school so that he could construct this epic triple-chamber glass billy. He called it 'Bongus Maximus' and drew skulls and crossbones on it with permanent marker.

'Check this out.' Martin opened a small cupboard to a crawl-space under the house.

The lights from a heat lamp reflected off a cardboard diorama covered in foil and nearly blinded me. I blinked. There was one three-foot plant, fat and glistening with sticky resin.

'Oh, wow!' I breathed out.

'Beautiful, huh?' Martin fingered one of the tightly wound bud heads. 'So juicy.'

'When's she due?'

'Not for a bit. Getting there. Gotta be patient.' Martin snapped the cupboard shut and put a padlock on the door, paranoid like most chronic stoners.

Martin put a bottle of wine on the table in front of the television and poured us two glasses.

'Fancy,' I joked, clinking my wine glass against his. 'It's usually goon straight from the cask with us.'

'Lol,' said Martin. He had this habit of saying 'lol' instead of actually laughing, probably caused by spending too much time on MSN and Facebook chat.

'So, wanna play some PS3?'

We played *Killzone* on PS3 but I hadn't played it before and Martin was just owning it, so that got pretty boring fast.

'Hey, you still got Bongus Maximus?'

'Bongus Maximus smashed.' Martin actually looked a bit sad. 'I've just got this ceramic one now. You know Pete Matthews? He had this insane party, we had, like, probably a half to smoke between four of us ...'

'Four people? Not much of a party.'

'Naw, there were, like, over a hundred people there, I'm just telling you what we had between four of us.'

'Oh, okay.'

'Yeah, so we had a half pound of chronic, three or four pills each and a ton of goon and beer. It was off tap.' Martin shook his head, grinning. 'Yeah, so we nicknamed this little beauty,' he pointed to the ceramic bong on his coffee table, 'Bongus Chronicus.'

I faked a little laugh. 'Ha ha.'

Yeah. Humour wasn't Martin's best asset, but he was really good-looking. Bright golden brown eyes framed with dark lashes and nice skin. Even when he was baked he looked healthy and glowing. That was one of the worst things about having blue eyes like mine. When I got stoned or maggot my eyes went all glassy and bloodshot, like one of those droopy-eyed St Bernard dogs. Not pretty.

'So, you got any weed?' I prompted him.

'Yeah. Chop up?'

'Defs.'

While Martin mulled up I drained my glass of red wine and then topped it up. I was still restless and keen to get a buzz on.

Martin clocked me guzzling the wine. 'Whoa, slow down, wino.'

I wiped my mouth. 'Sorry.'

Martin grinned. 'Kidding. Go for gold. My dad has so much wine, he won't even notice shit is gone. Top me up, too.'

We punched a couple of cones each through Bongus Chronicus. My head felt light and my body went limp. Martin leaned into me on the couch and put his hand on my knee. I felt weak, but my heart started beating super fast.

Martin's mobile rang.

'Hello? Yeah. Nothing. Jez is over here. Yeah. Fuck yeah, that sounds awesome. Yep, yep ... I will. Okay. Lol. See ya, bye.'

'Who was it?'

'Kid named Jimmy, you wouldn't know him.'

'Jim Eggles?'

'Nah, Jim Newton. You wouldn't know him.'

'Oh, okay.' I was so stoned I could feel my eyeballs losing

moisture. I imagined them cracking if I blinked. I stared, eyes wide open.

'He's just bought a bunch of pills, we've gotta go over there.'

'How much?'

'Thirty each.'

'I've got fifty, but I don't know if I want a pill tonight.'

'Why the fuck wouldn't you want a pill tonight?'

I tried to move my tongue around in my mouth, but it, like my eyeballs, had dried right out.

'I dunno. Maybe I do.'

Martin laughed, snorting. 'Fuuuck, Jez. You're fucked.'

I laughed helplessly. 'So fucked.'

Martin put his face over mine and kissed me, pushing his tongue hard into my mouth. He didn't taste like spearmint Extra this time, more like cigarettes and peanut butter. My mouth was so dry I could hardly move my lips. I pushed Martin away.

'What's wrong?'

'Dry mouth.' I took a long sip of wine.

'Top up?' Martin drained the bottle of wine into my glass and I took another big gulp.

He started kissing me again.

'I always wanted to hook up with you.' Martin slid his hand under my shirt. 'Remember the Year 10 formal?'

'Yeah,' I said. 'I was so wasted.'

'You spewed all over my new shoes.'

'Sorry about that.'

'All good.'

When Martin leaned in to kiss me again he was like a lizard, feeling his way around with that big ropey tongue of his. Seriously, the worst kisser. I macked on with him for a bit longer, but then, all of a sudden, I just wasn't feeling it. I wasn't feeling *anything*. My fingers were cold and numb and my toes were curled inside my sneakers and I felt my throat go all tight. I had to get out of here.

'Fuck!' I pushed Martin off me and stood up. 'Fuck. I'm fucked.' I stepped over his legs and went for the door which led back up to the house.

Martin came after me. 'Lie down for a bit, Jez. You can use my bed. You'll feel better if you just lie down.'

I could hear the desperation in his voice as he followed me to the front door. I fumbled with the dead bolt.

'Jez, wait.' Martin tried to give me a hug, but my hands were up around my neck. 'You're just greening. That hydro is fucking mental. Just come lie down for a sec, you'll be fine.'

I breathed and leaned against Martin's shoulder. I was glad he was being nice to me, but I wanted to get the fuck out of there. I didn't even know what I was doing there anymore, why I'd even called him up in the first place. All I could think about was closing myself into my bedroom and lying on my own single bed and riding out the high.

'Thanks, Martin,' I whispered, and kissed him close to his ear. 'I'll catch you another time, hey?'

'You want me to walk you home?'

'Nah, nah …' I figured out the deadbolt and flung his front door open. 'I'll catch ya.'

'See you, Jez.'

I looked over my shoulder to wave and saw Martin standing in the doorway, hands shoved deep in his pockets, looking as confused as I felt.

EIGHTEEN

Mum and I argued about me going to Dana and Joanie's house for dinner right up until we rang their front doorbell. I'd been losing my rag all that arvo, like, really putting my foot down and saying, 'I'm not going,' but Mum was worried we'd look, like, homophobic if we didn't go. I don't know specifically *who* she was worried would think we were homophobic. She reckoned since Dana and Joanie were new in the hood and they'd gone to the trouble of inviting us we had to 'embrace our new neighbours'. I didn't really care about welcoming them, since their daughter had already muscled her way into my best mate's boxers. Mum would have to drag me kicking and screaming to get me over there for a meal. In the end she bribed me. No dishes or laundry for a fortnight and replacement guitar strings 'cos I'd broken two that morning playing power chords and screaming, 'I'M NOT GOING TO THE HOUSE OF LEZ!' It was sort of ironic.

Laura's house looked different from the last time I'd been over. Boxes had been unpacked, all the shelves were full of hardcover books and trinkets, the modular lounge was covered in beige-coloured faux fur throws and embroidered cushions and Asian art hung on the walls. Not tacky Asian art like the little Buddhas Mum had in her bedroom that she'd bought at the Dollar Shop, but Japanese-looking paintings of Koi fish and lotus flowers. Their house wasn't much bigger than ours, and it was so crammed full of stuff it might have felt really small, but everything was so colourful it felt warm. It looked like the 'after' photo of one of those Oprah interior design shows. And whereas our house smelled like dust, ciggies and cheap washing powder, theirs smelled like some sort of spicy incense and freshly baked bread. Mum acted like she was in a museum, oohing and ahhing and fingering fabrics, her eyes having sex with the exotic souvenirs.

'I travelled quite a bit in my earlier years,' Joanie explained, apologetic. 'I've hoarded a lot of junk.'

'No, this is . . .' Mum was stupidly impressed. 'I love your home.'

Home. I'd never really used that word when talking about our house. It was a house.

'Dana and Laura are in the kitchen, they're the chefs around here. Good for me, since I work so much.'

'Something smells amazing!' Mum flung her bag onto the sofa and collapsed alongside it.

'Are you hungry, Jez?' Joan turned her eyes to me.

'Not really.' My stomach gurgled. All I'd eaten that day was a bowl of soggy cereal topped up with warm UHT milk from the cupboard.

'Take a seat. Can I get you ladies something to drink?'

'Oh, we brought some ...' Mum fished in her bag and pulled out two West Coast Coolers, still frosty from our fridge. 'Sorry it's not much ...'

'I'll put it in a glass for you?'

'No, it's fine.' Mum held up her keys. 'Always carry a bottle opener.'

I sank into the sofa next to Mum as she cracked a Cooler open and took a swig.

'Do you want a Coke, Jez? Or a Sprite?'

'Water?'

Joan smiled at me. She was pretty when she smiled. Deep, soft crow's feet framed her eyes at her temples. 'No problem. Just be one sec, then. I'll grab Laura for you, Jez.'

A moment after Joan disappeared into the kitchen, Dana stuck her head into the lounge room and grinned.

'Hey! I heard somebody mention drinks,' Dana boomed and held up a half-drunken beer. 'Seems like we've been a little too ambitious in the kitchen. Laura's elbow deep in bread dough. Come on through.'

Mum and I obediently raised ourselves from the couch

and went through to the kitchen. Laura stood at the kitchen bench, rolling out a sticky dough, flour dusted on her cheeks and fringe.

'Hey, Jez, Helen.' She smiled shyly at my mum.

I hung back in the doorway while Mum squeezed her way into the small kitchen space, stopping close to Laura and surveying the platters of food spread across the benchtop.

'What a feast!' Mum's eyes widened, looking from Joan to Dana.

I craned my neck to see. It was all fancy stuff. Vegetables cut into strips, dips, cheeses and olives all arranged in coloured ceramic bowls.

'You really didn't need to go to all this trouble! We're sausage roll girls, aren't we, Jezza?'

'I'm vegetarian,' I said quickly.

'We remembered,' Joan's voice was smooth and soft. 'No meat in this dinner, Jez. We kind of went for a Greek theme.'

I felt embarrassed. 'Well, thanks. I'm really not that hungry —'

'Except none of us are Greek,' Dana continued. 'So we're kind of winging it.'

'I'm attempting flat bread.' Laura met my eyes. 'It might be an epic fail.'

'Well, you've tried your best, and that's what counts,' Mum said loudly, patting Laura on the shoulder. I think she was trying to be all 'Mother-wisdom' but she sounded like a complete dick. 'We can't cook for squids, can we, Jez?'

I shrugged. 'Never tried. Mum doesn't cook, so I never learned.'

Everyone fell silent for a moment.

Joan broke the awkwardness. 'Dana and Laura have a bit of fun with it.'

'Have you tried the Kambah Village Chinese?' Mum asked. 'It's one of our favourites.'

'Actually we did,' Dana replied. 'I didn't mind it. Joan is a bit of a food snob.'

'Oh, so is Jez!' Mum exclaimed. 'For years she'd only eat the bloody Mongolian lamb. Such a fussy eater.'

'It was good,' I defended myself.

'Joan's actually been to China,' Dana continued. 'I think that's where she got her pickiness about Chinese restaurants.'

'Ugh. Those sugary orange sauces.' Joan screwed up her face. 'Reminds me of the sweet-and-sour my mum used to make when I was growing up. Height of sophistication back then, of course.'

'Right.' My mum nodded even though I could tell she didn't know her arse from her head at that point in the conversation.

We sat outside on the patio to eat. The outdoor table was set with a colourful tablecloth and matching place settings, each with a white square dinner-plate, side-plate, a serviette made out of material rolled in a plastic holder, wine glass and cutlery. A shallow glass bowl of pink camellias sat in the centre of the table, next to a frosty pitcher of yellow drink with ice and lemons and herb leaves floating in it. The heaped platters of food looked like enough to feed a football team. It was totally OTT, I reckoned. I'd never been to a dinner like this in my whole life.

'Dig in,' Dana said, sitting at the head of the table, waving her arms across the spread.

I couldn't hold back. I was suddenly mega-hungry. My diet of oven-baked tofu nuggets, Mi-goreng noodles, microwave meals and hot chips from Maccas hadn't prepared me for this moment—proper food, like I'd seen people eat on the telly. I piled my plate with colourful things and cheese I didn't even know the name of.

'Thishispregood,' I mumbled to Dana, chewing on a kind of salty-rubbery-cheese stuff.

'Haloumi,' Dana said. 'We just put it under the grill for a couple of minutes.'

'Try some of the bread,' Laura said, showing off. 'I hope it's okay.'

I took some. It was moist and chewy and delicious.

'It's okay, yeah,' I said, not wanting to be too generous.

As we ate the conversation flowed easily, mostly because me and Mum ate like starving orphans while Dana and Joan chatted away. Dana and Joan, both in their late forties, despite looking around Mum's age, had travelled the whole world before they had Laura. Joan had a university degree in Law and Dana had once managed a lowrider bicycle store in the mid-nineties. Mum was wide-eyed and obviously impressed. I would have been more impressed if I didn't feel so annoyed.

Annoyed that my mum shopped at Kmart instead of Myers, that we'd never been out of NSW, that our fridge contained a six-pack of Bundy rum and Cokes instead of hummus and freaking haloumi.

'Have you travelled, Helen?' Dana asked Mum.

'Oh, no.' Mum laughed. 'Busy raising a kid on my own.'

'It's a tough business. We've struggled at times with Laura.'

Mum continued, nodding her head, 'Yeah, her father split when she was five or six —'

'I was six,' I interjected, but nobody looked at me. 'And you left him.'

'So it's been really hard. Cash has been tight. But I've managed.'

'*We've* managed,' I said between gritted teeth. Laura blinked at me across the table.

'Single mothers are the unsung heroes,' Joan said in her sincere, lilting voice.

Mum nodded, her eyes downcast, all modest. You'd think she was Mother fucking Theresa the way Dana and Joan were carrying on.

'Extra tough when the single mum has a drinking problem.'

Everyone turned and looked at me. Mum forced a laugh and waved her hand in the air.

'If you really had a parent with a drinking problem, you'd know all about it!'

'I do know all about it,' I said.

She shot me a look that said 'shut the fuck up'.

'Oh, Jez,' Dana squeezed my forearm, which was resting on the table next to her. 'Cut your mum a bit of slack, hey?'

'Sure, whatever,' I muttered.

'It's tough, alright,' Mum continued, oblivious to my ultra-hairy eyeball deathrays that were sending telepathic stab wounds into her face. 'I dreamed of travelling. I was right into music, too, just like Jez is. I played guitar and smoked dope and listened to all that grunge. Ha!' Mum shook her head. 'I was so naïve.'

'We all were at their age!'

'True, but I never had a mum either. I wish I had.'

Here we go. I twisted the cloth serviette in clenched fists in my lap.

'I was fostered from an early age. My real mother didn't want anything to do with me after that.'

'Oh, gosh,' Joan murmured, rubbing my mum's back. 'Helen ...'

'Maybe if I'd had a mum, a proper mum, I wouldn't have made the mistake of getting pregnant so young.'

Mum took a deep sip from her wine glass, and Dana and Joan followed suit, as though all three were contemplating the terrible mistake—*me*—that my mother had made. My face burned.

'So what brings you to the proverbial backwaters of Canberra?' Mum was trying to sound all clever. I had never heard her say 'proverbial' before.

'We thought it would be better for Laura,' Dana said at the same time Joanie said, 'My job, mostly.'

They looked at each other and laughed.

'We needed a change,' Joan said.

'I wasn't keen, I have to admit,' Dana said.

'How are you settling in, Laura?' Mum asked.

'Okay.' Laura hesitated, glancing at me. I looked down at my plate. 'It's quiet. Real quiet.'

I shoved back my chair. 'I'm going to the dunny.'

'Toilet, Jez,' Mum corrected me, smiling at Dana and Joan apologetically as if to say, *I didn't raise her that way.*

I was so tense and angry at Mum, I couldn't piss. I just sat on the toilet for ages, wringing my hands together and cursing under my breath.

When I came out of the bathroom, wiping my wet hands on my jeans, Laura was on the couch in the lounge room, the television flickering, reflected in her black-rimmed hipster glasses.

'Hey,' she said. 'Telly?'

I shrugged. 'Better than being out there.' I jerked my thumb towards the backyard as I threw myself onto the other end of the couch.

'Totally.' Laura gave a curt nod. 'I hate it when they get all, *Look how much I've sacrificed for you.*'

'You've got nothing to whinge about. Your parents are okay.'

'Ha!'

'What're you going on about?'

'I didn't want to move here, did I? This place is *bullshit*,' Laura hissed. 'It's like a fucking hick country town. Except

worse! A hick town might have some character, this is just ...
suburb upon suburb. It's just ... nothing.'

'Oh, not as good as *Melbourne*.' I found myself getting defensive. 'You're just too up yourself, that's your problem.'

'I'm not! It's just what I'm used to. I had *friends*, I had a
boyfriend!'

'Really?' I was interested. 'A boyfriend?'

'Yes. I loved him. He loved me. That was part of the
problem. My fucking *lesbian* man-hating mothers didn't
approve of him. Thought he was a fuckstick or whatever ...
So they up and move me out here!'

'Serious? Is that the reason?' I raised my eyebrows. 'Joanie
said it was because of her work.'

'Yeah, it helped that Joan is in the public service. Easy
transfer. And I think she really wanted to move and just focus
on her career anyway. I guess I was just the clincher.'

'So what happened?'

Laura took a deep breath. 'Well, you can't tell anyone ...'

'Yeah, sure.' I shrugged, trying to hide my curiosity.

'Oh, bull. I can't fucking trust you, who am I kidding?'

'Look,' I said, 'you've obviously got something grinding your
gears so spit it.'

Laura took another big breath, puffed her cheeks out and
then exhaled. 'I got pregnant.'

'No waaaay ...'

Laura spoke quickly. 'Yeah, I did. Dana hit the fucking *roof*
'cos I was only fifteen at the time. You'd think she was cool,

hey? Like she thinks she's so cool with her fucking butch-dyke-hair-spike thing. She's so not cool. She wanted me in a freaking chastity belt.'

'Fifteen. That's pretty young.'

'They both wanted me to "consider all the options". I just wanted to keep my baby. We both did, me and my boyfriend, Trent. We wanted to keep it and raise it. Dana and Joan just kept saying how smart I am, and so young, and how I have such a bright future and how I'd never get to travel or go to parties or finish school. And they didn't like Trent. Dana kept saying stuff about how he couldn't support a pair of tits if he was a push-up bra.'

'So what happened?'

'Abortion.'

Laura said it so bluntly, I think I flinched.

'Wow,' I half whispered, my eyes still wide. 'That's …'

'Fucked, I know.'

'Well, maybe. Maybe not. Look at my mum. You wouldn't want to be her.'

'I dunno. I really wanted to keep it.'

'You get to finish school now. You're going to uni, aren't you?'

'That's what Dana and Joan were most upset about. She said I'd never get to go to university. I always wanted to be a writer or a journalist. But I would have gone to uni eventually.'

'You can have a baby eventually. Look at my mum. She's thirty-three and working behind a bar, never been anywhere, never done anything.'

'She's got you. You turned out fine.'

'Don't you think she wishes every day she never had me?'

'Oh, my God, Jez. You are kidding, aren't you?' Laura snorted.

'I'm not kidding.'

'You don't see it, do you?'

'See what?'

'See how much she loves you!'

'Then why does she drink so much?'

'I have no idea. Maybe she's lonely? Depressed? Bored? Guilty? You're so busy feeling sorry for yourself —'

'Oh, right!' I snapped. 'I'm feeling sorry for myself.'

'You really embarrassed her out there. Bringing up her drinking.'

'She embarrasses herself.'

'I don't think so. Dana and Joan like her. She's got a lot of character, she's very genuine. And plus she loves you, you can just tell.'

'So do your parents. I reckon they probably had the best intentions or whatever.'

Laura sighed and pushed her glasses up her nose. She was silent for a long moment.

'Yeah, yeah. I know Dana and Joanie love me, too. That's why I can see now why they wanted me to give up the baby.'

'Really? So you're not mad at them?'

'I was mad. Now I'm just ... It's confusing. They say one day I'll thank them.'

'You reckon?'

'Maybe. And maybe one day you'll thank your mum.'

'For *what*?'

'Nobody's perfect, Jez.'

I pulled my legs up to my chest and rested my chin on my knees. 'She doesn't mean to be so hopeless. She's just an epic life fail.'

'I think she's pretty great.'

'Really?'

I stewed on that for a second, trying to see my mum through Laura's eyes. It was good how I could pretty much do whatever I wanted. She didn't nag me too much, she let me have a few drinks and durries every now and then.

'You should see the way she looks at you. She's so proud,' Laura continued. 'Sort of the same way Lukey looks at you.'

I snapped upright at the mention of Lukey. 'What'd he say?'

'Nothing. He doesn't talk much. You can just tell.'

I could feel my cheeks tingling with a blush.

'... you're his best friend.'

'Yeah. Best friend,' I echoed.

My mobile vibrated in my pocket. I fished it out; the screen flashed with an incoming call: Casey. It'd been nearly a week since we'd spoken.

'Hey,' I answered, trying not to sound deflated.

'Got your voicemail! Come over!'

'Why?' I perked up a little at the thought of seeing Cash. 'What's happening?'

'Party in the city tonight, wear something hot.'

'Hot?'

'Yeah! Aitch. Oh. Tee. Haaaawt! Something slutty but classy, y'know? Dressed up to get messed up! Frocked up to get fucked up!'

'I don't have any dresses, really. Hey, is Cash there?'

'I'll lend you a dress! Just come over! Cash just left. He said to say hi.'

'Oh, okay.' My heart sank a little. 'Where'd he go?'

'Down the caravan with my parents.'

'Batehaven? How long for?'

'JEZ!' Casey screeched so loud down the phone I had to hold it away from my ear. 'COME OVER!'

'Casey,' I explained to Laura as I shoved the phone back in my pocket. 'We're gunna go to a party in the city.'

'Oh. Sounds fun.'

'Hey ... Did you wanna come?' I felt a flush of niceness come over me. 'If ya want ...'

'Really?' Laura pushed her glasses up her nose. 'Do you really want me to come?'

I shrugged. 'Meh. No dramas, either way.'

Laura hesitated. 'Sure, I guess so.'

'Cool.' I nodded. 'Should be fun.'

NINETEEN
• •

I sat in a suite at James Court Apartments in the city, in a small living area crammed with people, who alternated puffing on cigarettes and swigging from bottles. I was wedged on a couch between two girls in teeny satiny material dresses and strappy-heeled sandals. One of the girls was Lee, a bony Asian who talked broad bogan crossed with Valley girl; every second word was 'loike', 'fark' and 'totally'.

'So this bitch, roight, loike, totally disses my mates in front of me and I'm loike, *Fark you, cunt! Don't you be farkin' dissin' my mates or I'll rip your farkin' eyeballs out.*' Lee fluttered her dagger-like acrylic nails in front of my face to illustrate her point.

I tugged uncomfortably at the hem of the black cotton tube dress that Casey had convinced me to wear. When I tried it on at Casey's house it had seemed sexy, kind of daring. But at the party, seated on the low-slung futon sofa, the dress kept riding up my thighs. I had to keep my legs clamped together. I hugged myself and took a long swig of my gin and tonic. So far the party was a total fizzer. Muscled guys with rat's tails and designer trackpants and girls with spray-tans and whitened teeth. Not really my sort of crowd. It was going to be a looong night. I seethed inwardly, while plastering this silly smile on my face and trying to follow what Lee was saying.

'So ... um ... did you fight her?' I asked.

'Nah, I totally wanted to, but I'm a softie really.' Lee grimaced, twisting her face into a sneer. 'I'm just real loyal to my mates. No cunt disses my mates.'

'Totally,' I agreed, without any enthusiasm.

It looked as though the party had been going for several days; empty bottles of beer were crammed on every flat surface, pizza boxes were piled in a corner behind a floor lamp. I kicked absently at a bottle top that was resting near my foot and craned my neck to see if I could locate Casey through the cluster of bodies crammed inside the apartment. She was in the kitchen doing Jager Bombs with a bunch of dudes in polo shirts and blue jeans. They lined up plastic cups full of Red Bull along the benchtop and on a count of three dropped shots into the bubbling guarana drink. I badly wanted in on the next round. The can of gin and tonic pre-mix Casey had given me when we arrived was a dud on the buzz front.

Laura was standing by the door, arms folded across her chest, looking really uncomfortable. I don't think she'd moved from that position since we got here. Casey hadn't been heaps happy about Laura tagging along. She'd pulled me aside at her house.

'Why'd you invite her for?' she'd hissed. 'She, like, totally stole your guy and now you're, what, BFFs?'

'Lukey's not *my guy*,' I'd hissed back. 'I like Cash!'

Casey paused and gave me a superior smile. 'Oh, Jez.' She shook her head. 'Don't *like* Cash. Fuck Cash, but don't *like* him.'

'What do you mean?' I wanted to know, but Laura had returned from the bathroom and our conversation moved to dresses and make-up.

Now Laura was desperately trying to wave at me across the party. 'COME HERE!' she mouthed, motioning with a frantic arm.

''Scuse me,' I said to Lee and the other girl.

I struggled to my feet and tottered across the room, my heels sinking and snagging on the thick pile carpet. I stood at Laura's elbow.

'What is it?'

'Some guy just tried to grab my *tits*,' she said. 'This isn't ... this isn't really my sort of crowd, hey.'

'This isn't *Melbourne*, Laura. Just get drunk.'

'Come home with me, Jez? I rang Dana. She said she'd pay for the taxi.'

'We just got here!'

'Pleeease come with me.' Laura clutched at my forearm. 'I don't even know where the taxi rank is.'

'It's, like, just across the road. You'll be fine. I'm gunna stay out.'

Laura looked unconvinced as she surveyed the crowd in the apartment, her face all sad-sack.

'We could watch Foxtel. I've got ice-cream,' Laura tried again.

'I want to get maggot.' I shrugged.

'Yeah, okay ... I guess I'll stay a bit longer.'

'If you want to go, go.'

'I don't want to leave you here. I'm getting a dodgy vibe.'

'Sure, whatever,' I replied, annoyed.

I turned from Laura and squeezed into the tiny kitchen area and tried to edge my way into the group that was standing shoulder to shoulder around the kitchen bench.

'Hey!' I leaned in towards Casey, yelling over the thumping house music.

Casey snapped her head towards me and grinned. 'Great party, huh?' She put her lips so close to my ear I could feel the wetness of her breath. 'Where's little Miss Buzzkill?'

I gave a tight-lipped smile. 'Being a buzzkill by the door.'

'Ugh! Why'd you even bring her? She's so fuckin' blah.'

'She's okay.' I surprised myself by feeling a little defensive of Laura. 'She doesn't know anybody in Canberra.'

'So many hot guys here!' Casey was still slurring into my ear.

'Totes.' I nodded. *Whateveeeer.* 'Fix me up with a shot?'

Casey nodded towards a guy with a pencil-thin strip of facial hair that ran along his jawline from ear to ear, and over his top lip. He was talking animatedly to a guy directly opposite him, waving a half-full bottle of Jagermeister.

'It's Damien's bottle,' she yelled.

Beard-guy turned at the sound of his name and ran his eyes over me. I stuck out my chest and tossed my hair back a bit, blinking through the thick eye make-up that Casey had applied to my face. I felt like a total fraud, like a freaking android trying to pass for a human being. Beard-guy was too drunk to notice my insecurity.

'I like your piercings,' he said.

'I like your ...' I paused for a second, trying to think. *Don't say Jagermeister, don't say Jagermeister.* 'Jagermeister,' I said.

He looked surprised for a second, then laughed. 'Jager Bomb?' he said, already grabbing a plastic cup.

He poured shots for himself, Casey and me.

'I'm Damo,' bearded-guy introduced himself.

'Jessica,' I replied. I felt like saying, *I don't give a fuck what your name is, just gimme the goddamn shot.*

'What should we cheers to?' he shouted, holding up his shot between thumb and forefinger.

I shrugged.

'To getting fucked uuuup!' Casey yelled and dropped her shot into her Red Bull.

I dropped my shot and tipped the liquid down my throat in two gulps, enjoying the sweet syrupy taste. I licked my lips.

'Another?' Damo asked, not waiting for a reply as he stepped around Casey and poured the rest of a Red Bull can into my cup.

I grinned; free alcohol was good alcohol. Maybe this wasn't going to be such a shitty night after all.

After three bombs I began to feel good. The alcohol was warming my limbs and the conversation began to fall easily from my lips. My head was like a balloon, lolling around on the top of my neck, swinging from side to side in attempts to follow the conversation. I couldn't take in everything at once, so I smiled and pretended I was listening, which didn't really matter because nobody was really talking to each other anymore, just yelling random drunken observations then hooting with laughter.

'Where's the bathroom?' I leaned into Casey, yelling over the thumping techno music.

'Ensuite,' she replied, throwing a hand towards a door, not even bothering to meet my eyes as she continued her conversation.

As I turned away from Casey and headed towards the bathroom, I nodded at Laura who had taken up my old position on the couch next to Lee. She was smiling. It looked like she'd dislodged whatever was stuck up her arse.

As I pushed my way to the bedroom door an older guy— maybe in his late twenties or thirties?—with black slicked back hair wearing a light-pink polo shirt turned up at the collar, stepped in front of me, met my eyes and gave me a wink.

'Hey, baby,' he said, putting his arms on either side of the doorframe, blocking my path, tossing a sideways look at his mates to see if he was getting their approval. They sniggered loudly.

'Excuse me,' I muttered, head down, and pushed past him.

'Hey, hey …' The guy grabbed my forearm. 'Where're you going?'

'To the toilet,' I said, and shook him off my arm.

'Can I come?' The guy grabbed me from behind, his hands on my hips, and rubbed himself against the small of my back.

I turned quickly and looked desperately to where Casey was standing in the kitchen, distracted, lining up more shots.

'Just fuck off, okay?' I didn't sound confident. The guy stepped in and closed his arms around me.

'How 'bout a dance, then?' he whispered so close to my ear I could feel drops of spittle land on my neck.

I pushed him backwards with my elbows. 'I need to go to the toilet, okay?'

'Can I come?' the guy said again and laughed. 'Give me a little head job, okay? Just a little bit of something, okay?'

'You've got to be kidding.' I narrowed my eyes, trying to get my bitch on. 'Gross.'

As I turned towards the ensuite bedroom, I felt the sharp pinch of fingers pulling at the flesh on my butt cheek and an involuntary shiver of disgust shot up my spine. I snapped around and swung, driving my open right palm up into his nose as hard as I could and then followed it with a kick to his crotch that found air because the guy was already stumbling backwards from the surprise force of the blow.

'FUCK! You fucking cunt!' the guy screamed, clutching his face. When he opened his hands in front of him there were smears of blood from the trickle that ran over his lips.

'Jez!' Casey was at my side. 'What the fuck did you do?!'

I shrugged, and straightened myself on my strappy heels. I could feel the eyes of everybody in the apartment, bodies jostling for position to cop a load of the skinny girl in the too-tight black tube dress who had just slammed her hand into some guy's nose. Laura came from the other side of the room and was tugging at my elbow.

'Let's get out of here, Jez, please, let's just go,' she pleaded urgently.

Casey looked from me to the guy and back at me. 'Jez! What the fuck happened?!'

I didn't get a chance to explain. The guy's friends pushed Laura and Casey out of the way and grabbed me by the arms, one on either side, so hard I knew it would leave bruise marks, and steered me towards the front entrance to the apartment.

'You're out, missy,' one of them sneered. 'Violent little bitch.'

Casey circled us, skipping back and forth, slapping the guys over the head with her purse. 'Let go of my friend, you wankers!' She was clearly enjoying her role in all of this, which made me grin in spite of myself.

'Fuck you, fucking wankers!' me and Casey screeched as they tossed us out on the street, and we clutched each other and laughed till tears came to our eyes.

TWENTY

• •

'You are so fucking loose, Jezza,' Casey cried, and I beamed with pride. 'Can't take you anywhere!'

Laura joined us a moment later. 'Sorry, I had to get my purse!' she gasped, out of breath. 'What the hell ...?'

'The guy totally deserved it,' I declared. 'The wanker asked me to give him a *head job in the toilet* and then pinched my arse when I told him to fuck off!'

'So you punched him?!' Casey crowed. 'Oh, my God, Jezza, why didn't you just suck him off, it would've been a lot easier.'

'Gross!' Laura cried. 'He was a greaseball.'

'Total greaseball,' I agreed.

We crossed the road towards the city, skipping in and out of the Saturday-night traffic that waited at the intersection lights.

'But, Jez, you can't go round king-hitting every guy who cracks onto you!' Casey squeezed between me and Laura, and slipped her arm through mine. 'You'll end up in jail or something! Sometimes it's just easier to give 'em what they want.'

'Sure!' I laughed. 'Like I'm gunna give some ugly wog guy a gobby in a toilet at a party.'

Casey shot me a quick look. 'It was a good party.'

I stopped walking and stared at her in disbelief. 'So what are you saying? You would have done it just to stay at the dumb party?'

'It was a really lame party,' Laura said.

Casey tossed her hair. 'Maybe if I was drunk enough. Not that big a deal.'

'Serious?' My mouth fell open.

'That's so wrong, Casey.' Laura shook her head.

'Look.' Casey put her hands on her hips authoritatively. 'I'm not saying you *should* have done it. I'm just saying that if you *did*, it wouldn't be that big a deal. It's just a blowie.'

'Fucking hell, Casey.' I shook my head. 'That is so trashbag. That is full sluz.'

'Oh, Jez.' Casey sighed impatiently. 'You don't know anything. It's not slutty, it's just what happens.'

'She shouldn't have to do anything she doesn't want to do.' Laura stepped between Casey and I. 'Especially not just to stay at a really bullshit lame party full of freshies.'

'Who the fuck asked *you*?' Casey got all up in Laura's grill. 'Why are you still here? Don't you have some cake to eat or something?'

Laura just blinked and turned to me. She swallowed hard and then let her mouth hang open, like she'd been slapped. I felt sick to my stomach and my head swam with drunkenness.

'I'm leaving, Jez. You coming?'

I looked from Laura to Casey. 'I dunno,' I hesitated.

'Stay out with me, Jez.' Casey slung her arm around my waist and gave me a peck on the cheek. 'We've hardly had a chance to hang.'

'Are you sure, Jez? Dana will pay for the taxi.'

'She's *sure*! Some of us actually would like to have some fun tonight, and since we're not going to any dyke clubs ...'

'I'm not a dyke.'

Casey ran her eyes up and down Laura's sundress and ballet flats. 'Whatever you reckon.'

'See you later, then.' Laura gave a half-hearted wave, her eyes lingering on mine for a moment as though trying to convince me to change my mind. I stayed silent as she turned and walked away.

'Bye!' I called after her.

'So anyways, as I was saying before I was rudely *interrupted*.' Casey jerked her thumb in Laura's direction.

'That was so harsh, Case,' I began, my eyes still following Laura.

'As I was *saying*,' Casey interrupted me. 'You shouldn't be so frigid! Sex is not gunna kill you, and it might actually get you places. Proper women know how to use their sexiness to their advantage.'

Laura disappeared from sight. I turned back to Casey.

'Case, I don't think I wanna use my sexiness. I don't even know if I *am* sexy.'

Casey scrunched her face as she looked me up and down. 'Yeah, you're not really. But you could be if you tried, and that's my point.'

'Yeah, I dunno ...'

'Jez.' Casey shot me a pitying look. 'Didn't your mum ever teach you anything about sex for fuck's sake?'

'My mum doesn't have sex. She hasn't had a boyfriend for like ... forever. Except she does now,' I remembered. 'Jeremy from the club.'

'Jeremy?!' Casey hooted. 'You're kidding?! That is too funny ... and kind of gross.'

'Tell me about it.'

'He's friends with Cash, y'know.'

'Yeah, I know.' I searched my bag for a piece of gum. 'So when you said forget about Cash ...'

'Forget Cash!'

'I was just wondering ...'

'What is Jeremy, like, ten years younger than her?'

'Eight, maybe.' I gave up searching for the gum and folded my arms across my chest.

'So gross.'

'I know, right?'

'But that proves my point! Everybody is having sex, Jezza. Everyone except you. You're like an old woman. Don't you have the internet?'

'What's the internet got to do with it?' I asked dumbly.

Casey let out a loud lungful of air. '*Porn,* you twat. If you'd been looking at internet porn you'd know that these days, as far as sex is concerned, anything goes.' She raised her eyebrows with authority. 'And I do mean *anything*. Think bondage, domination, S&M, DP, midget porn ... beastiality might be going a bit far ... *squid porn*, for fuck's sake.'

'You're making this up.'

'I'm not! You're so naïve, Jez. People are doing all sorts of shit, all the time, for fun. Haven't you ever heard of the sexual revolution? It happened, like, fifty years ago before our parents were even born. And *you*,' she waved her hand airily at me, 'break a dude's nose for asking for a gobby. Bit extreme, don't you think?'

Casey spun on one heel and stalked across the road. My face burned.

'Excuse me?!' I cried after her. 'A guy asks for a head job and I'm supposed to just go, *Ooooh, okay then*.' I put on an airhead type voice for effect. 'What if I didn't *want* to, Casey? The dude was groping me and it was really gross and sleazy, okay?'

Casey pirouetted on her heels to face me. 'Look, Jez. It's not gunna kill you,' she spoke slowly and mildly as though she were already bored of the topic. 'It's a penis. And you can't even get STIs from oral anyways.'

I couldn't believe my ears. 'That is fucked up, Case,' I muttered.

Casey snorted and stamped her foot impatiently, signalling an end to the conversation. 'Well cool, then. You didn't want to. So now look where we are.' Casey threw her hands up in the air. 'In the city with no money, no way home, no alcohol, no bud ... So what do you suggest we do?'

'Maybe we should call it, hey? We could probably catch up with Laura, share a taxi home?'

'No freakin' way.' Casey shook her head. 'Laura bailed because she is a zero. If we bail that's a bullshit end to a perfectly good night.'

I studied Casey, taking in the way she distractedly tugged at her hair extensions, simultaneously giving every female that paraded past us a critical assessment that I could read on her face: *Fat thighs ... ugly dress ... oooh nice hair.* Strangely, I felt grateful for Casey's company, when I probably should have been mad at her. I had been so sure that I was doing the right thing, smacking that guy in the face. I didn't want to be desperate like my mum, no sex for years and years. I wanted in to Casey's world. Casey was sexy. She was powerful and confident and always seemed so full of life and plans and fun; she was like an ocean—waves of enthusiasm crashing onto the shore, then drawing back and crashing in all over again. Whereas I felt like a stagnant little pool. I wanted to ride a wave.

'Okay, I'm in. What are we doing?'

Casey paused at the street corner, her face calculating as she scanned our surroundings. Clubbers and pubbers ambled up and down the bars and nightclubs of the interchange, along the footpaths under the white arched awnings of the 1920s buildings, arms linked, with skips in their step and the off-balance lean of tipsiness. The city looked pretty: strings of fairy lights were hung from the deciduous trees and Christmas decorations lit up many of the shopfronts and cafes. Couples and groups in their thirties and forties spilled out of restaurants and into the balmy summer night, faces lit up, intoxicated with silly-season cheer. Suddenly I felt infected by their optimism.

'I've got a great idea,' Casey said

I followed her eyes to a nightclub where a cluster of people were slowly shuffling through the double doors. 'We're gunna go into that nightclub over there and get our flirt on and get some free drinks from some guy's wallet,' Casey said. 'Stick your tits out and follow me. Don't stop or they might ask for ID. Just walk in like you own the joint.'

TWENTY-ONE

• •

When I woke up my eyes were glued together with crusted mascara and liquid eyeliner, and I had to pry them apart with my fingers and then give my throbbing temples a quick massage. I sort of peeked hesitantly out from under the smelly old sleeping bag, remembering that I'd crashed at some random guy's house that Casey had picked up the night before at the club.

As soon as we got into the nightclub she'd had her full flirt on, getting guys to buy us round after round of alcohol. She would kind of tease them with a kiss or a hand on the leg when the drinks started to slow down, or do that thing where she let her hand slide from her hair down to her boob, real casual like. The weird thing was, the more drinks I got into me, the more comfortable I felt getting my own flirt on. I got sick of Casey getting all the attention (and getting more drinks than me) so I hitched up my hemline a few inches and squeezed my cleavage together and tossed my hair around a little and the drinks started rolling in and then before I knew it I was outside the club with this guy (whose name I couldn't even remember), a Rugby player, his heavy arm draped over my shoulders, stumbling down the street after Casey and her own football player. So mental.

So anyway, we all got in a cab together and went back to one of their apartments, and we all sat around drinking Bacardi for a while and Football Player #1 was trying it on with me on the couch while Casey and Football Player #2 went into the bedroom and had really loud, grunting sex. Suddenly I was really panicked because I realised, whether I really wanted to or not, there was no backing out of the situation I'd got myself into. The flirting, the hair tossing, all fun and games at the nightclub, had all led to this moment and this guy was seriously, seriously expecting to get his end in. Not just expecting but demanding, with his hands on my breasts and fingers poking into my panties trying to rub my clit.

'You're hairy,' he grunted, pulling his hands out of my undies. 'You some sort of hippy?'

'I'm not hairy!' I snapped, defensive. 'It's called a "landing strip".'

'Most girls shave it all off.'

'I'm not most girls. And I don't want to look like a little girl.'

'Whatever. I don't go down anyway.' He grabbed me again and started kissing my neck and sliding his hands roughly down my body.

'Hey, hey,' I protested, trying to pry his fingers from my underwear again. 'Slow down.'

He kept kissing me, his five-o'clock shadow grating against my jaw bone, his weight on top of me. I could feel him move to pull down his jeans and then grind his hard-on against my pubic bone, which is when, I feel ashamed to say, I felt a little bit turned on, and sickened all at the same time.

As he thrust his alcohol-laced tongue in my mouth again I gave him a sharp shove and forcibly pushed him off me with all my strength and ran into the fluorescent lit kitchen and threw my guts up into the sink, heaving and choking and fighting back tears, while the prick stood behind me and went, 'Fuckin' hell. Gross.'

And when I finally raised my head from the sink, stomach emptied, face wet with tears, I turned around and he was gone and the apartment was still. I breathed a huge sigh of relief. I filled a mug with water and curled into a ball on the couch and slept.

When I caught the bus home it was already mid-Saturday afternoon and I was still in my heels and tiny black strapless dress, all panda-eyed and sticky and stinking with sweat. *The walk of shame.* I had to beg my way onto the bus because I spent my last few silver coins trying to ring Casey from a payphone in the city, my mobile out of credit. I just kept getting her voicemail. 'Hey bitches, I'm not answering because I'm having a better time than you. Leave me a message and I might ring you back.'

The bus driver, a youngish guy with tattoos and a buzzcut, found it really amusing to heckle me.

'Big night?' He grinned. 'Invite me next time.'

'Sure.' I played along, leaning over so my cleavage showed a little. 'Let me on for free?'

'Nothing's free.' He blinked at me, keeping a straight face for several seconds before grinning again. 'Kidding. Get on.'

I pulled off my heels as soon as I got off at my stop. I sucked in a sharp breath as the concrete burned my sore feet, and hobbled over to the prickly dry grass and sat down in the shade of a grey gum to inspect my blisters.

FML.

My mobile rang. Casey.

'Hey,' I croaked into the phone.

'Where're you?' Casey demanded.

'Where're *you*? I had to catch the fucking bus home.'

'I was out with Danny getting food!'

'Fair enough. I'm nearly home now.'

'Danny spoke to Mick this morning and reckons you were being a total prick tease last night.'

'Who the fuck is Mick?'

I could hear Casey exhale impatiently. 'The guys we went home with! Danny and Mick!'

'He was being a creep. Like, trying to force me to have sex with him on the couch.'

There was a long silence on the other end of the line.

'Hello? Casey?'

'I just dunno what your problem is, Jez. Mick is totally hot. He plays under-nineteens for the Raiders, you know.'

I'd had enough of the conversation.

'Look, Case, I gotta go. I'll catch ya, okay?'

I hung up the phone and let my head droop between my knees. The summer smells of cut grass and flowers burned in my throat and sinuses, and I was so dehydrated I could hardly swallow. I closed my eyes and imagined the skies filling with black clouds, rolls of thunder and then sheets of rain pouring down on my face. I pictured myself wandering out into the street, splashing in puddles and opening my mouth to catch the raindrops on my tongue. My eyes snapped open as I felt an insect biting at my ankle. A red ant. I squished it hard between my thumb and forefinger ... *You little fucker!* My ankle was already swelling and the pain was searing.

'Jez?!' I heard a young girl's voice giggle. 'OMG. Lukey, it's Jez!'

Lukey and his little sister, Ashleigh. Lukey slid down next to me, his back against the tree, his arm touching mine. Ashleigh knelt in front of us, her mobile glued to her hand, as usual.

'Oh, my God, Jez.' Ashleigh hung her mouth open as she stared intently at her mobile screen. 'We almost didn't recognise you.' She slid her phone in her pocket and grinned at me. 'Why're you all sluzzered up?'

'You look …' Lukey began.

I held up my hand to his face. 'Don't even.'

'You look nice.' Lukey pinched my leg gently.

'Argh! No pinching! An ant just bit me!' I stuck my ankle out to show him.

'Ouch. Saliva is meant to help, want me to spit on it?' He puckered his mouth as if he was going to spit.

'You do it, you die!'

'Ha ha, okay then. So what'd you get up to last night? That looks like a Casey type of outfit.'

I sighed. 'Yeah, went out with Casey. Such a full-on night.'

'You look better in Jez clothes. I don't get why you'd want to look like Casey.'

'Something different. Casey was all like, "Dress up! Wear something sexy!", so …'

'Meh.' Lukey shrugged. 'I don't really dig on that whole look. I mean, you do look nice. But you don't look like you.'

'Hey, I totally decked this guy at a party.' I laughed, changing the subject. 'It was off tap.'

'Serious? What the fuck?'

'Yeah, he was coming on to me or whatever and I just,' I demonstrated with my fist, 'SMACK!'

'You go, girl,' Ashleigh muttered, her phone back in her hand. 'Hey, Lukey, I'm gunna go over to Chantelle's house, okay?'

'You spending the night there?'

'Probs. Dunno.' Ashleigh got to her feet. 'Laters.' She fluttered her fingers over her shoulder as she strutted off.

'Teenage girls.' Lukey shook his head. 'What were you like at thirteen?'

'You *knew* me at thirteen.'

'I dunno what Ashleigh's up to these days. She doesn't tell me shit anymore. She's never at home, always at her friends' houses.'

'Sounds pretty normal.'

'Not that I blame her. Mark and Dad got into a fuck-off fight last night. It was mental.'

'Shiiit. What happened? Who won?'

Lukey shrugged. 'They were just drinking and then, bam, argument. Me and Ash just stayed in my room all night. Did you know she's started smoking ciggies?'

'We were smoking at thirteen.'

'Yeah …' Lukey stared off into the distance. 'But she's my little sister.'

'So?'

'You wouldn't understand. You're an only child.'

'Doesn't mean I don't understand.'

'I want to leave, I feel bad for leaving her there, though. She's, like, already starting to fuck up. I'm the only kinda normal person in her life.'

'So are you gunna leave?' I swallowed, my mouth dry.

'I kinda have to.' Lukey put his arm around me. 'It's Mark. He's the world's biggest derro.'

'He's gotten worse.'

'Yeah, tell me about it. I remember even when I was about ten or eleven, just before Mum got sick, he wasn't so bad. One time at the skate park this big group of guys were trying to pick on me, trying to roll me for my shoes or something, and Mark just walked over, real calm, and picked up a deck and just started swinging. It was fuckin' awesome. Then he even bought me Maccas after ... back when I still ate meat 'n that.'

'What happened to him?'

'I dunno. Mum died and then he was just always fucked up. Ha, not like I can talk, huh? I'm always maggot on something.'

'You're not a jerk, though.'

'I'm a different kind of jerk.'

'Yeah.'

'Hey!' Lukey gave me a shove. 'Anyway, I thought you could look out for her. For Ash. After I'm gone.'

'Me?' I wriggled away from him so I could look him in the face. 'She's *your* sister.'

'As a favour. For me.'

'Maybe I was gunna come with you! You asked me to come, didn't you?'

'Yeah, but that was before ...'

'Before what?'

'I dunno. You're being weird. You've barely even spoken to me for, like, two weeks.'

'Ooooh, two whole weeks!' I sargasmed. 'What would happen if I didn't see you for, like, a month! I'd be practically dead to you!'

'Well, why haven't you called me or anything?'

'No credit on my phone.'

'Facebook?'

'Why haven't *you* called *me*?'

''Cos you've been a mega bitch lately. Like fully losing your rag at me for no reason. Getting jealous if I hang out with Laura and all that.'

'I'm not jealous.'

'Could've fooled me. What's your problem with her anyway?'

'I don't know. Nothing, I guess.'

'She thinks it's because you like me. Like, *like* like me.'

'Oh! Sure!' I scoffed.

'She said she doesn't want to cut your grass.'

'There's no grass!'

'Yeah, well ...'

'There's no fuckin' grass!'

'She tries hard when she's around you, extra hard when you get all up in her stuff, talking smack.'

'Talking *smack*?! Ha ha, where do you get this shit from?'

'The internet mostly.' Lukey grinned. 'But serious, Jezza, she's just trying to get you to like her.'

'But why does she care?'

'Because she wants friends here, and she likes you. She told me so. She said, "Jez is so fun when she isn't losing her rag."'

'I can't imagine Laura saying "losing her rag".'

'Something like that. Give her a chance.'

'Maybe. Did I tell you we went over there for dinner last night? Me and Mum with her family?'

'No shit.' Lukey laughed. 'How was that?'

'Not as bad as I thought it was gunna be,' I told him. 'The food was awesome.'

'So you're thinking about coming, then? To Melbourne?'

'Definitely *thinking* about it. I kinda wanna finish school, too.'

'Serious? I didn't know that.'

'I passed all my subjects this year.'

'Fuckin' hell, Jez. You got brains, hey? That's rad.'

I shrugged. 'I dunno. Like, what are you gunna do for money?'

'I dunno, hey. Just anything I can get really.'

'I don't want to end up working in Woolies or something crap like that.'

'Nah, me neither. Fuck that. I'll get a job in a pub or something once I'm eighteen.'

'My mum works the bar. Turns you into an alco.'

'Ha ha. I wouldn't care. Free drinks are free drinks.'

'Yeah, I guess so.'

Lukey looked at his digital Casio. 'I gotta bounce. See if Dad and Mark have killed each other yet. Cross fingers.'

''Kay.'

'Call me later?'

'Yep.'

I started to walk towards my house.

'Hey, Jez!' Lukey called, about twenty metres away. 'Do you?'

'What?'

Lukey's voice cracked a little. *'Like* like me?'

My heart did little flips as I saw his hopeful eyes searching my face.

'Laura should shut her fat pie hole!' I yelled, and grinned so he could see I was joking.

I turned around and dashed across the melting-hot tarred road.

TWENTY-TWO

• •

I slept late into the night and woke up, bleary-eyed and head-fucked, to Mum rapping loudly on my bedroom door.

'Fuck!' My head pounded with dehydration. 'Can you give it a rest?'

'I've just had Dana on the phone.' Mum put her hands on her hips. 'She reckons you and Casey ditched Laura in the city last night!'

I pulled my pillow over my face. 'Not true,' I mumbled into the pillow. 'It wasn't even like that.'

Mum snatched the pillow off my face. 'So you and Casey didn't take off and leave Laura by herself? In a strange city she doesn't know?'

'She left! She said she wanted to go home!'

'Oh, *Jez*! Why didn't you walk her to the taxi? Apparently she was wandering around lost for half an hour, hassled out by a bunch of drunks.'

'I don't know! Is she okay?'

'She's fine. Dana isn't too impressed with you, though, letting her daughter roam the streets by herself when she was supposed to be out with her friends!'

'Oh, Mum. This is Canberra, not the ghetto. Melbourne would have been tons more dangerous.'

'That's not the point —'

'Well I don't know what the point is then.'

'Just … The point is …' Mum lost her parental nagging rhythm. 'Look, just apologise, okay?'

Mum threw the pillow back in my face and left the room.

The next day I went over to apologise to Laura. I kept picturing the look on her face when Casey told her to fuck off.

Dana answered the door.

'Jez!' Her voice sounded friendly, but her mouth was pressed into a straight line. I don't reckon I was her favourite person in the world at that moment. 'Laura's just popped to the shop for some munchies. I'm all greasy hands.' She held up her black-slicked palms as evidence. 'We've been working on one of my bikes. You want to take a look?'

'Sure.' I half shrugged and followed Dana out to the backyard.

'Here we go,' Dana gestured. 'What do you think? A vintage lowrider. Needs a new paint job and then she'll be right to sell.'

'That is awesome!' I breathed. 'I would totally ride that.'

'Thanks.' Dana smiled. 'It's a lot of fun.'

Dana raised a hand to her short, spiked blonde hair and then remembering her dirty hands, wiped them on the back of her bib and brace overalls.

'What colour are you going to do it?'

'Hm ... not sure yet. What do you think?'

'Red! Or maybe electric blue and black!'

'Like your hair?' Dana smiled.

'My favourite colours,' I admitted.

'I've always been a bike lover. Since I was a kid and me and my friends would ride around the neighbourhood together. I guess I never grew out of it.'

'I've never had a bike,' I told her. 'I'm more of a walker.'

'Canberra's so spaced out, though. You need a bike.'

'Maybe ... Look, I just came to say sorry for ditching Laura the other night in the city. Well, we didn't really ditch her. But she really wanted to go home, and I probably should have gone with her.'

'I appreciate your apology, Jez. She's my only daughter. I'd like for her to have some good friends who will watch out for her, and she can watch out for them. That'd really give me some piece of mind.' Dana spoke in a low gruff voice, but I could tell she really cared heaps about Laura. It made me feel guilty.

'Yeah …' I swallowed. 'Well, sorry.'

'So who is this Casey girl who was out with you?'

'My neighbour. She's okay.'

'Not according to your mum.'

'Mum doesn't like her much,' I admitted.

'Why's that?'

'I dunno. I guess she's kind of loose.'

'Loose? Like, sexually?'

I felt a blush in my cheeks. 'Nah, loose just means off tap. Like, a bit wild. But yeah, I guess sexually … That, too.'

'Sorry.' Dana grinned. 'Not up on the kid lingo.'

I shrugged. 'I hate it when my mum tries to talk young.'

'So you want to help me with this bike? I could do with an extra set of hands until Laura gets back. She's not that into the bikes anyway.'

'Yeah!' I was pretty keen, in spite of myself. 'What are you doing?'

Dana showed me this ripped old banana seat that she was going to re-pad and cover with a sheet of thick sparkly silver vinyl. It looked super rad. I helped her hold the padding in place while she fitted the base back onto the seat. I was so busy asking Dana questions about how she was going to customise the bike that I didn't notice Laura come into the yard until her shadow fell over us.

'Hi,' she said, all moody and flat, munching from a bag of Kettle chips.

'Hey,' I said.

'Hey, baby-doll.' Dana's face softened when she spoke to her daughter. 'Nice walk?'

Laura shrugged and perched herself on the edge of a sun lounger near the above-ground pool. 'It was alright. What are you doing here, Jez?'

I straightened myself up, shaking out my leg that had gone to sleep from sitting on the grass. 'Came to say sorry for the other night. Sorry I didn't bail with you.'

'Really?' Laura looked from me to Dana. 'Or is it because my mum rang your mum?'

I shifted, mega-uncomfortable. 'Nah ...'

'She treats me like I'm five years old!' Laura nodded to Dana and then stood up. 'I'll be inside. Too hot out here.'

'What are you doing now, then?' Dana asked. 'Why don't you offer Jez something to drink?'

'I'm just gunna watch telly,' Laura said dully, and dangled her hand in her packet of chips. 'If that's alright with you.'

The light had gone from behind Laura's eyes. I'd seen it happen to heaps of kids that'd grown up round here. One minute they're kids and they have a sparkle and they're laughing and playing games and then their fire just fizzles out. Next time you see them they're chaining durries and sinking Bundy Cokes at the Village and there's just nothing there anymore but blank, bored, stupid expressions on their dials. I wasn't surprised it'd happened to Laura, but I was surprised it had happened so fast. And surprised that it made me sad.

'Look, Laura,' I began. 'I'm really sorry about ditching you, and that party being so shitty and ...'

'Did you have a good night?' Laura didn't sound annoyed, more distracted.

'No,' I said. 'It was really shit. I probably should have just caught the taxi home. But then I would have been ditching Case, so ...'

'You could have walked me to the taxi rank. I got lost.'

I put my hands up in defeat.

'I'll be inside.'

Dana and I watched as Laura crossed the yard, sandals scuffing through the dry grass, then across the patio, into the house.

'She's not coping well,' Dana murmured, inspecting the bike seat. 'With the move and everything else.'

'It must suck for her. 'Cos in Melbourne there's so much to do, and here it's like ... dead.'

'It'll be good for her. I grew up in a neighbourhood like this. I loved it. We knew all our neighbours, and I was friends with all the kids in my street.'

'I think probably times have changed.'

'Yeah.' Dana gave a short laugh. 'Maybe I'm out of touch, huh?'

'No. You're cool for a parent.'

Dana smiled half-heartedly. 'I wasn't always a parent. Sometimes I forget that's what I am.'

'I'll go cheer Laura up.' I started towards the house.

'Jez,' Dana called after me. 'Thanks. You're a good kid. Don't let the bastards drag you down, if you know what I mean.'

I kind of knew.

'Sure,' I replied.

'And if you ever want me to fix you up with a bike ...'

'Sweet as.' I nodded. I locked eyes with Dana. We were kind of having one of those 'moments' like you see on the telly. I wondered if people had telly moments before telly was invented, or if telly had invented the moments thing and now people were trying to live like the lives of people they saw on the TV. I was no good at telly moments so I just hurried into the house extra quick, suddenly starving and hoping Laura hadn't finished all those chips yet.

Laura was in the kitchen pouring some Maltesers from a bag into a bowl.

'You mind?' I gestured towards them. 'I'm wasting with hunger.'

'Go ahead. I shouldn't be eating this shit anyway.'

'Cheers.' I popped a few chocolates in my mouth and chewed thoughtfully. 'You're upset about what Casey said, huh?'

'Casey's a fucking bitch.'

'Casey is a bitch,' I confessed to her. 'But she's okay once you get to know her a bit.'

'If she's a bitch, why do you hang out with her?'

'I dunno. I don't really. I don't really have female friends,' I told her. 'At school I'd just hang round with Lukey and Martin and a couple of other guys. Casey's sort of the same. She's not a girl's girl. She likes hanging with the boys.'

Laura narrowed her eyes a little. 'You know, girls who say that, it always makes me cautious.'

'Say what?'

'That they don't like other women.' Laura folded her arms and leaned back against the kitchen counter. 'How can you just rule out fifty percent of the population based on their gender? And then hang out with Casey even though she's so nasty?'

'I dunno.' I was flustered. 'Girls are just mean, hey. Guys don't dog each other the way girls do.'

'I've never dogged you, Jez. Not on purpose anyway.'

She had me there. Laura had really tried to be my friend. It was mostly me who'd been a cow to her.

'Start again? I am sorry, hey.' I looked her in the eyes. I was totally sincere.

Laura just stared. Then she grabbed the bowl of Maltesers from my hands.

'It doesn't matter, Jez,' she muttered before she turned towards the lounge room. 'I really don't care anymore.'

I let myself out the front door.

TWENTY-THREE
• •

I hate Christmas. Even when I was a kid, I never got the presents I wanted, it was always hot, and while I imagined every other family crowding around one of those perfect silver-and-blue baubled trees like I saw in David Jones, oohing and ahhing over their perfectly wrapped presents, then sitting down to eat one of those turkeys the size of a VW beetle, my Christmases never turned out like that.

I don't even bother getting presents for people. When I was about eight, maybe nine, I saved up my pocket money for twelve weeks, a dollar a week, to buy Mum an oil burner. It was a ceramic dish with a hole underneath where you could light a tea light candle and make your house smelly. I paid four bucks for it at the Dollar Shop and then bought a tiny bottle of rose oil to go with it. I hid it in an old shoebox under my bed, and was nearly sick with anticipation and excitement to give it to my mum. I kept picturing her face light up, and then her drawing me into a big hug, saying I was the best daughter ever.

Then about a week before Christmas me and Mum were in the Dollar Shop stocking up on plastic Christmas-themed tableware and serviettes and we walked past the shelves filled with the ceramic oil burners and I decided to test Mum out.

'These are real pretty.' I picked one up and showed it to her.

Mum wrinkled her face and took it out of my hand and put it back on the shelf. 'They stink. Give me migraine headaches.'

Later that night after Mum went to bed I took the oil burner out into the backyard and threw it against the concrete, smashing it into little bits and then scooped up the pieces with my hands and put them into the outside bin along with the little bottle of oil.

I thought about it every Christmas after that, and it always made me sad. So I never bothered buying presents.

I walked into the kitchen Christmas morning wrapped in my kimono robe. Mum was making a store-bought barbecue chicken dance while stripping off its skin and putting one bit on a plastic platter then tilting back her neck and dropping a fatty bit of chicken skin into her mouth, then smacking her shiny lips. Mum'd moved her telly from her bedroom to the kitchen table so she could watch Christmas specials while she cooked.

KISS Saves Christmas was playing on a table loaded with plastic tubs of Woolies creamy potato and pasta salads.

Mum clocked me standing in the doorway and gave me a wink.

'I bought that haloumi you like!' She held up a packet. 'Like we had over at Dana and Joan's. We can stick it under the grill as a starter.'

I shrugged. 'Yeah, it was alright. Shouldn't you put these salads in the fridge? It must be forty degrees already.'

'Fridge is too full!'

I opened the fridge door. It was stacked with six-packs of Bundy and Coke, Vodka Cruisers, bottles of wine and cans of soft drink.

'Santa's been, love!' Mum plopped the chicken down and wiped her hands on a teatowel. 'Come and check under the tree!'

I smiled in spite of myself. 'You're a dag,' I told Mum.

I knelt on the carpet next to the three-foot tall green plastic tree that Mum had put up and draped a few scraggly bits of tinsel over. There were two presents underneath, both had JEZ written in permanent black marker right across the wrapping paper.

'Remember I gave you that fifty bucks at the shops the other day, so just a few small things for Chrissie morning.'

I opened the biggest present first. It was a family-sized box of Cadbury chocolates.

'Yummo.' I faked a big smile.

'We'll share them after lunch, ay?' Mum looked pleased as punch with herself. 'Now open your other present. You're gunna love this.'

I tore the wrapping off the smaller gift.

'Oh … wow.' My mouth fell open.

I lifted up a delicate silk-and-lace camisole and matching boxer shorts. They were royal blue, the same colour as the streak in my hair. They were beautiful.

'Mum!' I was speechless.

'Real silk!' Mum was dancing from one foot to the other, practically exploding.

I felt a horrible lump in my throat. I had been such a bitch to my mother, I didn't think I deserved such a nice pressie.

Mum knelt next to me and stuck her arm around my shoulders and gave them a squeeze.

'A proper adult gift for a beautiful woman,' Mum said softly, de-tangling my bed hair with her fingers.

I wanted to hold her, like really really hold her and squash my face into her breasts like I did when I was a little kid and I'd skinned my knee and was crying, but I had to push her away because I was getting all choked up.

'You usually have such shit taste!' I laughed. 'This … is so … *me*!'

Mum beamed. 'Who'd have thought?'

I nodded, trying to control myself. 'Thanks, Mum. It's a great pressie. Sorry I didn't get you anything.'

'Bah, I'd rather you save your money and spend it on something for yourself. You want to help me set up the table outside?' Mum asked.

'Sure.'

I thought maybe my Christmas that year wouldn't turn out so bad after all.

TWENTY-FOUR

. .

'What is *this?*' Sharon held up a slice of grilled haloumi with her fork.

'We had it at Dana and Joan's last week, didn't we, Jez?' Mum said brightly.

'The lesbians?' Shaz raised her eyebrows.

'It's called haloumi, Shaz,' I said. 'It's a type of cheese. It's good. Eat it.'

'I'm from Kambah, honey. I don't eat bloody parmesan let alone bloody *halowmi*!'

I narrowed my eyes at her purposeful mispronunciation. *Stupid old cunt,* I seethed. She'd heard of haloumi, she wasn't that dense. Okay, so I'd only first tried it the week earlier, but I had definitely *heard* of it before.

I plopped myself down in a chair and lit a smoke.

'Yeah, it's just salty cheese, Shaz. La de da, hey. I saw it on Jamie Oliver so thought we'd give it a whirl, but Bega's the go, hey?' I said, dripping sarcasm.

'You can't beat a good tasty.' Shaz nodded.

Mum felt sorry for Shaz having to be alone at Christmas, but personally I thought it wasn't any wonder that Shaz was an old spinster with cobwebs growing over her vag. She had a permanent sneer on her face, lips like a cat's arsehole, with deep lines all around her mouth from years of sucking down the durries.

Across the table from me and Shaz, Mum was sitting between Barry and Greta, who both worked with her at the club. Barry was the groundskeeper. He had one of those craggy complexions made up of lumps and craters that formed the appearance of desert rock and gave the impression they might crumble and fall off his cheeks at any moment. He wasn't holding back on getting stuck into the booze. As he tipped beer into his face he kept burping loudly and saying, 'That was a good one!' like he wanted us to congratulate him.

'You know how to make a bush vibrator?' he asked Mum, loudly, making sure the rest of the table could hear. 'Put a blowfly in a Coke bottle!'

'Good one, Baz,' Mum said weakly and took a long sip of her white wine.

Greta was just as bad as Barry. She was a miserable old cow. Mum said it was because she'd had a divorce the year before; her husband had been rooting some other chick behind her back and now she was all depressed. I found it hard to believe she'd ever been happy-go-lucky. Even when she 'smiled' her mouth was turned down at the sides. She got on a storm with Shaz. Everything Shaz whinged about—which was *everything*: the weather (too hot), the food (tastes a bit weird … was the cream in date?), the beer (could be colder, is your fridge working alright?)—Greta humphed in agreement and snorted, 'Too right!' while looking down at her nose, avoiding everyone's eyes.

Mum was doing that thing she did when she started talking loudly and drinking fuckloads of wine to try to convince everyone that everything was awesome.

'Where's Jeremy?' I asked Mum.

'He'll be here. He's with his family for lunch and coming over here after that.'

'Jeremy!' Shaz scoffed. 'I still can't believe you're going out with *Jeremy*!'

'Going out with? So he's like your proper boyfriend now?' I interrupted, but everyone ignored me.

'Jeremy's a nice bloke,' Mum said mildly. 'He's sweet.'

'Sweet?!' Shaz crowed. 'Who cares about sweet? Can he … y'know … satisfy you?'

'Yeah.' Greta raised her eyebrows. 'Is he good in the sack?'

'I don't wanna know.' Barry held up both hands.

'Me neither!' I raised my voice. 'This is my mother we're talking about!'

'Your *mother* had a very good sex life once upon a time.' Shaz fluttered her acrylic nails at me.

'Alright, alright, change of subject.' Mum clapped her hands. 'Jez is here.'

'Tell us more about *Jeremy*,' Shaz insisted and turned to me. 'You know your mother blew me off last Saturday night for *Jeremy* ...'

'I didn't blow you off, Shaz, I was working,' Mum said, getting up. 'Who wants another Cruiser? Bundy?'

'No, you did, 'cos what time did you finish work?' Shaz leaned back on her chair legs, yelling after Mum.

'Two in the morning!' Mum screeched from the kitchen.

'And I wanted to kick on and what did you want to do?'

'Shaz.' Mum reappeared with an armful of Bundies and Cruisers. 'I was dog-tired. I went to Jeremy's but we went to sleep.'

Mum pressed a Cruiser into my chest as she passed my chair. I think she wanted me on-side that day. *Schaweet*, I thought, popping the top and taking a big gulp. It tasted like a strawberry Chupa Chup.

'Oh, sure! Youse went to sleep! I seeeee,' Shaz sargasmed.

'Settle down, Shaz. Helen's got a new love, of course she'll be wanting to please her bloke,' Barry said.

'Love?' I mumbled.

Mum patted my hand. 'Early days, Jez. Baby steps.'

'Love?!' Shaz hooted. 'With Jeremy! He's got a mug only a mother could love! Of course, you *are* a mother.'

'Settle down, Shaz.' Mum frowned.

'Nearly old enough to be his mother, too!'

'Lay off, Shaz.' Barry rounded the table and gave Shaz a squeeze around the shoulders. 'We're all mates. Now, where's the dunny, Hel? I gotta strangle a brown snake.'

I closed my eyes for a second.

'Yeah, Shaz, enough out of you,' Mum said firmly. 'He'll be here soon! Oh and Linda and Davo said they might drop by with their kid. What's his name again? Jordan? Jayden?'

'Who knows!' Shaz flicked her wrist dismissively. 'Haven't seen either of 'em in yonkers.'

'Linda was at the club a few weeks ago having dinner. I thought it might be nice to invite her over, for old time's sake.'

'Bah! Old times ...'

'Remember how we all used to have single girls' Christmas? We were like those *Sex and the City* women, hey, Shaz? That's what we always used to say. Which one was I? I was Charlotte —'

''Cos you're the most pear-shaped ...'

'Because I was always the arty one. And Kaye was Carrie because of her curly hair, and Linda was Samantha because all the boys wanted to root her!'

'Which one were you, Shaz?' I asked, wanting to say she should have been Samantha because she was a giant sluzza.

'I was Miranda, the smart one.'

'Ha ha! No, it was because you were flat-chested!' Mum hooted. 'Sorry, Shaz, but it's true. If you don't have the chicken fillets in your bra, there isn't a lump or bump. The boys at our school used to call her "Flapjacks". Oh, God, they were so cruel. Sorry, Shazza. You have to admit it's kinda funny.'

Shaz folded her arms across her chest and pursed her lips. 'It's better than your nickname in high school, *Helen Breville*!'

'Breville? What does Breville mean?'

'Don't, Shaz. Seriously. Just shut up.' Mum's face started reddening. 'It's gross.'

'*Breville*,' Shaz announced loudly, for the benefit of me and Greta. 'Because opening up her legs was like pulling apart a toasted cheese sanger.'

'Oh. My. GOD!' I clutched my head in my hands. 'First of all, TMI. Second of all, that is probably the most disgusting thing I've ever heard.'

'Thanks for that, Shaz. Thanks for telling my seventeen-year-old *daughter* that. It was only a few stupid boys anyway.'

'You're welcome!' Shaz smiled archly and settled back in her chair.

'Shaz, you know you are *such* a bitch —' I began.

'Jez! Enough!' Mum smacked her palms lightly on the table. 'Let's just have a nice Chrissie, no bitching, no fighting.'

'Hmph,' I grunted.

'Party games? Cards, maybe?'

'Goon of Fortune?' I joked, grinning.

Mum and Shaz cheered and laughed. 'GOON OF FORTUNE!'

Goon of Fortune is one of those games that people cracked out at parties when everyone was already too maggot to realise what a pointless game it was. A bunch of people circle the Hills Hoist and you peg a bladder of cheap wine to the line. People take turns spinning the clothes line and whoever the wine sack lands in front of has to scull for five seconds. Me and Lukey were playing Goon of Fortune at a party at Martin's house once and the goon kept stopping in front of Lukey, like, every single time. He ended up having mad voms in the bushes that night. Then the next day when we woke up and stumbled into Martin's backyard for a durrie we noticed the Hills Hoist was totally busted and on a slant, bound to stop in the same place every time no matter how you spun it, and Lukey'd been standing at the lowest point in the slant all night.

'Hello?! You out here?' Jeremy called over the side gate.

'Come in! Come in!' Mum leapt to her feet, but her fat arse was wedged in the lawn chair and it travelled halfway across the yard with her before it fell off and thunked onto the lawn. I snorted a little and Mum shot me a look, *Don't you start . . .*

'Hey, everyone! Baz, Greta, Jez, Shaz.' Jeremy beamed as he crossed the yard, one arm slung around Mum's shoulders and the other carrying an esky and plastic shopping bag.

'Jez!' Barry boomed, stepping onto the back porch and I looked up sharply. Jeremy and I looked at each other awkwardly. 'Other Jez!' Barry laughed. 'Sorry, Jessica, at the club we've got Jeremy who we all call Jez.'

Fuckin' hell ... I plastered a stupidly grim smile on my face. *Everyone's nickname ending in 'z'. So shamefully bogan.*

'True that.' Jeremy laughed, pulling up a seat beside me. 'Your mum has to talk about you as Jessica so we don't get confused.'

'She'll always be my first Jez.' Mum was practically crying with happiness. It was so gross. 'Jeremy is Jeremy to me.'

'I got you both a little something.' Jeremy reached into his bag. 'Sorry they're not wrapped. I'm not a good wrapper.'

'Not a good wrapper,' Shaz snorted behind her Cruiser, her eyes fluttering backwards into her skull, pissed as fuck.

'Here you go, Hel ... and you, Jez,' Jeremy said shyly.

I stared blankly at the box in my hands, it was a coffee mug with Harry Potter on the side.

'Your mum said you're a bit of a fan,' Jeremy explained.

'Thanks, Jeremy,' I said, putting the unopened box on the table.

'Oh, nice one, Jeremy.' Shaz picked up the box and turned it over in her hands. 'I saw these down at Kmart Tuggers. Bargain.'

Fuckin' Shaz, the Queen of the Moles.

'It's really awesome, Jeremy,' I said loudly and leaned across the table to snatch the box out of Shaz's hands. 'I'm a huge Harry Potter fan. I love it.'

Jeremy blinked at me and swigged from his beer nervously.

'Oh, my God, Jeremy, you shouldn't have!' Mum exclaimed over her little stone-coloured Buddha statue. 'How did you know I collected Buddhas?!'

'I saw the collection on your drawers,' Jeremy said. 'Thought one more couldn't hurt.'

Wait, I thought. *Jeremy had been over here?! When was this? Where was I?* I tried to catch Mum's attention so I could give her the hairy eyeball, but she carefully avoided my stare.

'So, so thoughtful,' Mum gushed, hopping up to give Jeremy a peck on the cheek.

'When are we gunna be seeing you down at the club, Jez?' Greta asked.

As if I would hang out at that shithole . . .

'She'll be eighteen in June,' Mum answered for me.

'Thursday nights are best,' Greta advised, her mouth turned down at the corners, staring at a point somewhere behind my head. 'Meat tray raffle on the chocolate wheel.'

'Right.' I nodded. 'I'll keep that in mind.'

'What's this? Little Jez gunna join us at the club?' Barry boomed loudly. 'Tell you what, when are you turning eighteen?'

'June,' I said, cringing as Barry came up behind me and put his hands on my shoulders. *Oh. My. God . . . I hope you washed your hands after the toilet.*

'I want her to go for a job at the club,' Mum said. 'Maybe pulling beers behind the bar.'

'A couple of the girls in the bistro are around your age, Jez.' Jeremy cracked a beer. 'Do you know Marika? She's got the eyebrow piercing and the crazy hair?'

'Yeah, I know her.'

'You know Sarah Richards? Short little chubby thing?'

'Yep.'

'They're waitressing in the bistro now.'

'Awesome.'

'Tell you what,' Barry said, pulling his chair up so our elbows were touching. 'You come see your old Uncle Baz on your birthday, I'll fix you up with some nice Scotch and Cokes on me. And I'll introduce you to a few of the lads from the club, how's that? You got a boyfriend, darlin'?'

'Not really,' I mumbled.

'A few real nice lads down at the club. Be stoked to have a nice little lady like you for company.'

'Alright, Barry,' Mum said. 'You're embarrassing Jez. She doesn't need you to fix her up. She'll do fine on her own.'

'Weren't you seeing Cash? Cash Holland?' Jeremy said innocently. 'He's a mate of mine. He said youse were getting a bit friendly.'

I could feel my face redden and my throat get all tight. The warm creamy pasta salad I'd eaten for lunch turned over in my belly.

Mum laughed loudly. 'Cash?! Cash Holland!' she hooted. 'Cash, our neighbour?!' Mum continued. 'He's the same age as you, isn't he, Jeremy?'

'Well, yeah. We went to school together.'

'Jez!' Mum turned to me and clocked the expression on my face. 'Jez … you're not seeing that Cash Holland are you? … Jez?'

'We just hung out a few times. Went swimming.'

'Right, but he's not your boyfriend, is he? I mean he's way too old for you.' Mum picked up her fork and started stabbing the scraps of food on her plate.

'He's not even that much older than me, Mum.'

'Oh, my Gaawd! Jez has gone so RED!' Shaz hooted. 'Look at her face! Like a freakin' fire engine!'

'Shut up, *Shaz*,' I hissed.

'Don't tell Shaz to shut up.' Mum dropped her fork. 'So is this boy your boyfriend or what? Why are you so embarrassed?'

'Why do you even *care*, Mum?!' I half shrieked. 'You didn't bother telling me you were fucking Jeremy for however many months, did you?'

'I'm not talking about *me* …'

'But you're a hypocrite! You reckon Cash is too old for me, but you're seeing Jeremy who's like, eight years younger than you!'

'That's true, Hel.' Shaz nodded. 'Double standards there. Jeremy isn't even old enough to be *her* dad.' She jabbed a finger in my direction.

'I had a younger lady once. Turned up at her house and she had nothing on but a Dire Straits record …' Baz squinted against the sunlight.

'Change the subject, ay?' Jeremy sort of coughed and shifted in his chair. 'Everyone goin' down the club for New Year's?'

''Course,' Shaz drawled, fanning her face with a paper plate.

'Yep, I'll be there,' Greta agreed with the same measure of boredom.

'Actually, I might have to join you lot later in the evening.' Mum forced a smile. 'Dana and Joan, who had us over for dinner the other day ... They're having a little do.'

'Whaaaaat?!' Sharon sat bolt upright. 'Helen, we always do New Year's at the club! You're gunna skip out on us for a fuckin' dyke party? What the fuck?'

'A dinner party.' Mum's face dropped again. She looked tired. Her mouth was starting to go all slack from too many Bundy and Cokes. 'Be nice. You're invited, too, Jeremy.'

'I'm not going,' I said.

'You're not invited!' Mum replied. 'Adults only. I think we might get a bit too naughty for kids' eyes.'

'Right.' I raised my eyebrows. 'Whatever.'

'You hardly even know those lesbians!' Shaz was fuming. 'You're gunna ditch your good mates for a couple of dykes you just met!'

Shaz was giving Mum full death-ray stares. Mum fidgeted around uncomfortably, sliding down in her seat and hitching herself back up with her elbows, and then attempting to cross her legs then realising her thighs were way too fat. Eventually she sighed and slid down in her seat again and drank deeply from her can of Bundy, tipping the last drops down her throat.

'Helen!' Shaz demanded. 'What about Jeremy? You'll be going to the club, won't you, Jeremy?'

'Yeah, I was gunna. But if I'm invited to this dinner, I could pop along ...'

'Oh, for fuck's sake, Jeremy!' Shaz snapped. 'Grow some balls.'

'They're good peepo.' Mum stood up unsteadily, swaying like a tree in the breeze. 'I'm gunna get another ...'

'I'll get it, Hel.' Greta got up but mum waved her to sit down.

'Yep.' Shaz raised her half-full Cruiser to her lips and sculled the rest in a few gulps, her eyes still fixed on Mum.

I followed Mum into the house.

'You wan' another?' Mum spoke into the refrigerator. 'Ah, Gawwwd, it's so nice 'n cooool. Bloody stinker today.'

'Yeah, chuck us one of those Cruisers. Shaz is being a total bitch today.'

'Ahhh, we're all a bit hot 'n bothered. I might have a dig in the shed to see if I can find that old shade umbrella.'

'So if lunch is finished, can I go?'

Mum turned around and handed me a Cruiser. 'Yeah, I guess so. Where're you going?'

'I dunno. Lukey's probably.'

Mum frowned. 'Stick 'round just a bit longer? Jeremy just got here.'

'Muuuum. Please. I'm frying into a little crisp out there and I'm fully gunna just punch Shaz in a minute, she is being so annoying. Barry's a dirty old man and Greta's just creepy —'

'Alright, alright!' Mum cracked a Cruiser and raised it to her lips. 'Go on then! Bring Lukey over here a bit later, though. I haven't seen him in ages.'

"Kay. Thanks. I'll help clean up tomorrow, I promise.'

I went to my room and pulled off my sweaty clothes and stood in front of the fan for a few minutes to cool off before changing into some denim cut-offs and a black singlet top. My hair was damp and prickly on the back of my neck and my throat was already dry with dehydration. Through my bedroom window I could hear the crackle and rumble of a motorbike approaching from down the street. My heart leapt with excitement. *Cash.*

I didn't even have time to reapply my melting make-up. I tugged on my sneakers and flew out the front door then dug my heels in to slow down as Cash's motorbike pulled into the Hollands' driveway. I stuck my thumbs into the pockets of my shorts and tried to look casual as I walked across the front lawn.

'Hey!' I smiled as Cash undid his helmet and dismounted the bike. 'What's been going on?'

'Hey yourself. I just rode back from the coast,' Cash said, coming over and giving me a little hug. 'I've got some friends in town I need to catch up with.'

'Casey down the coast still?'

'Yeah, she drove down yesterday. I think she's gunna stay till New Year's. Perfect life for her. Sunbathing, reading magazines and flirting with coasties.'

'Heaven for Casey.'

'Pretty much. How's your Christmas going?'

'Oh, great …' I trailed off for dramatic effect. 'My mum and a bunch of the drunks from down the club.'

'Hey!' Jeremy called from over our back fence. 'I thought I heard your bike. How's it goin', mate?'

'And Jeremy.' I jerked my thumb. 'I forgot to mention Jeremy.'

'Cash, mate, happy Christmas and all that.' Jeremy let himself through the gate and clapped his hand into Cash's palm, looking back and forth between us, kind of embarrassed-like. 'Does your mum know you're … erm … out here, Jez?'

'Yeah.' I leaned against Cash's motorcycle seat, trying to be casual. 'It's fine.'

'She's not in the best mood now, ya mum.' Jeremy shifted and kicked at a clump of crab-grass with his sneaker toe. 'Shaz is goin' off tap …'

'Fuck me.' I sighed. 'Shaz is always off tap.'

'Yeah, she's all bent up about the New Year's thing.'

'Hey, you guys hear?' Cash leaned back next to me against his motorbike, our arms touching. 'Our parents are staying down at the caravan for New Year's. We're gunna have a party at ours, me and Casey.'

'Fuck yeah!' I was excited.

'You gotta come, too, Jeremy.'

'Yeah, I dunno. See what Hel wants to do, eh …'

'Ohhhhoho …' Cash whooped. 'Pussy-whipped already.'

'Naw …'

'Um, I don't really want to party with my *mum* on New Year's.'

'Ha ha, yeah, fair enough.' Cash grinned. 'Your mum's alright though. A bit of a MILF.'

'Fuck OFF!' I gave Cash a hard shove in his side.

'Joking! Geez!'

'That's my lady your talkin' about, mate.'

Cash held up both palms. 'Jokes! Sorry!'

'Not funny.'

Jeremy shook his head. 'I better go check on your mum, hey, Jez ...'

I could hear Mum and Shaz's shrieks before the front flyscreen crashed open.

'Oh, fucking hell.' I stood bolt upright, like one of the meer-kats on those animal docos.

'I told you! I'm comin' to the friggin' club later!' Mum stumbled off the front step, bending back and forth like long grass in a breeze.

'It's the principle!' Shaz shouted. 'You're s'posed to be my best friend! Mates before dates!'

'I'm not talkin' 'bout this anymore. Jeremy! Jeeerrr-reeemmmy!' Mum slurred. 'Shaz's had enough. You're cutting her off.'

'Jeremy! Jeremy!' Shaz echoed in a high-pitched voice. 'Tell Helen I'm a fuckin' grown woman and I've had enough when I've fuckin' had enough!'

'Jez!' Mum clocked me and then looked at Cash and then

back to me again. 'Jez, what're you doin' over there with that boy?! He's too old for you, I already told you. How old are ya?' Mum stood a metre in front of Cash, squinting her drunken eyes, jabbing a finger in the direction of his chest.

'Twenty-five,' Cash said, kind of smirking, which I found both annoying and sexy at the same time.

'You dating my daughter?!'

'We're just good mates,' Cash replied, punching my arm casually. My heart sank a little.

'Yeah, we're just mates, Mum,' I said, kinda hollow.

'Right.' Mum stood up a bit straighter as if to say, *Well, that's that, then*. She turned around and swayed again, facing Shaz who was rocking back on her ugly black suede ankle boots. 'And, Shaz, you're cut off! Jeremy, cut Shaz off!'

'Cut yourself off, *Helen Breville*!'

'What does Helen Breville mean?' Cash asked.

A blue Holden Commodore pulled up on our front lawn. Linda and Davo. Their son—Jaxon? Jason?—peered out of the back window, curiously assessing us with wide child eyes. Davo stepped out from the driver's side and rested his elbows on the roof of the car.

'This a bad time?' he said, looking at our red angry faces, everyone facing off across our driveway. 'What's going on?'

Everyone just kind of looked at each other. Mum and Shaz were faced off like two bulls wearing crochet knits and elastic-sided jeans, Jeremy and Cash watched on, kind of fascin-ated, I looked at Linda and her son, who still hadn't got out of the car, and Davo looked at all of us, waiting for somebody to speak.

'This Christmas is OVER,' Mum shrieked, before she spun on her heel and dashed inside the house.

Mum couldn't even finish an argument. Fucking hopeless. I guessed it was up to me to sort out shit.

I walked over to Davo and Linda wound down her window. 'Um, I think everyone's just had a bit too much wine and sun,' I said, trying to sound adult. 'Maybe drop back another time?'

'Sure, Jez,' Linda said. 'No problem.' She looked strangely relieved as she turned to Davo. 'Let's go, honey.'

'Do you reckon you could give Shaz a lift home?' I asked Davo. 'I know she lives near you guys.'

I turned back to Shaz without waiting for Davo to reply. 'Shaz! In the car. Now.' And to my surprise she staggered over and fell into the back seat next to the kid, her face slack and sour with booze. Davo wasted no time in driving away.

'Jeremy,' I barked. 'Go check on Mum for fuck's sake.'

'Right, sure thing.' Jeremy loped, shoulders hunched, towards the house.

I met Cash's eyes, which were twinkling with amusement.

'Are all your parties that good, Jez?'

'Oh, yeah ... better,' I tried to joke, but I felt absolutely sick in the stomach.

'You were pretty awesome just then, hey? Bossing everyone around.'

'Yeah,' I said weakly, realising that my legs were shaking.

'Hey, hey …' Cash put his arms around me. 'Don't be upset. It's no big deal.'

I wanted to explain that I'd had enough of my mum and her gross friends, I'd had enough of living in a shitty little grey-brick box house in a suburb that felt like it was fixed on a cliff at the end of the earth, that I'd had enough of booze, and fighting, and this whole scorching claustrophobically hot summer.

'Can I come with you?' I met Cash's eyes, I was testing him. 'When you leave? You said I could come with you.'

Cash flinched. I already knew the answer.

'Yeah, about that. It's probably not such a good idea.'

'I gotta go.' I wriggled out of Cash's arms.

'Jez! JEZ!' Cash called after me, but I was already halfway up the street, running towards Lukey's house.

TWENTY-FIVE

• •

Even as the last light moved over the Tuggeranong Valley, you could have fried an egg on the tin roof of the high school gym where Lukey and I sat, dangling our legs over the side, sharing a fat joint. I kept having to rock back and forth so the backs of my thighs wouldn't burn.

Our pingers were just about to kick in and even though everything was mostly peaceful except for a few cockatoos and kids playing out late on their bikes, the noise of Christmas Day was still clanging around in my head. The first waves of the pill made me feel anxious instead of euphoric. There was a horrible warmth in my lower guts like I needed to 'strangle a brown snake', as Barry would say.

'I got an Xbox game from Dad. That was alright,' Lukey said, even though I hadn't asked. 'We just mostly spoiled Ashleigh today. She still expects stuff, y'know? Like, she hasn't got to that age where you realise Christmas is a capitalist thing. Like, just a boost for the economy.'

'Economy? Where're you getting this stuff from?'

'Josh, my cousin, reckoned that on Facebook. I reckon he's right, though.'

'Oh, okay.' I swallowed hard and clenched my jaw.

'You okay?'

I exhaled with a breathy *whoosh*. 'Full on today. Mum 'n that. Fucked up, really.'

Lukey nodded and jumped to his feet, picking up a tree branch that'd fallen onto the roof. I scratched at a mosquito bite on my elbow.

'I booked a bus.'

'Really? When do you leave?'

'New Year's. Like right on midnight.'

'Serious? Why?'

'All-ages show on New Year's Day that I'm going to with my cousin.'

'You'll miss Cash and Casey's party.'

'I'll come. Just have to leave a bit early.'

'You got much money?'

'Yeah, I've been making a motza in pills. Everybody wants one for Newies.'

'How many'd you sell?'

'Heaps. I'm nearly out. Saved a handful for us.'

'I'll come to the bus station with you.'

Lukey nodded and sat back down next to me, real close so our legs were touching. I shivered involuntarily and my hands felt all clammy.

'Full-on pills.'

'Yeah.' Lukey brushed his fringe out of his eyes. 'Listen ... I booked two seats.'

'Two seats?'

'In case you change your mind.'

'Oh.' My head swam. I really wanted to lie down. I rested my head on Lukey's shoulder and closed my eyes and reminded myself to breathe.

'If you don't come ... well ... more leg room for me.'

'It's a long bus ride, hey?'

'Eight hours I think. Maybe nine.'

'What are you taking? What about your bike and games and stuff?'

'I might take the Xbox. I dunno. See how much room's in my bag. Hey, Jez?'

'Mmmm?' My eyes were still closed.

'I got this for you.' Lukey gently pried my balled fist open and pressed a small tissue-papered package into my palm. 'For Christmas and that.'

I sat upright, woozily. 'Hey, you got a smoke?' I felt out of it. Fucked up.

'Open that first.'

'Okay.' I unwrapped the tissue paper. Inside were two silver rings.

'For your snake bite,' Lukey explained. 'When it's all healed up, you can take the studs out and put these in, if you want.' Then he took my face in his hands and ran his thumbs along my bottom lip.

'See, it feels much nicer ...' Lukey kissed me, his silver piercings smooth and cold against my skin. 'When you've got rings in your lip.'

Whooosh. I let out another huge lungful of air.

'Thanks,' I whispered. 'Sorry I didn't get you anything.'

'No worries.' Lukey smiled and dug in his pocket. 'Smoke?'

'No.' I leaned in closer. 'Kiss. Again.'

And we spent the rest of the night just like that.

TWENTY-SIX

• •

On Boxing Day I got up early and cleaned up the backyard. Mum came out of her bedroom at some point and took a glass of water and some panadol back to bed with her. I dumped stinking plates of creamy salad, empty bottles and cans and ashtrays into the bin and hosed off the outdoor table, turning the hose on myself and slurping straight from the end of it when the morning sun crept up a little too high.

'Mum?' I knocked on Mum's bedroom door and carefully pushed it open. I didn't know if Jeremy had stayed the night. 'You awake?'

'Yep,' Mum rasped, her voice croaky. 'What is it?'

'I want to talk. Can I come in?'

'Can it wait till later? I feel like hell.'

'I'll be quick.'

'What?' Mum hitched herself up on her elbows. 'Come here, sit.'

I switched on her water cooler fan and sat next to her on the bed. She fluffed up her pillows and sat up a bit, her chin still resting on her chest. There were puffy circles under her bloodshot eyes and her hair was all mashed on one side.

'So what's going on?'

'I just wanted to tell you that I think I'm going to move out.'

'WHAT?!' Mum sat up a little bit straighter. 'What? When? When did you decide this?'

'Last night. Well … sort of … I mean I've been thinking about it for ages but I guess … Yeah. Last night.'

'Where are you going?'

'To Melbourne. With Lukey.'

'Lukey talked you into this?'

'No! He's going and I want to go, too.'

'This is crazy, Jez. You're not even eighteen. What about school? How are you going to afford this?'

'I don't want to live here anymore. It's just no good.'

'You're not answering my questions.'

'Lukey's gunna spring a bus fare for me and we've got friends to crash with until I find some work and then I guess I'll rent a room or something.'

There was a long silence, just the whirring of the water cooler fan. Mum and I looked at each other dead in the eyes.

Hers were narrowing a little, studying my face. I didn't want to back down. In the end, she looked away.

Mum shrugged. 'Okay.'

Now it was me narrowing my eyes. 'What do you mean, "okay"?'

'Like, okay, when are you leaving?'

'That's it? You're okay with this?'

'Yeah. Did you want me to throw you a going away party, Jez?' A note of sarcasm crept into Mum's voice. 'Okay. Go. Just go.'

'WHAT?!' I jumped off the bed as all the blood in my body rushed to my head, then I sat back down almost immediately, dizzy as hell. 'What do you mean?'

'You should go. Just go, then.'

I felt sick to my stomach. *She's been waiting for this moment for seventeen years . . .*

'What do you mean, *just go*?!' I repeated, hissing. 'Oh, so you've got Jeremy now so you want me out of the way, is that it? You can't wait to get rid of me?'

Mum straightened her neck. 'Jez, didn't you just tell me a minute ago that you wanted to move out? I'm not kicking you out.'

'Yes, but now I know that you don't even care if I leave! You never even asked me why I'm leaving!'

'Because you want to move to Melbourne?'

'No! I'm leaving because of *you*! Because I'm sick of you drinking and being down at the club all the time and spending your time with that bitch Shaz and that loser Jeremy instead of with me!'

'Oh, turn it up, Jez.'

'NO! I want you to LISTEN to me.'

'Jez, I offer to spend time with you. You're busy with your friends.'

I was caught out. It was true. I nearly always blew Mum off.

'That's not the point. You always do this. You turn it around so it's all about you.'

'What is the point? That I drink too much? Yeah, I do.' Mum rubbed her temples. 'You know that's something I really want to change. Especially after yesterday. Worst Christmas ever, right?'

'Mum, don't try to change the subject, seriously.'

'Sorry, the subject is?'

I was floundering like a fish out of water. The conversation wasn't going the way I'd planned it in my head.

'That … that … you don't want me here. That you want to live with Jeremy now.'

Mum laughed. 'Oh, Jez … I'm not moving in with Jeremy. Not for a long time yet. We're just getting to know each other.'

'Then why do you want me to leave?'

'Why do you want to leave?'

'I told you! Because of YOU!'

'I don't know what you want me to say, Jez. I mean, you've fed yourself on a diet of telly and movies to the point where you seem to think I should be some sort of television mum.'

Oh, fuck.

'And the thing is I've tried, Jez, I really really have. I want to go out to the movies with you, or to dinner, or go shopping. I would love to. But you're a teenage girl and you'd rather be dead than seen with your fat old mum, I get that.'

My face burned. 'I'm sorry ...'

'You have a room here. You have free rent, free food, a mum who loves you more than anything. You don't even realise how hard it is out there. You don't even realise how lucky you are.'

Mum was unbelievable. She could totally manipulate whole conversations so quickly I found it hard to keep up. I was determined not to back down this time.

'Are you serious? Food? There's some two-minute noodles and a jar of fucking Chicken Tonight sauce from 1991!'

'God, you exaggerate. I haven't had time to do groceries this week, I was busy organising bloody Christmas, wasn't I?' Mum was in full defensive mode now. 'That was bloody expensive, too. And there was HEAPS of food at Christmas.'

'What about the other fifty weeks of the year?' I raised my voice to match Mum's. 'And there was that time I asked you to buy shampoo and you kept "forgetting" for, like, two weeks. I ended up shoplifting some because I was sick of wiping the grease off my roots with toilet paper!'

'That never happened.'

'Yes, it did,' I hissed. 'Not that you would have noticed.'

'And what did I tell you at the time?'

'MUM! You can't wash hair with *SOAP*.'

'Fine, so you're moving out, then? And I suppose it's all because of me?' Mum was switching gears, I could already sense it. She was moving into self-pity mode. This was usually the one that got me.

'Mum …'

'You don't even know how lucky you are just to have a mum who loves you! I never even had a proper mum! Foster families! And then I was living with Paulie's family.'

'Mum, I know. I've heard this a thousand times.'

'And then there was you. My little Jez. My own daughter. And now she wants to abandon me, too!'

'Oh, Mum … It's not you …'

Wait a second … It was totally her!

'It is me, Jez.' Tears began to slide down her cheeks. 'I'm a drunk … I'm pathetic …'

'Mum, please, don't —'

'No, it's true. And I'm sorry I kept forgetting the shampooooo!' Mum began bawling.

'It was just that one time with the shampoo. I don't know why I brought that up.'

'And you've always had food, right?' Mum blinked at me through her tears. 'You never went hungry?'

'Yeah, it was fine. Just that other families …'

'We aren't other families. We're just us two. You and me. You're all I've got.'

I sighed and edged a bit closer and put my hand on top of Mum's.

'I'm sorry, Mum. But you know I've got to leave sometime.'

'Can it be later rather than sooner? Please, Jez? I'm really, really going to try. No more late nights. Lots of groceries. Lots of shampoo.'

I laughed in spite of myself.

'Serious, Jez. I'm really gunna try not to drink anymore.'

I'd heard this before. But it's not like Mum wasn't being sincere. That was part of her problem. She totally believed all her own bullshit.

'Do you drink because of me?' I asked suddenly. 'Do you think you might even be better, like, without me around?'

'Christ, no. You're the best thing ...' Mum gripped at her pillow, her face all bunched up.

'Oh, Mum, don't cry.' I climbed under the doona and gave her an awkward hug.

'Please stay, Jez,' Mum was bawling again. 'Please stay ... I'm so sorry. I don't really want you to go, I was just try-ing ...' Mum started gasping, hardly even able to talk through her tears.

'Mum! Breathe!'

Mum gulped in some air. 'I can't stop you from going to Melbourne. If I tried then you'd hate me even more. I hate that you hate me. I hate that I've been a bad mother.'

'Oh, Mum. I don't hate you.'

'I want you to stay here! Please, please stay here. I still need you!' Mum sobbed. 'Please don't go, Jezza ...'

'I'll think about it,' I said.

Mum grasped for the glass of water on her bedside table and choked down a gulp and then collapsed back against her pillows, staring up the ceiling, pulling her best sad-sack head and all I could do was kind of pat her hand and say, *It's okay . . . It will all be okay, Mum . . .*

She'd done it again.

TWENTY-SEVEN
• •

Lukey and I started hooking up.

That day we were hanging around an abandoned shop that we liked to break into. We didn't even need to break in anymore. Nearly all the windows were smashed and nobody'd bothered to come fix them; maybe the shop was going to get demolished. We dumped a couple of pills each to get really off tap, and then smoked a fat joint straight away. We were both in destructive moods, just fucking shit up and kicking over shelves, then getting out cans of spray paint and drawing dumb pictures and slogans all over the walls. FUCK THE PIGS. MEAT IS MURDER.

When the pills kicked in we calmed down a bit and slouched in a corner and smoked durries in silence, side by side, our backs against the back wall of the shop, surveying our damage and having a good laugh about it. We didn't talk much. I didn't want to think about the future. The future seemed to me like just this black hole. The only thing I could really picture myself doing the next year was going back to school to finish Year 12, but I reckoned that was because I knew what my school looked like, and I didn't know what Melbourne looked like, or what I looked like in Melbourne, what I'd be doing, or where I'd be living. So I didn't think about it. I dug around in my pocket and pulled out a berry-flavoured Lip Smacker and slicked it over my lips.

'Fuuuck. These pills.' I looked sideways at Lukey, not daring to move my head in case it fell off my shoulders.

'Fuckin' oath.' He sighed. 'So hectic.'

'Maybe I should have only done one.' I felt a bit panicked. I concentrated on breathing, but the waves of the drug were crashing through me like a stormy ocean, knocking me over and under.

'Jez? Jez, you right? Your face is like ... white.' Lukey rubbed my back. 'You want to go for a walk? Get out of here?'

I nodded.

'Let's go, then. Back to mine.'

When we got to Lukey's bedroom he pulled off his t-shirt. His armpits were shiny with sweat, all the stringy, black hairs twisted together in little clumps.

'Do you mind if I get naked?' Lukey tugged down his shorts and kicked them across the room. 'I mean ... do you want to, like, mess around a bit? It'd be fun, like ... I've never done it on pills before.'

'Sure,' I said, like it was no big deal. 'It's so hot, hey?'

I was nervous. I eased my t-shirt over my head. My skin was so pale I could see all the blue veins running down my ribs, and I had a t-shirt line, the skin on my arms pink and dry from a fading sunburn.

I climbed onto the bed next to Lukey. I was in my bra and undies. He was in his boxers, satin ones with Peter Griffin from *Family Guy* printed on them, and he was still wearing his socks.

'Are you gunna take your socks off?'

He reached down and peeled off his socks. His feet looked all spongy and smelled like rotten garbage.

'What's with your feet?'

'I dunno. I think it's like, whatdyacallit? Some fungus thing? 'Cos Dad never cleans the shower.'

'Why don't *you* clean the shower?'

'Are you serious? Who cares?'

'It smells.'

Lukey shrugged. 'Does it bother you?'

'I guess not, no.'

We started kissing.

Lukey pulled back. 'You taste funny.'

'It's berry lip gloss. Is it gross?'

'It doesn't matter.'

We kissed again. Lukey angled himself so that he was half on top of me and reached around to undo my bra. He struggled with it.

'Do you want me to ...?'

'I nearly got it.' He kept struggling. 'Here, just turn around for a sec.'

I turned around. He got the bra undone and pulled it off my arms. I lay there, bare-chested, both Lukey and I looking down at my breasts. They were relaxed in the heat, two small swells of tissue topped with pink-brown puffy nipples. I felt they were totally uninteresting compared to breasts I'd seen on telly, which were big, hard, balloon-like with long erect nipples. I wondered what Lukey was thinking, but didn't want to ask.

'You have really nice breasts,' he said finally, massaging one of them.

It was hot, uncomfortable, sweaty. Writhing around on his stinking sheets, which probably hadn't been washed for months, our clammy skins gripped and pulled on each other stickily. Not the way you imagine when you see sweaty people having sex in the movies, sliding over each other, all oily. Our bodies, both mostly skin over bones, jutted and jabbed like we were all knees, hips and elbows. For the first time in my life I wished I had some soft fatty flesh on me.

Lukey took off his boxer shorts and then pulled down my underwear and flung them onto the floor. I wondered if I was supposed to have removed his shorts for him. I stole a look at his crotch. A soft pear-shaped penis, broad at the base, narrow at the tip, hung like a sock on a doorknob under a surprisingly large bush of black hair. It wasn't ugly, but it wasn't anything that nice to look at, either. I could see big blue veins twisted like rope under the surface of the skin, and a gathering of darker skin at the tip, ruffled and wrinkled.

'You're not hard,' I said.

'I'll get there,' Lukey said, guiding my hand down to his penis while he gently kissed my face, neck and lips. 'It's the pills.'

Lukey got an erection. The soft, gentle kisses turned into hard tongue pashes. He avoided my eyes in favour of my breasts or vag and started poking his fingers in down there. I could feel how dry I was. When he opened his palm and started rubbing at me, hard and then harder, it felt like sandpaper.

'It's the drugs,' I whispered, shifting his hand away.

'Maybe.' Lukey frowned for a second and then flopped back onto his pillow with a frustrated sigh. 'I'm gunna get blue balls now.'

'What?'

He stared at the ceiling, one arm crooked behind his head and the other hand pulling at his cock. 'I just really need to come.'

'Oh, okay ...'

'I'll just wank, okay?'

He half knelt over me, one arm by my shoulder supporting his weight, the other hand pumping away at his cock, his eyes avoiding mine, fixed on my breasts, until he came, hot and thick over my belly. He fell back onto the bed next to me, a little breathless, his fringe sticking to his forehead with sweat.

'Oh,' I said. 'You got a towel or something?'

He leaned over the side of the bed and handed me a t-shirt. 'It has to be washed anyway.'

I wiped myself and handed the t-shirt back to him. He threw it back on the floor and turned to me.

'You want me to do anything for you?' He gestured vaguely towards my crotch.

'Nah,' I said. 'It's okay. I'm feeling kind of sleepy anyway.'

'Yeah, fuck.' Lukey nestled his face into my neck and slung an arm and a leg across my body. 'Me too. So tired …'

Within minutes his breathing grew deep and heavy and he was asleep. The light was still on. I got up and turned it off and lay in the dark, fingering my clitoris. I was still dry. As dry as old leather. I gave up and, eventually, fell asleep.

I woke up to the smell of cigarette smoke. Lukey was sitting up in bed, a durry clenched between his lips, Xbox controller in hand.

'Hey.' I pulled the sheets to my neck and propped myself up on my elbow. 'Give us a drag.'

'Want one?'

'Nah, just a drag.'

He took another quick puff then passed me the cigarette. I smoked it down to the butt and then dropped it in an empty beer can on his bedside table. Lukey put down the Xbox controller.

'How're you feeling?'

'Meh.' I felt like shit. My head felt hollow and my stomach ached with lack of food.

'Comedown is harsh, hey?'

'Totally. I hate the comedown. I always cry,' I confessed.

'Serious?'

'Yeah. It's not like I'm always sad or anything. It's more like … I just don't know what to feel. It's just like … nothing.'

Lukey slipped his arm underneath me. 'Weird times last night, hey. I mean, it was good. But weird, too.'

'Yeah, I know what you mean.'

'I feel bad I didn't make you … y'know …'

'Oh. That's okay.'

'I was just tired.'

'No worries.'

'I could try again?'

He kissed me. His breath was sour and stale with cigarette smoke. I turned my head away so his kisses landed on my cheek and neck. His hand found its way in between my legs and his fingers touched my clit and he began to rub gently. It felt nice. I sighed.

'You like that?' Lukey began to rub harder.

'No, like you were doing it before,' I said. 'Softer.'

'Oh, okay. Most girls like it hard.'

I ignored him and closed my eyes. 'I like it better soft.'

Lukey shifted on top of me and I could feel his fringe tickling my belly as he kissed further and further down until his head stopped between my legs. His tongue and mouth worked over my folds, softly sucking and licking. Minutes seemed to last for ages, until my hips began to buck up and down and my hands went numb and I didn't know what the fuck was happening. Lukey held my hips with both hands and bore down on me, his whole mouth covering all of me until it felt as though every feeling in my body and every bit of warmth rushed to that one spot between my legs and I cried out with the fucking brilliant pleasure of it all, *Ooooh. My fucking. God!*

Lukey emerged and wiped his mouth with the back of his hand.

'Good?' He looked smug.

I let out a shaky breath in reply. Lukey flung himself back on the bed.

'So is now a good time to ask if you're gunna come with me to Melbs?'

'Ha, yeah, probably.' I wiggled my numb toes.

'So are you gunna come?'

I squeezed my eyes shut. 'Mum is gunna kill me.'

'YEEESSSSSS!' Lukey leapt on top of me and wrestled me into a hug. 'Fuck yes! This is gunna be so fucking good we'll crash at my cousin's until we get jobs and then when we have enough money we can get a really sweet place just us on our own and I'll start selling pills and we'll have a ton of cash to party and ...'

I rolled onto my stomach and switched on Lukey's electric fan and enjoyed the breeze brushing my naked skin. Sometimes life could be pretty fucking sweet, I decided.

TWENTY-EIGHT
• •

I practically skipped home, still moist between my legs and smelling of Lukey's sweat and Lynx deodorant. My cheeks were raw from Lukey's stubble. *Pash rash*. I grinned to myself.

'Fuck, YEAH!' I exclaimed spontaneously, the sound of my voice surprising me. I broke into a run towards a low branch of gum and swung from it monkey-style. 'Yeee-haw!'

One of our neighbours appeared at his flyscreen and bashed with his fists. 'Get out of the tree!'

I dropped to the concrete and brushed my hands on my jeans.

'WHAT'RE YOU GUNNA DO ABOUT IT!' I yelled back and stuck my finger up at him. I smiled all the way home.

'Mum?' I called, crashing through the screen door. 'You home?'

'Here!' her voice was muffled, coming from the direction of her bedroom.

'Mum?' I stuck my head in her door. 'What are you doing?'

Her arse was hanging out her closet door, her head buried somewhere inside. Around her ankles were mounds of clothes, towels, elastic-shot knickers and tangles of bras.

'Spring clean.' Mum emerged from the closet, her face red and sweaty. 'Chucking a bunch of shit out.'

'Why?' I hesitated. Something was up. Mum almost never cleaned like this. 'What's going on?'

She glanced at me quickly, grinning like a maniac, wiping her brow with self-satisfaction.

'New start. Out with the old and all that,' she said, sweeping a hand across the mess of books, knick-knacks, tape cassettes and shit on her bed. She picked up a book, a Stephen King novel, and flipped through the pages absent-mindedly.

'I might start reading again,' she murmured and squinted at the back cover. 'I remember enjoying this when I read it years ago. You don't get much time to read when you're a mum.'

'I've never seen you read.'

'I used to read. Where d'ya think I got all these books from?'

'So read, then. I've never stopped you from reading.'

'Maybe I will,' Mum said optimistically. 'Put this in the lounge with the paperbacks, will you, Jez?'

'Tell me what's going on first! Are we moving house?'

'What? No! Nothing like that. I'm cleaning.'

I took the book from her. 'This is a horror. I thought you didn't like horror stuff.'

'It's more like a thriller.'

'Fine.' I waved the book at her. 'I'll put it with the other books, the ones you never read. But you're gunna tell me what's going on!'

I went down the hallway to the lounge room and Mum followed me. There was an ugly old brown shelf behind the velour couch which held plastic-framed photos—mostly of me as a kid, a few of me and Mum, Mum's dusty collection of Happy Meal toys, which was pretty much her pride and joy in life because she'd been collecting them since I was born, and about a dozen paperback novels. I shoved the Stephen King onto the shelf.

'There,' I said. 'You can *not* read that for another twenty years now.'

'Don't be like that, Jez,' Mum said mildly, collapsing back on the couch. 'Here, sit.'

'Aren't you hot in that thing?' I sat next to her and tugged on the sleeve of her long-sleeved dressing gown.

'I haven't showered yet. I got too excited.'

'About cleaning?'

'No, not about that,' she murmured, being all mysterious.

'TELL ME!' I couldn't take it anymore. 'Excited about what?'

'About ... my new job!'

'New job? What?'

'I got a freaking PROMOTION!' Mum squealed. 'No more bar work. No more late nights. You are looking at the new bloody nine-to-five front desk receptionist at the club!'

'Get FUCKED!' I shoved her, feeling a jolt through my body. 'MUM!'

'I know, I know!'

'Why didn't you tell me when I got here? Jesus, you had me worried.'

'Sorry, sorry ... I don't get to give good news that often. I wanted to tell you properly.'

'Just tell me next time.'

'I think this is gunna be really good for us. You'll be in Year 12—I'm so bloody proud of you by the way—YEAR TWELVE! And I'll be working during your school hours, so we won't be passing each other like ships in the night anymore. A whole new start, Jez. Things are really gunna change.'

'When do you start?'

'Straight after New Year's! Second of January, baby!' Mum was wiggling with excitement. 'No more beer-soaked clothes. I might even have a new uniform! A nice little skirt and jacket with the club logo on there.' She gestured towards her chest. 'No more late nights ... and Jez, I'm really gunna cut back on the drinking, hey? No time for hangovers anymore with this new job.'

I nodded. 'That's great, Mum. So good.' My mind had started to wander back to earlier that morning. *Lukey. Melbourne.*

'The pay is so much better, too. We can finally fix this place up a bit. Get one of those pergola-shade thingos for the back-yard, eh? You know what? Maybe even a dog, what do you reckon? That dog you always said you wanted!'

'Yeah ...' my heart started twisting in my chest.

'You know what? I didn't even realise how sick of the bar I was. Those bloody drunks and sleazy old fellas. Greta whingeing in my ear about her divorce. Depressing. Funny, though, I didn't even realise how miserable I was until Big Boss asked me if I wanted to work reception. Then suddenly I was like, yes! I'll be behind a desk instead of on my feet. And the nights off to spend with my Jez!'

'It'll be weird having you around all the time. Good weird.'

'Good weird. You've got a way with words, Jez.'

I laughed. 'I mean it will be weird at first, but it will be good. We can eat dinner together and stuff.'

'I'll have to brush up on my cooking skills, won't I?'

'You have cooking skills?'

Mum and I both laughed.

'Ooooh! Speaking of which, look what I bought on the way home yesterday!' Mum hurried from the room and came back holding up a cookbook. 'I bought this at the newsagent, see? *Vegetarian Cooking.*'

'I've been thinking of going vegan, actually.'

'Oh, bloody hell, Jez, I can't keep up.' Mum flipped through the pages. 'Here we go, this pasta thing here. That looks yum, hey?'

'That's awesome, Mum.' I hugged her. 'Thank you so much.' Another stabbing pain in my heart and sinking feeling in my gut.

Mum heaved herself to her feet and shrugged out of her dressing gown. 'I'm gunna go shower, Jez. Then we are going to clean. And I'll pop to the shop and buy the ingredients for that pasta thing. A whole new start for the New Year, okay? Help me clean?'

'Sure.'

'Make me one of those awesome coffees you do?'

'Yeah, definitely.'

I sank sideways onto the couch, pulling a cushion under my head and curling my legs up. *Wow*. This was big news. I never considered Mum might get an actual proper good job. She'd been working the bar at the club for so many years I'd always kind of pictured her still there at fifty, gasbagging with the regulars and staying after close for staffies. I thought she was happy bartending. I thought she liked it because she didn't have to spend as much time at our shabby little house, with me. Stupid as it sounds, I never kind of realised she'd done it because we needed the money, that she'd done it for *us*.

We cleaned all day, sorting stuff into various bags, some for the charity bins, some for the garbage. We dusted and polished and vacuumed and washed and swept and mopped until we were covered in grime and then, sinking into the chairs on the back porch, we sipped on cans of Pepsi Max, and watched the last of the sun sink over the Brindies.

'Things are really gunna change, Jez,' Mum said, gazing into the distance. 'Really this time.'

I forced a smile, but I suddenly I wanted to cry. I was thinking about Lukey and the bright city lights of Melbourne waiting for me just hours down the highway. My stomach lurched with nerves and guilt and gassy soft drink bubbles.

'So I decided to cool things off with Jeremy.' Mum was still squinting into the backyard. 'We had a little chat at the club last night.'

'Serious?! Why?' I felt another sharp stab of guilt—guilty that I felt relieved and excited, so I tried to sound all sympathetic and concerned. 'I thought things were good between you guys?'

'I just was thinking, Jez. About me and you and how maybe I've been a slack mum and how it's your last year of school coming up ... and how you're probably going to want to get out of here as soon as you can after that.'

'Oh, Mum. You haven't been slack.'

'I have been slack,' Mum said firmly.

'No ...'

'I think it was you telling me about that crazy Melbourne idea. I realised ...' Mum twisted her hands in her lap. 'I'm not ready to let my baby go.'

'Mum —'

'No, no, no. I've made up my mind, Jez. New job, a new life for us. We'll get you finished up, get that Year 12 certificate. No distractions. It will be the year of Helen and Jessica versus the world.'

'Mum, about the Melbourne thing.' I took a deep breath. I had to tell her about me and Lukey. I had to tell her I was still going.

But then I hesitated. Did I really still want to go? If things were gunna be good from now on, with Mum's new job and a clean house and her not drinking, maybe I could stay just one more year. Get my—

'Have you noticed I haven't been staying at the club so late this week?'

'Not really,' I admitted. I'd been hanging out with Lukey most nights, dumping pills and wandering around the lamp-lit neighbourhoods, pashing on street corners. Fucking awesome times. Why'd she always have to make me feel so bad for having such awesome times?

'Well I haven't. Straight home to bed most nights.'

'That's really good.'

'I feel better for it, too. Might have even lost some weight.'

'Really? In one week?'

'Well, baby steps.'

'Yeah. Baby steps.'

Mum took a swig of her Pepsi and gave a little burp. 'Ooh.' She blinked. ''Scuse me.'

'Knock, knock!' The front door flyscreen creaked open and crashed shut again.

'I'll go.' I popped up and stepped inside.

Shaz was already in our kitchen, loading a case of cans into the fridge.

'What are you doing?' I asked.

'Drinks,' Shaz replied, not bothering to look up at me.

I stomped back out onto the back porch. 'MUUUM! Shaz is here!'

Mum met my eyes briefly and then hauled herself out of her chair. 'Coming!' she yelled.

Shaz appeared at the back door holding up a six-pack of Bundy Cokes in one hand and a bottle of white wine in the other. 'Hair of the dog, eh?'

'What do you mean, hair of the dog?' I asked.

'*Hair of the dog!*' Shaz emphasised, ripping a can of Bundy from the sixer and holding it out to Mum. 'We had a few last night, eh, Hel?'

'Only a few.' Mum eased herself back into her chair and glanced at me, nervous-like. 'To celebrate my job 'n that. I reckon I might give it a miss, Shaz. Me and Jez haven't had tea yet.'

'Just one, then.'

'Nah, me and Jez are gunna cook some vegetarian stuff.'

'Cooking?' Shaz laughed. 'I've seen your cooking. Get some take-away.'

Mum folded her arms defensively. 'I really want to learn to cook better.'

'Whatever.' Shaz snorted and cracked a can of Bundy, plonking the rest of the booze on the table. 'Don't mind if I do.'

'I do mind, actually,' Mum said, her eyes lingering on the grog. 'I was just gunna pop to the shop for some pasta.'

'Sand in your vag today, Hel?' Shaz slurped from her can. 'I'll just sit here and keep Jez company.'

Mum sighed. 'You know you never even apologised to me and Jez for wrecking Chrissie lunch.'

Shaz raised her eyebrows. 'Were we at the same party? I didn't wreck anything. Now why don't you just jump on the phone to Dominos, order some pizza, and we can all sit right here and enjoy the rum. My shout.'

Mum looked at me; I could tell she was caving. 'Up to you, Jez. Pasta tomorrow night instead? You feel like a rum?'

I nodded, reaching for a can, the guilt that had been racking my body all day starting to lift. 'Yep. Order me a vegetarian.'

'Cheers to Helen's job!' Shaz lifted her can.

Mum cracked open her drink and raised it, tinking it against mine and Shaz's.

'To my new job!' Mum beamed.

'And to things changing,' I snuck in before we all drank.

Mum looked the other way.

TWENTY-NINE
• •

Shaz was as pissed as a newt. I don't even know what a newt is, or how pissed they get. She was probably more pissed than a newt, to be honest, like, totally maggot. She lurched across our lounge room and threw herself facedown onto the couch.

'Put some music on, Hel!' she blathered into the couch cushions. 'Put on some Pearl Jam!'

'I better get you a blanket,' Mum said.

'Noooo!' Shaz howled, struggling to raise her head to look at us. 'We're just getting started! Put a CD on!'

'I reckon I'm about done,' Mum called from the hallway, pulling a blanket out of the linen closet.

Mum had taken it easy, sipping on her Bundy cans when she normally would have slurped them down. I was impressed. Maybe she really did want to get her shit together. I plopped myself down in the armchair opposite Shaz. I felt tired, dehydrated. Sick of Shaz and all the shit she talked. She'd gone oooon and oooon about Jeremy and how Mum was better off without him. *You need a real man, Hel. Not some young boy. Still lives with his parents, dun he?* Mum was quiet in her responses. *Jeremy's alright*, she said. *Still lives at home because he's saving up for his own place.*

'There ya go.' Mum threw the blanket over Shaz.

'Have another drink with me!' Shaz howled. 'One more!'

'Nah, nah. I'm beat.' Mum raised her hand at me in a wave. 'Night, Jez.'

'Night, Mum.'

Shaz humphed and pushed herself upright, grabbing her can from the coffee table.

'You'll have another with me, won'tcha, Jez? Keep yer Aunty Shaz company.'

'I'll finish this one.'

'What's with ya mum? It's the silly season! That new job gone to her head already?'

'The new job will be really good for her. It's a really good opportunity.'

'Ha! Well, as long as she doesn't forget where she came from. As long as she doesn't start thinkin' she's better than the rest of us.'

Shaz worked part-time hours at a supermarket, in the deli section. She reckoned it was a good place to meet guys because all the meat made them think about sex. I didn't reply to her comment because I didn't think there was much chance of Mum ever thinking she was better than anyone. That was part of her problem, really. She honestly didn't think she was good enough. I swigged the last of my Bundy, put the empty can down on the coffee table and got to my feet, a little shakily.

'Stick a fork in me,' I said wearily. 'I'm done.'

Shaz tightened her arms across her chest and narrowed her eyes at me. 'And don't you go thinking you're better than the rest of us either, *Jessica*.'

'What the fuck is that supposed to mean?'

'Your mum told me. About you going to Melbourne and all that. You think you're above all this, huh? I'll tell you —'

'I don't think I'm better,' I interrupted. 'Just different, maybe.'

'Different?!' Shaz gave a hollow laugh. 'Different! Jez, oh Jez, honey,' she crowed with a condescending sneer on her face. 'You *are* me.'

'I'm nothing fucking like you.' I felt like I'd been slapped.

'You think you're so different? You think you're special? You're gunna be old like me before you know it. I was you.' Shaz laughed again, plumping up the couch cushion. 'Helen, too. She was you. And in another fifteen, twenty years or whatever, you will be us. That's just the way life goes. So go ahead to Melbourne with ya boyfriend, 'cos it'd be nice to have my best friend back. See the thing about me and Hel is, I'm always gunna have her back. You're like a little parasite that's been feeding off her for the last seventeen years and —'

'Why don't you shut the fuck up?' I snapped. 'Seriously. You are such a booze hag alco.'

'Alco! Like you don't drink?'

'Not like you.'

'Oh, you just do it for fun, right?' Shaz slurred. 'Yeah, it's all just a bit of fun. Then you start wanting it.'

'Sometimes I want a drink. So what. I'm not like you.'

'Then soon you want it more days than not, right. Then soon you *need* it. And shit gets to the stage where you just gotta have it. That's just the way it is. That's like me and your old mum.'

'Mum hardly drank tonight. She's trying to change and you keep coming over and shoving shit in her face.'

'She wanted it. I could tell.'

'You're a fucking bitch!' I screamed. 'You don't want her to stop drinking 'cos that means you'll be even more pathetic drinking alone!'

'Look who's talking.' Shaz nodded at me.

I shook my head. 'No way. I'm not even —'

'Ooooh. Reality bites, dunnit?'

'You're a twisted old mole and you're full of shit.'

Shaz lowered her head onto the cushion and her drunken eyes fell shut. '*You are meee . . .*' she slurred again and cackled before passing out into a snore.

Fuck you! I thought, but she really got to me. I was seven-teen. I did drink a lot, but it wasn't like Mum drank. I drank because I was young and dumb and bored and wanted a laugh with my mates. I took pills because it made me happy. I smoked weed because it made me forget, and sometimes even made the world look strangely beautiful for a spell. What else was there to do? But there was no way I was gunna end up like *Shaz*. She didn't even have a life, that's why she was always over at our house trying to leech onto Mum. Fuck her. I could go to Melbourne if I wanted and things would be awesome. I'd have Lukey. Suddenly my heart lifted and I felt pretty pleased with myself, smug even. Yeah! I had Lukey. I was only seventeen and I already had a guy who was totally into me. *Fuck you, Shaz!*

The see-sawing of emotions made me feel dizzy. My head swam and I thought I was gunna puke. Lying on my bed with the electric fan aimed right into my face, I managed to keep from hurling, but the room spun round and round until I fell into a horrible nightmare-ridden sweat-fest of a sleep.

THIRTY
• •

I woke up New Year's Eve morning with a jolt and a sudden rush of excitement coursing through my veins. *New Year's! Party! Melbourne ...*

It occurred to me that it could be the last time I woke up in my bed, in my bedroom, in this house. I looked around my messy room, strewn with clothes and comics and CDs, Mum's laptop still open on the floor. Flopping back onto my pillow, I clutched the sheets up around me and stared at my posters, remembering when I had blu-tacked them to the walls. I wondered what Mum would do with my room if I left, if she'd pull down the posters and put my things into the cupboards, or even out in the shed. Maybe she'd throw my stuff away. I wanted to take it all with me. It was all I had in the world, the contents of this one room. My trinkets and boxes and cheap jewellery. My clothes. My music. My cherry-red fender strat guitar.

I sighed and flopped out of bed and took a couple of old school backpacks down from the top shelf of my cupboard. I didn't even own a suitcase or a travel bag. I'd never been anywhere, never seen anything. I emptied one of the backpacks out onto my bed. An eraser, some pencils and pens, an exercise book—Year 8 Maths. On the cover of the exercise book was a conversation in blue pen—two different sets of handwriting, mine and Lukey's:

    — Mr O'Brien looks like an emu.
    — Ha ha. His nose has its own postcode.
    — Soooo bored.
    — Me 2.
    — No fuckin' idea what the answers are. You?
    — Lost.
    — Lunchtime bongz?
    — YES.
    — I'm gunna buy an iced donut for lunch.
    — Halfsies?
    — Nah.
    — Fatty.
    — Okay then, J.

I smiled to myself, picturing us up the back of the Maths class, swinging on the back legs of our chairs, Mr O'Brien yelling, *Stop swinging on those chairs or you'll fall backwards and crack your head!* And us ignoring him, smacking our gum loudly and then him yelling, *Spit out that gum or you'll fall backwards and swallow the gum and it will get stuck in your throat!* What a wanker he was.

I threw the pencils and exercise book into my waste basket and began picking out some clothes from my closet to take with me. That wasn't hard. Two pairs of black jeans, four t-shirts, bras, undies, socks.

'Yooohoo, Jez! Wakey wakey! Last day of 2009!'

I shoved the backpacks under my bed just as Mum pushed open my bedroom door, and I could smell the instant coffee in the mugs she was carrying.

'C'mon, let's go sit out back, it's not too hot yet.'

'Just a sec, I'll be there in a sec.' I tried not to sound guilty.

'Whatcha doin'?' Even Mum, usually oblivious to everything but herself, noticed that it was a bit weird that I was kneeling on the floor next to my bed.

'Nothing, really. Just looking through some old junk.'

'You've got enough shit in here! Next big clean-up we're doing is in here. Not enough storage, I reckon. Just that one closet. I was thinking of making some storage boxes, actually. This thing I read about in a *Better Homes* mag last time I was at the doctor.'

'No way. Clean the rest of the house, but not in here.' I loved my little treasure cave. My stomach twisted. I was gunna miss it if I left.

'Just thinking out loud.' Mum wandered off down the hallway, calling back, 'Don't be too long, your coffee will get cold!'

I got the backpack out again and shoved in a few more items—hairbrush, make-up bag, MP3 player, the silk pyjamas Mum gave me for Chrissie. As an afterthought I picked up the little baby-doll Courtney Love dress that Mum had given me when I was thirteen and held it up in front of me in the mirror. *I'll wear this tonight,* I decided.

Mum was getting all guzzied up for New Year's, too. She was excited to go over to Dana and Joan's for the dinner party.

'You know, I never get invited to dinner parties,' she told me. I sat on the end of her bed watching her pull out dresses that she hadn't worn since the nineties. 'I know you think I'm old, but seriously, my friends just party, they don't dinner party. Dinner party sounds so adult, don't you reckon?'

It was nice to see her so happy, prancing about in her bra and stomach-holding-in knickers.

'Oh, God, Jez, I forgot to show you.' Mum ran to the bathroom across the hall. 'Look what I bought!' She held up a box of leg wax. 'Do you use this? You know I've never even waxed before! I thought we could do our bikini lines! Wouldn't that be funny?'

I made a face. 'I let Casey do mine once. It kinda hurts. Not as bad as you think it will, but it does a bit.'

'Oooh, let's do it, Jez. Serious. I want to do girly stuff this arvo. We could do facials!'

'With what? You need those cream masks and stuff.'

'I could run to the shop!'

'If you want …'

'Oh, come on, Jez! Well, at least help me wax, then.'

'I'm *not* waxing my mother's bikini line. No way! Why do you need to do your bikini line, anyway? I thought you broke up with Jeremy?'

'Yeah, I did.' Mum sighed and fiddled with the price tag on the box of wax, peeling it back with her fingers. 'I just want to do girly girl things with my daughter, can we do that?'

'Mum, I'm not exactly a girly girl.'

'Don't you wax?'

'I usually just shave,' I admitted.

'What about the … hard-to-reach areas?'

'MUM!'

'Well …'

'I'm not that hairy!'

'Look, are you going to help me or not? I'll give you five bucks. Consider it like a waxing apprenticeship. Beauty school.'

'Fifty bucks I'll give you a makeover.'

'Makeover? What do I need doing that's worth fifty bucks? What's wrong with how I look?'

I tried to be tactful, which really wasn't a very strong point of my personality. Mum could be mega-sensitive when it came to her appearance, even though she put fuck-all effort into her make-up. 'You're just a little decade impaired. It's the bushy eyebrow thing with the blue eyeliner. And the eyebrow bar makes you look like a dyke.'

'Alright, that's enough,' Mum huffed. 'I love how you've got metal sticking through every bit of your face, but I've got one eyebrow bar and it makes me dyke-ish.'

'You asked!'

'You're supposed to lie!'

'Sorry!'

'Are you going to help me with this wax thing or not?'

'Look, I'll watch you while you do it. You put it on, and I'll rip the strip off, okay?'

'Oh, forget it! I'm over it. I need a fag.' Mum rummaged around in her purse, finding her cigarettes.

My mobile rang. Casey.

'Hey.'

We hadn't talked since the night with the football players. She'd been down the coast at her parents' caravan over Chrissie, and to be honest, I'd been kind of glad to have a breather from her. She just could be so intense.

'What's doin'?' Casey sounded distracted; she didn't wait for me to reply. 'Come help me organise shit for the party, will ya?' She sensed my hesitation and added, 'Puh-leeeeese, Jezzy? With a cherry on top?'

'Yeah, I can a bit later. I'm not ready yet and I'm helping Mum get guzzied up for this dinner party she's going to.'

'Sluzzered up? Ya mum?'

'Guzzied up. Like, dressed up.'

'Oh.' Casey sounded annoyed.

'Hey, get this,' I said to lighten the mood. 'She asked me to help her wax her bikini line!'

'Ya mum?!' Casey snorted. 'Too funny. I gotta do mine, but last time I did a home job I got all these ingrown hairs on my vagina. Had to pick them out with tweezers, hurt like a mother.'

'Yeah, right.' I cringed, trying to shake the visual of Casey's spotty vag.

Girls chronically over-sharing information about their vaginas totally tugged my tampon. Shaz did it all the time. She'd come over and be like, 'I just want to claw my vagina, this thrush is so brutal.' It's, like, *I'VE GOT A VAGINA, YOU'VE GOT A VAGINA?! LET'S TALK ABOUT OUR VAGINAS*. I always felt like going, *TMI, bitch*. I dunno when that became a thing that women just publicly blurt out shit about, but I'm pretty sure women in the old days didn't sit around going on about yeast infections, dry holes and UTIs.

'So anyway, I'm sticking to salon waxes only. You should tell your mum that.'

'Will do.'

'Catch you later, like, how long you reckon? I need you to help me string fairy lights.'

'Couple of hours?'

'Fuuuck. An hour, okay? Puh-leeease, Jez. I'm totally freaking out as it is that nobody's gunna come and everyone's gunna go to the city. I neeeed you.'

'Soon as I can. I got shit to organise here.' I paused for dramatic effect. 'This might be my last night here.'

'What the fuck?'

'I'm taking off. To Melbourne. Tonight.'

'WHAT THE FUCK? When? How're you getting there? WHY?'

'With Lukey. He's gunna go live with his cousin and I'm going with him.'

The line went silent. For a moment I thought Casey had hung up.

'So you guys finally hooked up?'

'Yeah.'

'He your boyfriend now?' Casey questioned sort of nasty-like.

'I dunno,' I said, being honest. 'We haven't talked about it.'

'What about Laura?'

'Laura's history. That was just a thing. I think he's over that.'

'Oh, really?'

'I think so.'

'And he's not seeing anybody else either?'

'Nope. We started hooking up like a week or so ago, just around Chrissie.'

'Oh, Jez,' Casey clucked. I could almost see her shaking her head. 'Jez, Jez, Jez,' she continued, all smug. 'We need to talk.'

'About what?' I demanded.

'You better come over here.'

I sighed. I wanted to spend time with Mum. If I left for

Melbourne, I was gunna miss her and because I couldn't even bring myself to tell Mum I was planning to leave, I wanted some Mum–Jez time before I left for Casey's.

'Soon, Case.' I rubbed my forehead, feeling headachey. 'I'll be there soon.'

I swore through clenched teeth. It couldn't be good news. Casey wouldn't save up good news to tell me in person. She was a bitch; she would save up bad news to tell me in person so that she could enjoy it more when she saw my face fall. Suddenly I had a bad feeling about the whole night, like that extra Spiderman sense that the giant shit-pot of Kambah in the cesspool of Tuggeranong Valley was starting to stir up a big stink. It made me want to run out to the back porch and throw myself into my mum's arms and be, like, *Can we just stay in tonight? You, me, a six-pack of beer and some potato chips?*

I dressed in Mum's old white baby-doll dress, my hands shaking as I pressed pale foundation to my damp skin, and lined my eyes with black khol.

'You look like a doll.' Mum startled me, appearing over my shoulder in my full-length mirror. 'With that pale skin and red lipstick. Pretty.'

I spun around to face her.

Mum wore a shiny dress with fabric that swirled with peacock colours, like an oil spill. She looked at me with so much pride and so much kindness that I almost broke down and told her everything—the packed bag stashed at the top of my wardrobe, the midnight bus, Lukey, Melbourne. But

I hadn't seen her so happy in so long, as excited to be going to this dinner party as a primary school kid going to their first disco.

'You look beautiful, Mum.' I swallowed.

'You reckon?' Mum was chuffed, too flustered to notice that I was nearly in tears. She tugged at her bra straps and hoisted her stomach-holding-in pants up under her breasts. 'Yeah, I scrub up alright! We both do.'

We stood side by side in front of the mirror, me looking at Mum, and Mum looking at herself, adjusting and readjusting. I couldn't meet her eyes.

THIRTY-ONE

Mum convinced me to help her carry the plates of food and bags of wine and booze and chocolates over to Dana and Joan's house. She'd gone overboard at Woolies, buying cheeses and nuts and all sorts of shit. I was kind of embarrassed by it. It was sweet that she wanted to impress her new friends, but she was going totally OTT. Trying to tell my mum to settle down and play it cool when she's all worked up is like trying to nail mashed potatoes to a tree.

Laura answered the door.

'Hi,' she said, all sad-sack. 'Come in.'

Mum went straight through to the back of the house to find Dana and Joan, leaving me with Laura.

'I'm not staying,' I told her, handing over a bag of groceries. 'There's a party on at Casey's. You coming?'

Laura snorted. 'Ha. No way. I don't think I'd be welcome.'

Laura played with the hem of her pink candy-striped, black-lace-trimmed dress. I felt a little stab of jealousy. She always looked so cute, with the ultra-feminine dresses and the diamonte-pierced dimples sparkling below those black frames. Even though I was wearing a dress, too, I felt gangly and awkward next to her. All elbows and knees. My hand flew to my lips; I was thinking about my square, wide front teeth, too big for my mouth.

'So, what are you gunna do, then?'

'Watch telly, I guess. I dunno.'

'Okay, then, well … See ya.'

'See ya.'

But as Laura went to shut the door I found myself quickly sticking my hand out to stop her.

'I reckon you should come to the party,' I said. 'Beats watching telly.'

'I don't think so.'

'C'mon!' I urged her. 'It's New Year's. You can't hang out with a bunch of old ladies!'

'I'm just going to watch Foxtel.'

'You should come to the party. Definitely.'

'You think so? I don't think Casey likes me.'

'Probably not. But I want you to come. Lukey would want you there, too.'

'Will Lukey be there?'

'Yeah. Pretty sure he's keen.'

'Have you been hooking up with Lukey?'

'Oh ... yeah. We kind of have been.'

'I didn't know for sure, but I hadn't heard from him since before Christmas, so ...'

'I'm sorry,' I said again. 'I didn't know it was gunna happen. I didn't even realise I liked him. After years of being mates ... I dunno. It just kind of happened.'

Laura nodded. 'That's cool. I wasn't heaps into him anyway. Well, maybe a bit. But I'll get over it.'

I nodded back at her, seeing her in a totally different light. She was cool. Very cool. If the situation had been reversed and she'd moved on a guy I'd been seeing, I reckon I would have totally cut sick. Even though she was one of those chicks who I considered a 'girly girl', all into frilly dresses and painting her nails, I reckon she had my back like a proper mate.

'Actually ... we're going to leave tonight,' I confessed to her. 'Him and me. We're going to Melbourne.'

'Wow!' Laura's eyes widened.

'I know.'

'I'm glad stuff's worked out. And I'm really sorry about what happened. I mean, between me and him.'

'Look, it's not your fault, Laura,' I said. 'I know that now. I was a bitch to you and I'm sorry. Come to this party, okay?'

'Really?' Laura looked relieved. 'You really want me to come?'

'I reckon you should.' I nodded. 'Casey will be okay.'

'Thanks, Jez.' Laura leaned forward and squeezed my arm. 'I'll just go get my purse.'

Laura came back with her bag, yelling goodbyes over her shoulder.

'Ready?' I felt another big rush of adrenaline shoot up through my torso.

'Ready. You know, I think I might even miss you when you leave.'

Weird as it was, I felt like I might miss Laura, too.

When we got to Casey's the yard was already full of kids, drinking, smoking and standing around in bunches. The girls were in short, glittery dresses, miniskirts, short shorts and heels, the guys were shiny and showered, with gelled hair and bright t-shirts. Most of the crowd was sitting and standing around on the paved patio just outside the kitchen where dance music pumped from portable speakers hooked up to an MP3. There were fairy lights strung from the big old pine and they lit the ceramic garden animals. It was almost trippy. I wished I had some acid.

Up the back of the yard, on the lawn near Cash's tent stood Cash, Stu and Jeremy, beers in hand.

'Jeeez!' Casey clocked me and rushed over, clawing at my elbow with her ridiculously long acrylic nails. 'Oh, my God. I need to talk to you.' She ignored Laura and pulled me back into the kitchen.

'What? Sorry I didn't come help set up, I had to go with Mum to —'

'Forget that!' Casey waved her hand. 'Cash set up for me. You gotta help me get more people here!'

'There's gotta be, like, twenty, thirty people here already.'

'I know! Total fucking *disaster*. It's, like ... nearly eight o'clock. Why are you so late? And why'd you bring *her*?'

'I told you, I was helping my mum.'

'Yeah, right.' She arched an eyebrow at me accusingly. 'Well, I've been on the phone to Lee and she reckons heaps of people are going to the city. I can't believe it. I'm so tempted to go and just ditch my own party.'

'Don't go! I can't afford the city. I think Lukey's coming later.'

Casey perked up a bit. 'Really? Ring some people, Jez! What about Martin? What's he doing?' She fiddled with the rings on her fingers.

'I guess I could ring Martin ...'

'Do it! We need some *guys*. It's like a fucking fanny factory out there.' Casey jerked her thumb towards the backyard.

'I saw a bunch of guys.'

'Nobody worth hooking up with. If I don't get a decent root soon, my hole is going to close over.'

'What about Stu? You thought he was hot two weeks ago.'

'Been there, climbed that mountain. And it was no mountain. I've gotten more pleasure from inserting a tampon. Hey, you got any gum?'

'Are you on something, Case? Seriously, you're more mental than usual.'

Casey's mouth stretched into a smile. With her back to the light in the kitchen, little black shadows cast over her eye sockets. 'Dexies,' she told me. 'You want?'

'Nah,' I said.

I felt like if my heart pumped any faster it would squeeze its way up my throat and out of my mouth.

'So what did you want to talk to me about, anyway?' I asked her. 'Before on the phone, you said you needed to tell me something?'

'In a sec.' Casey stamped her foot impatiently. 'I've been a little busy here trying to organise my party, so I'm going to have a slash and freshen up. You get onto those calls, okay?'

'Right.' I pulled my mobile out of my pocket and pretended to type in a number until Casey left the room, then stuck it back in my jeans. I didn't have any credit on my phone anyway.

'Jez, hey.' Cash wandered into the kitchen and stuck his head into the fridge. 'Beer?'

'Fuck yeah.' I accepted the beer he held out for me and cracked it open. 'How've you been?'

'Not bad. You? Haven't seen you since Christmas. Things were a bit hectic over at your place. Awesome dress, by the way.'

'Thanks.' I gave my little baby-doll dress a bit of a shake. 'It was my mum's. When she was younger, obviously.'

Cash smiled. 'Your mum's alright, hey.'

'Yeah, sorry about running off like that on Christmas —'

'Nah, I'm sorry,' Cash interrupted, touching my shoulder. 'You must think I'm a huge prick, huh? It's just I got to thinking ... about how you're real young and stuff.'

'It didn't seem to bother you that night in the tent.'

Cash raised his eyebrows and laughed, then shook his head. 'Yeah, well. You got me there. It's just that after Casey told me how much you liked me ...'

'Casey told you?'

'Well, yeah.'

'Look,' I said. 'It's okay. You don't have to feel sorry or whatever. I'm not some dumb kid who's in love with you if that's what you think. You're not that cool.'

'Oh, gee, thanks.'

'You know what I mean.' I grinned. 'It was fun. I like you.'

'Even though I'm not cool? Even though I'm just an old prick?'

'Don't fish for compliments. You know you're good-looking.'

'So,' Cash said casually after a pause. 'I think I'm hitting the road tomorrow, if I'm not too hung-over.'

'Yeah? Looks like everyone's leaving, then.'

'Who else?'

'Me and Lukey,' I said proudly. 'We're jumping a bus to Melbourne.'

'You and Lukey?' Cash wrinkled his forehead. 'Really?'

I stopped short, unsure of myself. 'Yeah,' I countered. 'Why?'

'Fucking hell. Stop it you two!' Casey was back from the bathroom. 'Stop all this flirting bullshit. We need to be partying right now.'

Casey grabbed a glass and sloshed some vodka and orange juice into it. 'Cheers, cunts!' She tipped her glass back. 'Now.

Party.' Casey grabbed us both by the elbow and pushed us towards the back door.

'Wait, Case!' I waved Cash on ahead of us. 'I just gotta talk to Casey for one more minute.'

'What is it?' Casey said, impatiently, tapping her toe. 'C'mon, c'mon.'

'I just wanted to ask you ...'

'Why is *she* here, anyway?'

'Laura? She's cool,' I told her. 'No point in fighting with her. I'm taking off tonight, anyway.'

Casey rolled her shoulders back. 'Why the fuck would you do that?' She narrowed her eyes.

'To get out of here. Canberra's the biggest hole, you know that. And we're at the hairy-arse-end of the hole down here in Tuggeranong.'

Casey shrugged. 'Is this 'cos of Laura? You're gunna move to Melbourne and think you're better than everyone else.'

'What? No!'

'So why? Are you, like, *in love* with Lukey?'

'I don't know.' I swallowed. 'Maybe. I mean we only just hooked up, but —'

Casey gave a short, humourless laugh. 'Look, Jez. I'm the last person who would want to burst your little bubble. But you deserve to know the truth.'

'Truth?' I felt my mouth go dry. I swigged from my beer. 'What truth?'

'About Lukey,' Casey ventured, tapping her acrylics against

her glass. 'Well, it's not a huge surprise really, you know he's always had a horn for me.'

'*What?*' I pressed her. I could hear the blood rushing to my head. It sounded like when you held a seashell up to your ear at the beach. 'What happened?'

'We hooked up.' Casey shrugged like it was no big deal. 'So you see, Jez, maybe you should think twice about going to Melbourne with him. It doesn't seem like he's all that into you. I mean, it's not my fault entirely because he'd had a crush on me for YEARS and ... what *is* that dress you're wearing?' Casey gave my dress the twice-over and wrinkled up her nose.

I ignored her comment about my dress. 'When did this happen?' My voice dropped to a whisper. I felt weak.

'Only a couple of days ago. The same day I drove back from the coast. So you can't blame me, huh? 'Cos I didn't even know about you and him. Last time I checked you were with Cash. It's hard to keep up with you these days.'

'What is that supposed to mean?'

'It's like how you chased after Cash. Seriously. Did you actually think he was going to go out with you or what? You totally threw yourself at him. It was sort of desperate.'

'Whaaaat? I didn't. He was into me, too. It was both ways.'

'Ha! Oh, honey.' Casey patted me on the shoulder. 'One second you're a virgin and the next you're throwing yourself at every guy in the neighbourhood. It's a bit embarrassing.'

'Where the fuck is this even coming from?' I was turning red.

'Martin told me you went round to his house and practically begged him for it.'

Now I was angry. 'Martin is fucking lying, then.'

'Is he?' Casey said, all superior. 'Look, it's okay, Jez. Martin told me everything. I saw him over at Jim's house, like, that night. Everyone thought you were frigid, so now you're being all, like, slutty or whatever. So it's no wonder, once Lukey found out ...'

'Found out what?!'

'Once I told him how you've been putting it around. Well, he wasn't heaps happy.'

'Why the fuck would you tell him that?! You're supposed to be my friend, Casey!'

'Well, I'm Lukey's friend, too. I thought he deserved to know. See the problem with you, Jez, is that 'cos you dress all emo or whatever, and 'cos you talk smart and hang out with the boys, you think you're better than me. But the lesson I've taught you is that pretty girls will always win the guys. You should be *thanking* me.'

'Thanking you?' I managed to squeak.

'And look who your new bestie is! Laura! Even after she did the dirty on you with Lukey! 'Cos she's from Melbourne, she thinks she's better than us! And after hanging out with her for a month you're suddenly moving there?' Casey folded her arms across her chest. 'You've totally changed, Jez. I mean you always did try so hard, didn't you? Do you think you're a fucking rock star 'cos you dye your hair stupid colours and wear too much eyeliner? It's a bit sad, really.'

'You are such a bitch, Casey,' I choked out, not able to hold back my tears. 'I like Laura because she's a nice person. Unlike you.'

'Oh, my God! Are you, like, lesbians now or something?'

'No!'

'How come you're hanging out with that lesbian, then?'

'Laura's not a lesbian! She had a boyfriend in Melbourne and everything. She even got knocked up by him.' The words slipped out of my mouth before I could stop them.

'FUCK OFF! Are you serious?!' Casey's whole face lit up. 'What happened? Miscarriage? Abortion?'

'Abortion,' I hissed. 'Can you talk any louder? Fuck. You can't spread this.'

'Okay, okay. Tell me what happened, though!'

'I'm not telling you shit! Go fuck yourself!'

'Oh, get over it, Jez.' Casey sneered. 'I can't help it if I'm what guys want.'

Casey spun on her heel and went out to the party. I felt kind of dizzy, and gripped onto the kitchen bench for support, and then found a bar stool and fell onto it. I took a big long chug from my beer, and then I grabbed the bottle of vodka she'd left open on the bench and slopped some into a paper cup and chucked it straight down my throat. It brought more tears to my eyes. I felt pathetic. Standing in the Hollands' kitchen in my grungey little dress, my hair teased several inches high, make-up painted on thick. In front of my mirror, getting dressed that afternoon, I had felt like a rock star. I'd put on the

Misfits and smoked a joint and then several cigarettes out of my bedroom window and then when I was feeling really good and baked, I sat in front of my full-length mirror pouting at myself, admiring the way my lips shone with the glossy lipstick. Maybe Casey was right. Maybe I did think I was fucking awesome. But only sometimes. And only in little windows between hating my whole fucking life.

'Hey.' Laura squeezed through the sliding door. 'You gunna come outside?'

I hung my head. 'Yeah ... in a sec,' I said, all flat and sad-sack.

'What's wrong?' Laura put her hand on my back. 'I could see you talking to Casey. Is it because I'm here? Did she give you shit about that?'

'Nah, it's not you.' I looked up at her. 'She had a go at me.'

'Aw, Jez.' Laura squeezed my shoulders. 'Whatever she said, don't listen to her. She's just such a bitch.'

'She said I'm trying to be all slutty,' I said. 'Which is bullshit. And then she told me she hooked up with Lukey.'

'Omigod!' Laura's eyes widened. 'Like slept with, or just made out with?'

'I dunno,' I admitted. 'She made it sound like slept with.'

'He's a guy,' Laura said quietly. 'A nice guy. But still a guy.'

'That makes it okay?' I spat. 'I thought he liked me. Proper liked me.'

'I thought he liked me, too.'

Laura and I looked back at each other.

'Casey reckoned I was throwing myself at them. At Cash, and this other guy, Martin.'

'You thought I was throwing myself at Lukey.'

'Yeah, yeah,' I huffed. 'I get the point, Laura. I said I was sorry.'

'I know. Look, Casey is jealous of you.'

I laughed, all bitter. 'Yeah, right.'

'She is,' Laura insisted. 'She knows Lukey would never go out with her. She's been trying to get with him for ages now. He told me. Then I bumped into her at the Boxing Day sales and kind of let it slip that he'd hooked up with you. You should have seen the look on her face.'

'She told me she didn't know I was with him!'

'She totally knew.'

'What the fuck?' I shook my head, trying to take in this information. 'What the … That is so mental. Casey was never into Lukey. She always goes for big meaty footy player types.'

Laura shrugged. 'Everyone's fucking everyone around here, didn't you know? You've got your head in the clouds, Jez. Lukey's a nice guy, nerdish type. Like I told you, Casey was jealous. She was probably sick of the randoms and wanted a proper boyfriend.'

'Why didn't Lukey tell me this, though?'

Laura shrugged. 'Doesn't seem like you guys talk much about that sort of stuff.'

'I gotta go talk to him.' I polished off my beer and went to the fridge and stuck another couple in my handbag. 'For the road,' I explained to Laura.

'Jez, don't leave me here!' Laura pleaded. 'Talk to Lukey another time, when you're not so angry!'

'I'm not angry,' I said truthfully. I was shocked. I still couldn't believe Lukey would do that to me, hook up with Casey, of all people, behind my back. 'And I gotta talk to him now. We're supposed to be getting on a bus in a few hours.'

'Okay.' Laura looked glum. 'But you're coming back, right? I don't want to be here alone.'

'Half an hour, tops,' I promised. 'If I'm catching this bus I'll have to come get my bag from my house, anyway.'

'Can't you just call him?'

'No credit.'

'Call him from my phone?'

Impulsively, I gave Laura a little hug. 'I'll be back soon,' I said. 'Promise.'

THIRTY-TWO

• •

The sun was going down, the silhouettes of the Brindabellas slate-grey against the orange-tinged sky. I blinked back tears as I half jogged, then walked, then jogged again the two streets over to Lukey's house. It was a path I'd trodden hundreds of times over the past five years. To the end of my street, turn left, across a small stretch of dry yellow grass near the bus stop and then up the hill on Sinclair. It was a five-minute walk. I made it to his front door in under two.

The door was open, the screen door closed. I banged my balled fist against the flyscreen frame, briefly enjoying the clanging noise as the metal reverberated.

'Lukey!' I screeched. 'It's Jez!'

'Whatdafark?' Mark stuck his head into the hallway from the lounge room. 'Jus' come in, stop farkin' screaming 'n carryin' on.'

'Sorry,' I said. 'Lukey here?'

'Lukey? Fuckin' LUKEY.' Mark pulled up his singlet to wipe the sweat from his face. 'Faggot's in his room.'

I went down the hall. Last door on the left. I didn't bother knocking. Lukey was on his bed, cross-legged, shirtless, just wearing his tight stovepipe black jeans that he'd cut off just above the knee to make shorts. He was packing a bong, thumbing the mix right down into the cone piece. He looked up at me through his fringe and then lit the cone, eyes bulging as he struggled to hold the smoke in his lungs.

'You ready to go?' he managed as he exhaled.

I sat at the edge of the bed, breathing in the sweet smoke.

'Shut the fuckin' door!' Lukey spluttered, eyes watering as he coughed up the last of his lungful of smoke.

'Sorry!' I snapped. 'No, I'm not fuckin' ready to go. Kinda wondering if I'm gunna even bother,' I spoke quickly, not choosing my words, just letting the hurt and anger spill over my lips. 'You fucked Casey?! I can't fuckin' believe it. I had to hear it from you. Is it true? Say something! Don't just fuckin' stare at me. SAY SOMETHING.'

Lukey blinked. 'She tell you that?' And then he reached for the bong and the mix bowl. I wanted to knock them right out of his stupid hands.

'So it's true?' I managed, my throat tight.

He shrugged. 'Sort of.'

'What's that mean? What's "sort of"?'

'You want details?'

'Just tell me! Yes or no!'

'Well … yes, then.'

'After you and me?'

'Fuck, Jez! What the fuck do you want me to say? I fucked up,' he spat angrily. 'Like what about you and Martin?' He eyeballed my face through his fringe. 'Ha! Yeah, you thought I didn't know about that, huh? And Cash? So it's alright for you, all the while you're giving me shit about Laura and you were hooking up with all these dudes.'

'That was before you and me,' I choked. 'That's different.'

Lukey flicked his fringe out of his eyes. I could see his face. He wasn't guilty, he wasn't sad. He looked … absent. Stoned. And there was a puffy black ring around the edge of his right eye.

'What happened?' I asked, not sure whether I actually cared or not. 'To your eye?'

'Mark.' Lukey shrugged. 'We got in a fight over the remote.'

'Over the remote?'

'He was flicking channels. I was like, "Just choose a channel. One fucking channel." So he punched me.'

'Arsehole,' I murmured.

'Yeah,' Lukey said.

'I'm not going with you to Melbourne,' I whispered. 'Not now.'

'I never thought you would, anyway.'

It sounded like a challenge. But I didn't even have the heart to argue with him. Maybe he was right. I wasn't ready. I'd bitched and moaned about my house, Kambah and the shit-hole that is Canberra for years now. But every time I thought about leaving home it was like a punch in the guts. I wanted to stay. I wanted another year of school and teachers and home-work and normal teenager stuff. I wasn't ready to grow up yet.

'Why did you do it? Why Casey? You always said she was sluzza.'

'She's alright. Crazy girl.'

'Was it worth it? Didn't you think about me?'

'I was maggot. She threw herself at me. I didn't wanna hurt her feelings.'

'What about my feelings?'

'You're not my girlfriend, Jez! We never even talked about that. Do you want to be my girlfriend? Is that it?'

'Fuck, no!' I choked. 'Not now. I know I don't mean shit to you.'

I did want to be his girlfriend. I wanted to scream it in his stupid, stoned face. *YES, you stupid idiot! I want to be your girlfriend!*

'You do mean something, Jez.'

'Oh yeah? Like what?' I pressed. I wanted to hear that he loved me, that he couldn't live without me.

'You're my best mate. I like you. *Like* like.'

'And what about Casey? What's she to you?'

'Didn't mean anything.'

'If it didn't mean anything then why do it?' My throat hurt, and my eyes stung from the clouds of stale smoke in Lukey's hot little bedroom. I suddenly realised it might be the last time I sat there, in that room, on Lukey's double bed. I fingered his doona cover, dark and light blue checks, worn and balling. I thought about all the times I'd curled up next to him watching horror movies, and then fallen asleep to *Rage* video clips on his telly. I looked at his walls covered with posters of bands we didn't even listen to anymore, and his small set of shelves that held keepsakes and trinkets, his stuffed gorilla wearing boxing gloves that he'd won at the Canberra Show years ago.

Aren'tcha gunna give it to me? I'd said. *You're s'posed to give me the toy 'cos I'm a girl.*

Nah, Lukey had grinned. *He's mine. I'm gunna name him Mike Tyson.*

Give it to me! I'd insisted.

You're not my friggin' girlfriend, Jez!

I guess even back then I was one of those stupid romantic types. I wanted kisses with snake-bite piercings and holding hands in front of a sunset, while everyone else wanted fucking and blow jobs.

Lukey followed my eyes to Mike Tyson. He leaned over on his knees and plucked the gorilla off the shelf.

'You want to look after Mike Tyson for me?' He held out the toy.

I shook my head. 'Nah.'

'Oh …' Lukey looked down at the gorilla for a moment, and then chucked it to the corner of the room.

'I better get going. I kinda ditched Laura at the New Year's party.'

'Party any good? I don't reckon I'll go, hey. Reckon I'll just take off.'

I shrugged. 'Pretty average.'

'Well … Can I get a hug, at least? Even if you're mad at me?'

My eyes spilled over with tears. 'Fuck off,' I managed to choke out as I leaned over to grab him around the waist. He stroked my head as I sobbed into the soft downy strands of hair that circled his belly button. I wanted him to hold me like that forever, like we were still kids, like that time we got our tongues pierced and we sat so close together it was like we became one. I wanted to beg him, *Please don't go … please don't leave me here alone … please stay with me … please say you love me as much as I love you.* But I didn't say any of that. I lifted my head and wiped at the wet patch I'd left on his stomach.

'Snotty.' He half smiled.

'Sorry 'bout that.' I couldn't even look at him, I felt like my heart might crumble into dust inside my chest.

'Come visit?'

'Yeah.'

'Oh, hey, got something for ya.' Lukey pulled his bedside table drawer open and pulled out a baggie of E. There were four white round pills inside. 'Happy New Year's,' he said. 'Last ones.'

'Cheers, big ears.' I tried to smile.

'Not a wucka, motherfucker.'

I gathered my bag and rummaged in it till I found a stubbie and cracked it open.

'One for the road,' I explained to him, still unable to look at his face. 'I'll catch ya.'

'See ya, Jez,' he said quietly.

I waited until I got outside onto the street before letting my tears fall again and then I cried and cried and sucked on my stubby of beer like a baby on a bottle.

THIRTY-THREE

• •

The air was heavy with the scents of sizzling sausages and steaks on backyard barbies, and I could hear the buzz and shout of conversations from New Year's parties. Everyone was having a good time except for me. I trudged along the asphalt road, my sneakers scraping, hating life, blinking back the tears that stung my eyes and throat. The last of the sun disappeared over the mountains and I could see the neon-green glow of the Kambah Tavern roof through the trees that edged the Village.

My mind had kicked into overdrive, but just one thought buzzed around in there, like a scratched CD on a stereo. *Casey*. She had fucked me over. She'd gone after Lukey. My lovely, lame-brain, nerdy stoner emo fairy best friend. She was out of control. She'd gone too far this time. Was there any guy off limits to her? Why'd she have to go after every single fucking guy?

Back at Casey's the party had picked up. Hilltop Hoods blasted from the speakers, big clusters of kids stood around sinking beers, taking shots and lining up Jager Bombs. I scanned the backyard for Laura but couldn't see her. Cash was sitting at the picnic table under the old pine, surrounded by a group of girls in short shorts and strapless dresses, his arm hooked around the neck of Casey's friend, Lee, the hot bogan Asian. I felt my stomach lurch with jealousy. *Fuck him*, I thought angrily. But it hurt. It hurt so bad.

'Where's Case?' I demanded, marching up to the table and staring pointedly at Cash.

He hesitated for a second and blinked, kind of guilty-like. 'Dunno, Jezza,' he shouted over the music. 'Maybe inside. You know Lee?'

I nodded, not looking at Lee and held Cash's eyes for a few more moments, searching for something in them, one of those looks he used to give me with the crooked smile showing his chipped tooth. But he just sat there, his face not giving anything away, and pulled Lee closer to his chest. She tipped her head up at him and smiled, slow and satisfied. The cat that got the fucking cream.

'You right, Jez? Got a beer?' he asked.

'Fine.'

I spun on my heel and marched towards the house.

'Casey!' I screeched, my voice breaking. 'CASEY!' I slammed the glass sliding door behind me.

Her bedroom door was open a crack, the dim glow of a bedside lamp shining from inside. I could hear muffled sounds and a little giggle. I put my hand on the door and pushed gently.

'Casey? I need to talk to you …' I was angry, not thinking straight.

There was no reply. I could hear a male voice say, *Tell her to fuck off!*

'Casey! I want to fucking talk to you. NOW!' I pushed the door hard, wide open.

Casey was on her knees, in front of her bed, her face buried in Martin Carroll's lap. His hands were on the back of her head, pulling her onto his cock. I could hear her gurgle and gag, as Martin looked up and narrowed his eyes at me, a slow, smug smile stretching across his face. Casey snapped her head around and clocked me, her eyes bleeding black mascara.

'Fucking hell, Jez. FUCK OFF!' Casey gasped. 'Have you lost it?'

I stood my ground. I wanted it out with her. 'I want to talk to you. NOW.'

'FUCK OFF, JEZ!' Casey screeched. 'I'm fucking serious.'

Martin reclined on his elbows, not bothering to cover up his stiff and swollen penis, which bobbed up and down as he flexed his groin muscles. I stared in horrified fascination.

'Come and party with us, Jez,' Martin said, catching me looking. He gestured towards his crotch. 'I can handle youse both.'

'No way.' Casey stood up and gripped my arms, clawing at my bare skin with her acrylic nails. Forcing me back into the hallway, she gave me one last death stare before closing the door in my face. I stood there, breathless with anger. I could hear Martin laughing on the other side of door, before the muffled sex noises began again.

'FUCK YOU, CASEY!' I screamed, my voice strangled. 'FUCK YOU, SLUT!'

Casey was at the door in less than a second.

'What did you call me?' Her voice had dropped to a whisper. 'What THE FUCK did you CALL ME?!'

Over her shoulder I could see Martin sniggering, clutching at his cock like a monkey holding a banana.

'Lukey —' I began.

'Don't you ever—EVER—call me that again.' Casey leaned in so close to me I could smell the rum and Coke on her breath and the rich, earthy scent of sex on her skin. 'Now get the fuck out of my house.'

'You're supposed to be my friend,' I said, blinking tears. 'I trusted you. I loved Lukey.'

'Ha! You loved him? You loved him when you were fucking my brother? Did you love him when you threw yourself at Martin?' Casey jerked her thumb over her shoulder and Martin snorted.

'I've loved him for years.' I was crying openly now, hating my own patheticness. 'Why'd you do it? You're supposed to be my friend.'

Casey folded her arms tight under her breasts and circled my face with her eyes in cold scrutiny.

'Well I'm not now, bitch.'

Casey slammed the bedroom door so hard I could feel my teeth shake in my skull.

And that was that. There was no more to say. I left the party.

I let myself into my house. I was shaking as I yanked open the fridge, looking for some drinks. Half a bottle of white wine left over from the night when Shaz'd been around. *Wine! Yuck!* But I snatched the bottle and drank greedily. It tasted like grape voms. I stepped out onto the back porch and stood for a few seconds, staring beyond the fence to the party next door. Laughter and chatter over strains of some sort of rap shit, Jay-Z or something, I dunno, I hated all that pop-chart top-forty shit. *Lamest party ever, Casey*, I thought nastily. But I wished I was there. I wished me and Lukey were there, sitting at the wooden picnic table, sinking cold beers, poking each other in the ribs and taking the piss out of the freshies and their crap music. I took the ashtray inside and lit a smoke in the kitchen, still swigging from the wine bottle, desperate to drown my sadness.

My mobile rang in my pocket. Laura.

'Hey!' I answered eagerly. 'Where'd you go to? You're not gunna believe the fight I had with Casey ... Oh and I'm not going to Melbourne anymore either —'

'Slow down, Jez! You're not going? So weird, I had this feeling … I mean after the Casey thing. I'm at my house. You want to come over here?'

'Yeah! Sure! My mum still there?'

'Yep. The oldies are drinking still, listening to nineties music and being all nostalgic. It's pretty funny.'

'I'll be there in, like, ten.'

THIRTY-FOUR
. .

Laura was sitting on her front porch when I arrived, sipping from a small silver hip flask. I sat on the step next to her, pulled a Winfield out of my pack and lit it, enjoying the red crackling glow of the tip against the dark night.

'Vodka?' She held the flask out to me.

I took a sip, enjoying the feeling of the liquid burning in my chest. It took me back to the last time we'd drunk vodka at Laura's house, a few weeks earlier, after popping those pingers and swimming in her pool. Me, Laura and Lukey. We hadn't really even known each other then. It seemed like so long ago. So much had happened since.

'You told Casey about my abortion,' Laura spoke softly. She didn't accuse, she just stated it as fact.

'I'm so sorry,' I said quickly. 'Please don't be mad. It was a mistake. It just slipped out.'

'I believe you.' Laura looked me in the eyes.

I smiled, grateful. 'Thanks.'

'Casey called me a baby-killer,' Laura told me. 'Right in front of a whole group of kids. She really doesn't like me. For no reason.'

'Casey,' I spat. 'Don't even worry about her. You were so right about her.'

'Let's not talk about her. Let's just enjoy the rest of the night, okay?'

We sat side by side, sipping from the hip flask, enjoying the warm night breeze. I could hear the crackles and explosions from fireworks going off in the distance and people in back-yards and houses blowing on noise-makers, yelling, 'Happy New Year!' and singing 'Auld Lang Syne'.

'Happy New Year,' Laura reached out and squeezed my shoulder.

Five minutes later my mobile bleeped. A text message from Lukey. *I made it. I'm on my way.*

I showed Laura.

'You upset?' she asked, making a concerned face.

'Yeah. A bit.' I nodded. 'Actually, heaps.'

'Things happen for a reason,' Laura said. 'Everything will come out in the wash.'

'You reckon?' I swallowed hard, trying to get rid of the lump lodged in my throat. 'You really think that?'

Laura hesitated. 'Maybe. Just have to wait and see, I guess.'

'Yeah, I guess.'

'You know what I want to do?' Laura sighed. 'Foxtel and ice-cream. Maybe some really lamely happy Pixar animation.'

I snorted. 'Serious? I want to get fucked up. Like just get really messy.'

Laura shrugged. 'We can sneak some booze, for sure.'

'I've got pingers for later. Present from Lukey.'

There was laughter and music, Red Hot Chili Peppers' 'Under the Bridge' coming from the backyard at Laura's house.

'Should we go say hello?' Laura asked. 'Your mum might wanna see you.'

We went out the back. It was just Mum, Dana and Joan around a big table strewn with empty plates, wine glasses, party poppers and balled serviettes.

'Our girls!' Mum cried, her face glowing under the strings of fairy lights and Chinese lanterns. 'Happy New Year, baby!'

'Have a seat, girls!' Dana cried. 'A little bit of wine? A glass each for a toast.' She scraped back her chair and went into the kitchen and returned with two oversized wine glasses and filled them each about a third full.

'What happened to your party?' Mum asked. 'I thought you'd be out all night. Nice of you to come spend Newies with your old mum.'

I smiled. 'Yeah, the party was good,' I lied, 'but we wanted to come spend time with you guys. I thought you were going down to the club?'

'I've been having too good a time here!' Mum grinned. 'Shaz was ropeable.'

'Yeah? What happened?'

'Oh, she kept ringing and ringing and then when I ignored her calls she sent this.' Mum flicked through her phone until she found the message and read aloud. *You are a dog friend.*

'Oh, Mum. You're not a dog friend. Shaz is the dog friend.'

Mum shrugged. 'You know what it's like down there. Everybody would have been drunk. Shaz gets nasty when she drinks.'

'She's nasty anyway.'

'I think you might be right,' Mum agreed. 'You know, I don't reckon I really want to be spending a whole heap of time with Shaz anymore.'

'Fuck, yes!' I cheered. 'Let's drink to that.'

We raised our glasses.

'Joanie? You want to make the toast?'

'I think we should let Helen —'

'No, no!' Mum protested. 'No, you do it, Joan.'

'Okay.' Joan sat up a bit straighter in her chair. 'First of all, I've had way too much wine tonight, so I'm going to get sentimental.'

'Aw, Joanie, please don't.' Laura groaned.

'Let her speak!' Mum cried, loving it. She loved sentimental crap.

'I just remember when I was travelling and spending so many Christmases and New Year's Eves with strangers, or just being a face in a crowd on the Thames in London or once even on the Bund in Shanghai —'

'Get to the point, Joanie!' Laura was embarrassed.

'— and so many times I remember hoping that one day I'd have a family of my own to spend these types of occasions with. And now I have you, Dana, and our beautiful daughter, Laura.'

Laura groaned again.

'And our new friends with us, Helen and Jez …'

Mum let out a huge sigh of happiness and leaned in against me.

'And I just want to say that this moment couldn't be more perfect. Cheers and Happy New Year's.'

Mum started weeping openly, happy tears. I took a sip of my wine, and couldn't help but feel kind of nice and glowy. But it wasn't happiness exactly, it was something else. I'm not one hundred percent sure because it was something I wasn't used to feeling. It felt a little bit like hope.

Mum got totally maggot on New Year's and could hardly get out of bed the next day, but I didn't mind because everyone had been maggot. Me and Laura had popped a pinger each and went wandering around the neighbourhood for a few hours, and when we got back to Laura's the oldies were still sitting on the back patio, pissing on. It was dawn as me and

Mum stumbled back through the grey streets, the laughs of kookaburras pounding in our hollow skulls.

I helped Mum out with her hangover, shifting the DVD and telly into her room so we could watch *Dirty Dancing* while she sipped on water and nibbled vegemite toast. We both cried at the end.

I thought about Lukey all day. I missed him already. It didn't seem real that he was hundreds of kilometres away. When the doorbell rang later that arvo, I leapt up, half expecting to see him there on the doorstep, staring at his sneakers behind his curtain fringe, hands buried deep in the pockets of his black cut-offs.

I yanked open the door.

Jeremy.

'Muuuum!'

I stood to one side of the door as Mum emerged from her bedroom in her bright-orange camisole nightie, panda-eyed, hair sticking up in sixty directions.

'Jeremy!' Mum's mouth fell open as he stuck a bunch of pink gerberas under her nose.

'I missed you last night, Hel,' he squeaked. 'Wasn't a party without ya.'

'I missed you, too,' Mum murmured, sniffing the gerberas. 'These don't really smell like anything.'

'I just got them down at the petrol station,' Jeremy admitted, embarrassed. 'Nothing open today.'

'They're beautiful.'

'You look beautiful,' Jeremy said, which I thought was ultra-generous of him considering Mum's fright-wig hair.

Mum cast a quick sidelong glance at me. I gave her a small smile and nodded before she stepped into his arms for a kiss that involved way too much tongue than was decent. I made a show of sticking my finger in my throat and making gagging sounds, but I was secretly chuffed for her. She'd got her *Jerry Maguire* moment. Mum deserved to be happy. Maybe she had even found love.

I went back to my room and pulled Mum's laptop onto my bed and logged into Facebook. Lukey Johnson: *Melbourne I'm inside you*.

I miss you already, I typed under his status update, and made a little heart-shaped emoticon.

The reply came back almost immediately.

I miss you, too.

I smiled through my tears and logged off the computer.

THIRTY-FIVE

Six months later, me and Laura were at Skin Deep Tattoo in Canberra City, high on adrenaline and the triple-chocolate Oreo vegan thickshakes we'd just sucked down at a cafe. My eighteenth birthday and we were about to get our first tattoos; totally sweet.

'I feel like I'm going to wee my pants!' Laura giggled. 'So nervous.'

'It couldn't be much worse than piercing,' I said, running my tongue over the rings in my lip. 'Plus it's forever, so it's worth the pain.'

Forever didn't seem like such a long time to me. I was eighteen and I didn't think much further ahead than the next few days, and that weekend it was gunna be a party at Dana and Joan's all for me, in honour of turning eighteen, and then after that, my present from Mum, a bus trip down to Melbourne to visit Lukey. I'd kept my promise to him. I was keeping an eye on Ashleigh; me and her were hanging out regularly. She was cool, almost like my own little sister.

I hadn't seen Lukey since New Year's, but it wasn't so bad. We chatted on Facebook every night of the week and talked on the phone now and then. I saw photos that he'd posted online. He'd shaved his head and was dressing more punk and he had a whole heap more tattoos done, too. He looked good. I couldn't wait to show him my first tattoo. Freaking awesome.

But to be honest, I didn't miss him as much as I thought I would. The surprise was my new best friend: me and Laura became totally tight, really quickly. After Lukey left, she turned out to be totally solid, and was heaps of fun to hang out with. Plus our mums all got really close, so it was kind of like one big family.

The door to the tattoo place opened and this little hippy chick walked in, bells around her ankles. She walked up to the front counter, her long paisley skirt flowing.

'I want to get an "ohm",' she told the guy behind the counter.

'A what?'

'An "ohm". It's a Buddhist thing. And maybe a lotus flower, too, underneath it.'

'Are you a Buddhist?' he asked her

'Not really. It's more the symbolism.'

'The symbolism of being a Buddhist?' Laura interjected, sneaking a cheeky smile at me, her eyes sparkling.

The hippy chick turned and looked at us. 'Um, yeah.'

Laura leaned over to me and whispered, 'That is so funny. The other day I saw a forty-year-old slapper in a pub guzzling wine with a "Ganesh" tattooed on her foot. I was like, *Honey you're from Canberra, not fucking Raja.*'

I snorted loudly and the hippy shot us a hairy eyeball as she stomped out of the shop.

Laura collapsed into me, giggling. 'What a poser! I bet she's from Tuggeranong, just like us.'

'Tuggeranong like us? Are you a Kambah girl now?'

'Um, let me see. The other week I wore my Ugg boots down to the Village, smoked bongs in three separate backyards, drank my weight in Bundy and Coke and now we're getting tattooed. Is that Kambah enough for you?'

'You'll never be one of us,' I teased her. 'No matter how much you want it. See, you just made fun of that girl getting the "ohm" symbol, but everyone knows a good bogan has a least one eastern religion figurine in their house that they bought from the Dollar Shop.'

'Have you seen my house? Dana and Joan eat that stuff up.'

'Sorry, but if you pay more than two dollars it doesn't count.'

'Damn. I had to be born to the pseudo-yuppy-hipster family. You're right. I will never fit in.'

'It's never too late to start collecting McDonald's Happy Meal toys.'

'Was I pretentious like that? When you first met me?'

'Nah, you were fine.'

'You lie! You thought I was so up myself.'

'Maybe.' I grinned. 'Yeah, okay, I did.'

'And I thought I would hate living here. It hasn't been all that bad, thanks to you.'

'Don't get all mushy on me.'

'Never.'

We hugged tightly.

When I got home a few hours later my house was empty. I went to the kitchen and pulled open cupboards. The tattoo had made me starving. *Yeeeessss.* Mum had done the grocery shopping. I pulled down a bag of cheese-flavoured corn chips and a jar of pasta sauce, then I went to the fridge and found a bag of grated tasty cheese. I tipped the corn chips into a bowl and poured some pasta sauce and cheese over the top and then took the bowl onto the brown velour couch in the living room and ate with both hands, licking the sauce off my fingers, just closing my eyes and smiling like the cat that ate the mouse. *Om nom nom.* But that wasn't enough. I went back to the fridge and got a family-sized block of Cadburys and broke off two whole rows and crammed it into my face all at once. *Yuuuuuum.*

I heard the front door open and slam shut. Mum appeared at the kitchen door in her work uniform.

'Jez?' She looked at me standing in front of the fridge, mouth brimming with chocolate. 'My chocolate! Gimme some of that! What's with you?' she asked, eyeing me suspiciously.

'You look happy! Where's my daughter gone? Are you stoned?'

'No! I jush hungwee!' I choked out, grinning like a maniac, a big messy grin, chunks of melted chocolate stuck all through my teeth. Mum started laughing.

'You look like a hobo!' she crowed, baring her own chocolatey teeth at me.

'So do you!' And we both fell into helpless fits of laughter.

I threw my arms around her neck and gave her a big hug. 'I love you, Mum.' I looked in her eyes. They were the same shade of dark blue as mine. I could feel a lump rising in the back of my throat.

Mum looked hesitant. 'Are you sure you're not on something?'

I shook my head and swallowed my mouthful of chocolate. 'Nah, I swear.'

'So did you get that tattoo today?' Mum asked, popping some more chocolate in her mouth. 'What were you going to get again? A snake like Lukey's?'

I shook my head. 'I changed my mind at the last minute,' I told her.

'Oh, thank God. That's gunna be on there for life, you know. Piercings are one thing, but I wasn't heaps keen on you getting that tat.'

'I got a different one.' I lifted my t-shirt sleeve and held out my arm, still wrapped in plastic.

'C'mon, then! Show me!' Mum hopped up and down impatiently.

I peeled off the plastic. The tattoo was still moist and slimy with blood and ink, but the design was really bright, and really popped against my lily-white skin.

'Oh!' Mum drew in her breath. 'Oh ...' Her eyes filled with tears.

In beautiful red, gold and black ink, on my arm, a big heart with a scroll that just said 'MUM'.

Mum started to cry. 'What are you doing to me, Jez?' she said, wiping her eyes, laughing and crying at the same time. 'You never stop surprising me.'

And we stood like a couple of mentals in the middle of the kitchen, laughing and crying and hugging and cramming more chocolate into our faces, and it was the closest I'd felt to Mum in, well, maybe ever.

Later that night I sat on the back porch and cracked my birthday six-pack of rum and Cokes, a present from Jeremy, and lit a Winfield, enjoying the sounds of Mum and Jeremy in the kitchen, cooking dinner, laughing and joking. Jeremy was thinking about moving in soon, too. It would be a full house. It felt like more than a house lately. It felt like home. I took a long swig from my can. *Things are gunna be different now. Things are finally gunna change.*

In a place like Tuggeranong, the season's change creeps up slowly, then, bam, it's colder than a nun's fanny. The gums don't change colour, so autumn came and went. After the frosts set in, and the Brindies were speckled with white snow, summer seemed like an age ago, a different time and place. It seemed like years had passed since that night sitting on the hot roof of the school with Lukey, sweating out pingers, sharing sunset kisses. I missed Lukey, but I missed the feeling more: falling in love.

'Jeeeez!' There was a voice from the darkness. 'Jez, whatcha doin'?'

Under the moonlight I could see Casey's white-blonde hair glowing around her shadowy face. I walked over to the fence that separated our properties.

'Having a few rums.' I held up my half-drunk can.

'Drinking alone?' Casey asked. 'That's kinda sad.'

'What're you doing?'

'Having a fag.' Casey exhaled a cloud of smoke and butted her cigarette out on the fence. 'Hey, isn't it your birthday soon?'

'Yeah.' I nodded, sort of pleased she'd remembered my birthday. 'Today.'

'Naaww. Happy birthday, Jezzy!' Casey put on her best sugary voice. 'What you been doin'? Haven't seen you in ages. I've been sooo bummed.'

'Yeah? How come?'

'The parents found out about me stripping and Dad totally flipped balls. They said I had to quit or move out. So I quit. Fuck paying rent, such a waste of money.'

'Yeah.' I nodded. 'So what're you doing for cash?'

'I get by. Selling dexies and stuff. Doctor reckons I've got ADD so I get all these pills and then just sell 'em to people. Hey, you want some? I'll do you a cheap deal.'

'Nah.' I held up my hands. 'I'm good.'

Casey lit another smoke.

'You heard from Cash lately?' I ventured, all causal.

'Naw. Probably won't see him for another few years. He's like that. He liked you, y'know. But he's just —'

'Yeah, that's cool,' I cut her off. 'I get it.'

'So what's new? What did you do for your birthday?'

'Stuff,' I said, guardedly. 'Got a tattoo today.' I couldn't resist showing off a little.

'No waaay,' Casey drawled. 'Show me! I'm heaps into tatts now, too! Come over! Mum and Dad are down the coast. I've got Cruisers.'

I hesitated.

'Aw, c'mon, Jezzy. You don't still have your panties in a bunch over that Lukey shit, do ya?'

'Nah ...'

'What's the problem, then?'

'Mum and Jeremy are cooking dinner for me and —'

'Laaaame,' Casey groaned. 'C'mon over! We'll have mad hangs, fuckin' mayhem, fuckin' whatever.' Her eyes glinted and she tossed her hair. 'C'mon! Bring your rum. I'll ring up some hot guys.'

I felt a shiver of anticipation in the pit of my stomach and, in spite of myself, could feel a slow smile creeping over my lips.

But then, over my shoulder, I could see Mum through the kitchen window, smiling and laughing. And I knew it'd be warm in there, I'd get a good feed, and I could cosy up on that old corduroy couch in the lounge room and hug the heater and watch Mum cry over *Dirty Dancing* for about the bazillionth time.

'Maybe another night,' I told Casey, and smiled so she'd know everything was cool. Then I turned and went back inside.

ACKNOWLEDGEMENTS

I'm most grateful to my incredibly loyal parents, Bill and Marg Thompson. I love and respect you, and want nothing more than to make you proud of me.

Thanks to my supportive family—Justin, Erin, Dan and Sarah Thompson, Greg Murrie and Claire Murrie (Gran)—and the rest, extended, around the world.

Special thanks to my amazing friends Jessica 'Jess Mess' McQuade and Laura Conlon, for your unwavering friendship, and for lending your names to my characters (who bear no resemblance to the real women). My close friends Scott Rutar, Dan Hanford, Katie Saarikko and Komala Kyme—you all rock. And cheers out to the rest of my friends for all the shows, laughs, beers and good memories.

For your belief in my writing, and guidance in the early stages of drafting *Snake Bite*, thank you to Dr Adrian Caesar and Lucy Neave. Very fair to say my writing wouldn't have come this far without you both spending considerable amounts of your time helping realise my potential.

Professionally, thank you to Lyn Tranter, my agent, for taking a chance on an unknown writer, and Jane Palfreyman, my publisher, for the same reason. Belinda Lee, Alissa Dinnallo and everyone at Allen and Unwin, you are a pleasure to work with. Much respect to Alex Nahlous for doing the hard yards copy-editing the manuscript. Thanks Holly Granville-Edge, friend and incredibly talented photographer, for helping realise my vision for the cover of this novel, and to the models Alanna, Rhianna and Sarah.

Finally, thanks to my writing companion and beautiful little dog, Bettie.